Duane —
Stay Spooky!

513/1,000

This book is dedicated to all of the hotel and motel housekeepers who clean up our disgusting messes after we leave.

Give them an extra five or ten the next time you check out.

The
PALMER HOTEL

Stories by Rick Paulas
Art by Tiffany Silver Braun

This book was written in Brooklyn, New York—much of it in the back courtyard of Lady Jay's on Grand ave.—between March 1st, 2020 and October 31st, 2020.

The Palmer Hotel

Table of Contents

Human Remains Discovered After Historic Hotel Razed..12

1. Mary Falls to Her Death.
    Room 750 (2008).......................................16
2. Lloyd Dies the Next Day.
    Room 207 (1952).......................................24
3. Mrs. Abernathy Waits.
    Room 204 (1945).......................................32
4. Kimberly Finds a Fake.
    The Penthouse Suite (1990).....................40
5. Jacklyn Has Birthday Drinks.
    Apt. 8L (2015)..48
6. Gus Goes Home.
    Room 207 (1984).......................................56
7. Henry Finds Out Where to Begin.
    Room 460 (1988).......................................64
8. Vincent Retires.
    Room 579 (1960).......................................72
9. Lydia Meets a Bird.
    Room 680 (1980).......................................80
10. Graham Goes Through His Motions.
    The Fourth Floor (1897)...........................92
11. Leo Makes a Hit.
    Room 708 (1938)......................................102

Interlude I. *110*

12. Laurie and Fred Catch Up.
    The Anchor (1999)...................................112
13. Edie Debates a Score.
    The Penthouse Suite (1964)...................122
14. Eli Makes Believe.
    Room 489 (1993)......................................130
15. Joseph Palmer Jumps.
    Room 1150 (2008)....................................138
16. Natalie Cleans Up.
    Room 584 (1992)......................................148

17. Baldwin Rearranges the Furniture.
   Room 352 (1983)......................................156
18. Franklin Pieces It Together.
   Room 708 (1953)......................................164

An invitation. *174*

19. Sofia Starts Her New Life.
   Room 201 (2003)......................................176
20. Stroud's Night Shift.
   The Guts (1968).......................................184
21. Lukas Opens the Case.
   Room 699 (1965)......................................194
22. Mikey Gets a Scoop.
   Room 699 (1970)......................................202
23. The Crew's Last Ride.
   Room 450 (1998)......................................212
24. Abigail Closes the Case.
   Room 699 (1975)......................................222
25. Sally's Last Dance.
   The Tabor Hall (2011)..............................230

Interlude II: The Grand Dance *238*

26. Jimmy Price Cleans Up.
   Room 584 (1929)......................................244
27. Wendy Learns an Old Trick.
   Room 650 (1985)......................................254
28. Hoight Dies.
   Room 809 (2000)......................................262
29. Gertie Paints Her Masterpiece.
   The Penthouse Suite (1925).....................276
30. The Séance.
   The Lobby (2020).....................................286
31. Hoight's Long Night.
   The Palmer Hotel (∞)..............................300

Overnight Fire Guts Palmer *314*

1. Mary Wakes Up.
   #750-S (2020)..316

Human Remains Discovered After Historic Hotel Razed

by Michael Jervis,
special to The Chronicle

DOWNTOWN, November 1st, 2020

When the dust cleared after Saturday's demolition of the 122-year-old Palmer Hotel, workers predicted that they would find wood, concrete, and rebar.

What they didn't expect to discover were human bones.

"Old buildings have secrets," says Jamal Wright, foreman for TK&C Demolition, the company commissioned for the project. "But not usually like these."

During the clean-up that followed the successful demolition of the two buildings — the older, twelve-story southern wing, and the more modern, ten-story northern wing — workers made the grisly discovery.

"We've seen human remains, and other things that people might have hidden away decades ago," Wright says. "But skeletons are a new one."

While medical examiners are still sifting through the wreckage, which has now been declared a crime scene and cordoned off by police, early estimates put the number of bones or bone fragments in the thousands.

"It's upsetting this was discovered only after the demolition," says Dr. Grey Franklin, professor of archeology at nearby Tech University. "It's impossible to know which floor, or which room, this cache of remains came from."

As of publication there have not been any positive identifications, but Dr. Franklin said they appear to be from "a wide range of years."

The Palmer Hotel dates back to 1898, when local entrepreneur Jonathan Palmer was rumored to have won the building, then known as The Winthrop and set near the downtown crossroads, in a poker bet. The four-story hotel soon became a top destination for tourists and investors seeking opportunity in the burgeoning city. The space was profitable enough that, in 1910, Palmer added eight more floors, and then, in 1929, an entire second ten-story tower on an adjacent plot of land.

In its prime, The Palmer's grand ballroom played host to congressional banquets and proms, while in the 1950s and 60s, it became a hotspot for celebrity spotting — Cary Grant and James Dean were once guests. As investment departed downtown for the suburbs in the 70s and 80s, the hotel saw a drop-off in its clientele, and the glitz and glamor fell away.

Ownership stayed within the family for nearly a century, from Jonathan Palmer to his son Jack in 1953, to Jack's daughter Jacqueline in 1965, to Jacqueline's son Joseph in 1985. In 1994, Joseph sold the buildings to the investment group Latham Incorporated, who initially kept running it as a hotel.

"It was a fun, weird place," says Connie Harley, a

former desk clerk. "An old building like that had plenty of creaks in the night, and plenty of creeps too."

It was also the site of a particularly ghastly homecoming.

On October 31st, 2008, former owner Joseph Palmer returned as a guest, checked into a 10th story room in the southern tower, and fell out of the window to his death in the courtyard. Tragically, his body struck and killed another guest on the ground.

In late 2008, Latham Incorporated announced the hotel would be converted into condominiums, but that year's economic turmoil halted those plans mid-renovation.

The hotel remained vacant until New Year's Day 2013, when the conglomerate secured financing to convert the buildings into luxury apartments to be rented under a new moniker, The Palmer Arms. Tenants began moving in, but the high price tag continuously kept the occupancy rate low.

In late 2019, an unusual seismic event shifted the buildings off their bases, and subsequent inspections by the city found them structurally compromised and uninhabitable. Residents were given a one-week notice to vacate, and, after months of closed-door debates, the company ultimately decided to raze the historic buildings, citing cost concerns. A last-minute effort by an advocacy group to list the buildings on the National Registry of Historic Places failed. However, sources tell The Chronicle, not before the group broke onto the Palmer grounds before its demolition for one last all-night hoorah.

(***CONFIRM BEFORE GOING TO PRESS***)

It remains unclear how Latham Incorporated will use the land.

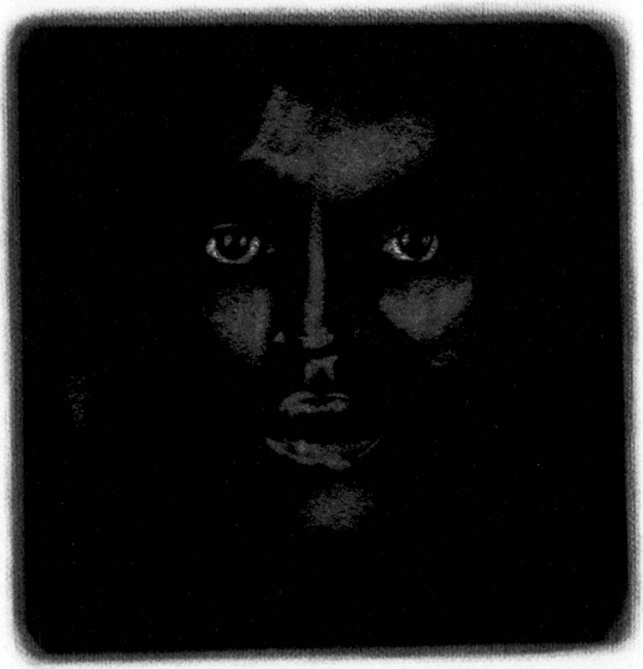

1. Mary Falls to Her Death.
Room 750

MARY WATTER WOKE to a tapping sound that rattled around and around in her brain.

She shook off her hazy drunken sleep and saw that the hotel's cheap flat screen TV, bolted to the wall, was broadcasting a commercial for some slick new generation of computer servers. She must have left the TV on.

The signal suddenly cut to black and Mary heard the sound again.

tap. tap. tap.

It came from above.

She sat up in bed and squinted her tired eyes at the ceiling. The sounds came again, louder this time.

Tap! Tap! Tap!

She huffed in annoyance and blew a raspberry with her lips, and when she did:

TAP! TAP! TAP!

The TV fritzed back to life and snapped to an image of a shiny man in a pristine blue suit behind a news desk. He was in mid-sentence.

"—e'll see here," he said, "a graphic that is surely on everyone's mind."

The next image showed an electoral map of the United States, in its chaotic puzzle of blue and red shapes, previewing next week's election between Obama and McCain. Then, a cut across the studio to a roundtable of political hacks filling time with simply speculation. Like uncles around the barbecue bullshitting their way through quantum physics, Mary thought.

The tapping sound came again through the ceiling.

It was fainter this time, but at a frequency that, once she'd tuned into its wavelength, was impossible to ignore, one of those sounds that once they get in they never get out, chipping away at the insides of your skull until you lose your mind.

With a huff, Mary twisted off the bed and planted her feet on the thin green carpeting. She grabbed the remote off the bedside table and muted the TV.

tap. tap. tap.

She walked to the light switch and bathed the room in a wash of yellow-orange that caught the full-length mirror outside of the bathroom. She paused to take a look at herself.

She ran her fingers through her long brown hair, a few more grey strands every time she looked, it seemed. She examined the cobwebs of wrinkles that flanked the outsides of her aqua blue eyes, squinted at the burst capillaries on the tip of her nose, then noticed she was still wearing her long red dress from that night's party.

It was the start-up's first Halloween shindig. They'd rented out the entire Palmer for the weekend, flown everyone in from the Bay, and given everyone their own rooms, all on the company's dime. It all meant, of course, that attendance was mandatory, even if it wasn't officially stipulated in the so-called invitation.

All employees were allowed one guest, and Mary

had considered taking Joel, a friend of a friend of a friend whom she'd met at a party and had just started more or less "seeing" a few weeks back. It'd been going well enough, with no immediate red flags, but she didn't need to be mixing her work with her real life so soon. That was what she'd told herself in any case, and so made the trip alone like usual.

Anyway, this whole weekend was a giant waste of money, an affront to Mary's accountant sensibilities. But what wasn't in this dumb industry? Everything in the tech world was basically a dick-measuring contest between founders, and these weekend parties were no different. Spend money to make money, or at least give the appearance that you were.

Tap. Tap. Tap.

"The fuck," she muttered and looked at the clock.

Twenty-eight minutes before midnight. The rest of her young coworkers were still partying away in the hotel's downstairs ballroom, but Mary's age-bestowed wisdom had impressed on her the benefits of a good night's sleep. And that wasn't happening as long as that fucking sound still pounded against the ceiling.

She picked up the phone and dialed downstairs.

"Front desk, this is Colleen, how can we help you," drolled the voice of a young woman.

Mary told her about the noise, and Colleen said she'd have someone check, so Mary turned off the light and crawled back into bed. The TV anchor was offering some more electoral analysis as Mary pressed OFF and drifted toward sleep.

Her mind recycled images from the party.

A band costumed in suspenders and checkerboard pants that took requests but played none well. Her kicking off her shoes anyway to dance with her coworkers, none of whom could keep up. Her boss Peter giving his blank-eyed smile as he commented on sales figures before skulking away in hopes of finding someone, anyone else. Now that she thought about it, it would've been fun to have Joel around, at the very least to make fun of these people, to keep her grounded.

TAP! TAP! TAP!

Mary opened her eyes and saw shadows like writhing demons on the ceiling, and spastically jumped out of bed with a slight gasp, only then realizing they were being cast by flickering red lights from outside.

She walked to the window and saw the neon sign on the hotel's rooftop, announcing:

PALMER HOTEL

It quivered and popped. It must have a short.
TAP! TAP! TAP!

She tried the front desk again, but now the line was dead. She'd have to take care of this herself.

She grabbed her key card and left. Halfway down the hall she realized she was barefoot, but continued ahead anyway and pushed open the stairwell door. Her feet hit the cold concrete, and she ascended one floor then pushed open the metal door into the Palmer's eighth floor.

It felt different up here. Colder, disinfected, sterile.

The walls had fresh coats of white paint, and instead of carpeting it was lined with beige tile. There was sawdust collected in mounds, and most of the rooms had their doors torn off and replaced with plastic sheets.

"Hello?" she spoke.

A white puff of breath spread from her mouth. Gooseflesh rippled on her arms and she rubbed her hands together for warmth.

"Hello?"

Another faint cloud puffed from her lips, then disappeared.

She steeled her nerves with a deep breath then

stepped forward once, twice, again, until her momentum carried her to Room 850, the one right above hers.

A plastic sheet floated in its doorway and billowed from wind of mysterious origin. Even so, Mary knocked on the door frame to be polite.

"Hello?" she called through the rippling plastic.

No answer.

She pulled the sheet aside, and her eyes adjusted to the new environment. Dark, lit only by the trembling red from the rooftop sign. She flipped on the wall switch and bright, white halogen light flickered then caught.

It was similar to her room downstairs in basic footprint, but the amenities were largely missing. No bed, no desk, and the bathroom was gutted, with stray tiles strewn across the floor and hieroglyphic pencil marks on the walls. A fridge and washer/dryer set-up were stashed in the corner, still wrapped in its factory plastic.

"Well, shit," she said, and flipped off the light.

She waited a moment, hoping to hear the sound again, but it never came, so she returned down the stairwell, her red dress fluttering behind as she descended.

She used the key card to unlock the door to her room, crawled back into bed, and thought about the sound for a moment, then another, but soon it all dissipated and she finally drifted off to sleep.

Tap! Tap! Tap!

"Son of a fucking bitch!" she screamed.

TAP! TAP! TAP!

That mix of static moonlight and shuddering red came through the window, and so she walked to snatch the curtains shut, but when she did, saw the black metal fire escape outside. It was part of the network that hugged the Palmer's courtyard, connecting the rooms of the hotel's two wings from the rooftop all the way down to the ground floor.

Tap! Tap! Tap!

Mary lifted open the window, pulled her hair back into a bun, and stepped barefoot onto the fire escape and into the crisp night air.

She looked across to the hotel's other wing. A few TVs were still on at this late hour, casting white vibrations against the walls and onto feet sticking out from the covers. Below, in the middle of the hotel's courtyard, she saw an all-glass enclosure, almost like a greenhouse with a small pyramid on top. That must be the dining hall she'd heard mention about.

She heard the nearby elevated train clatter along on its predetermined path, same as ever, tracing the same arcs through the city that'd been set in place so many years ago.

Mary climbed the fire escape steps to one floor above and was again outside of the curtainless window of Room 850. She pressed her hands against the glass and saw no movement inside—it was as barren as she'd left it.

She descended again back to her room, but midway down, she noticed a strange piece of glass embedded in the exterior wall of the building.

It was small and oval, like a portal, nearly indistinguishable from the brick. It was seemingly between the floors, somehow.

She stepped onto the fire escape's railing and leaned to get a better look, pressing her forehead against the glass. She felt its cold against her skin, but the reflected glare from the rooftop's red neon obstructed her view, so she cupped her hands around her eyes to block out the light—then saw movement on the other side.

It wriggled and squirmed in sweaty commotion. She saw an elbow, then a knee, an ankle, wrist, an entanglement of limbs, some hairy, some bare, writhing like a rat king of human appendages and wet flesh. She smelled something spoiled in the air.

She heard a soft tap on the glass.

Suddenly, the chaos of limbs parted with the speed of cockroaches struck by a kitchen light, and in their place appeared the face of a man.

He had a sheen of sweat, deep-set eyes, dark skin. His smooth forehead crinkled into a look of awed wonder, then new fresh fear, then pleading and desperation.

His mouth opened, and the cracked edges of his dry lips split and bled, producing twin trails of deep crimson that ran down the sides of his face and collected at the bottom of his chin.

The man breathed in deeply, and then let out a deafening scream. It shook the glass and turned his face into a ghastly blur.

Mary leapt back in terror and felt her foot slip off the railing.

She swiped a desperate hand, finding metal—but only for a moment, before she grasped at nothing but air, then wind as she fell.

She was somehow unafraid—as if she'd instantaneously accepted to her fate.

She saw the glow of a TV in a window across the way and watched its light create odd, mysterious shadows against the ceiling. Placidly, she used the span of her final moments to spin around and look up. She was hoping to see the stars, but her view of the night sky was blocked by the shape of a man above her, him falling too, only a moment behind.

Mary watched the man's arms flail then steady, and the sign's blinking red caught his face. He was older, distinguished looking, staring at her with a new look of serene calm in his eyes.

It seemed to Mary that for an instant he even made a slight smile.

"Weird world," Mary thought, and then she thought no more.

2. Lloyd Dies the Next Day.
Room 207

SWEAT BURNED Lloyd Farley's eyes as it dripped down his forehead like an open fire hydrant on a hot summer night.

He wiped it away with his forearm; the beads clung to its thicket of hair. The fresh scratch down the side of his face next to his bulbous nose throbbed in the new salt wash.

tap. tap. tap.

It took him a moment to realize the sound was from the gun he held in his hand, tapping against the desktop.

He grabbed his wrist and held it tight, urging himself to stop with the tapping. That damn tapping. Boss never liked that tapping.

It drove him batty, he'd tell Lloyd. Then, Boss would threaten to have one of the boys lop Lloyd's hand clean off if he ever heard it again.

Stop the yips, or lose the fist, Boss would say.

The taps stopped.

Lloyd pulled his left hand up to his face and examined the red scrapes and purple bruising across his knuckles. It looked like a cloudy sunset.

Oh yeah, Lloyd thought. The Boss.

He released his wrist and let his yips tap-tap-tap again from his gun, the one that had sprayed the Boss's brains against a brick wall alley between 5th and 6th Aves.

tap. tap. tap.

Years later, when researchers described this era of downtown gangland murders, they'd call Boss's murder a "hit." But it wasn't really like that, so organized and planned.

It was just one of those things.

One step too far.

Boss had been riding him all night, all week, all month really. He always had, but there'd been something different about this latest round. More taunting, more seeing how much his power could get away with, testing him. Like Boss had something to prove.

And when he'd mentioned Lloyd's kid earlier that night, well, that was the iron safe that came crashing down on the camel's back.

"Does Little Brian know he's got a lousy fathead for an old man?" Boss had said. "Does he know he's got the genetics of a verifiable white-livered piece of sh—"

Lloyd didn't realize he was hitting Boss until he was four or six or maybe eight punches deep, feeling those brittle cheekbones buckle inward against his knuckles as he felt moisture from the squirt of a popped eye.

Boss got in a good sharp swipe at Lloyd's face, but just the one before he fell in a clump against the wall, whimpering. Lloyd watched the bloodied man put a fist on the ground to hoist himself back onto his feet, and in that moment he considered his options. So, out came the gun, then two bullets through Boss's head.

Lloyd walked an hour to give him some distance from the scene, knowing that his earliest exit from the city couldn't realistically come until tomorrow's first train. Once he was a few cities over, he'd call Brian's mother, the two of them now living halfway across the country. He could hook them up with connects he still had back in St. Louis.

He'd been mulling over an exit plan in the back of his head for years, anyway. Everyone in his field of work had something like this simmering. But as this came unscheduled, he needed a place for the night before the morning train.

His basement one-bedroom on the west side was too hot, and all the usual safe joints would soon be getting word, hence the Palmer, known for its utmost discretion.

Lloyd set his gun on the desk and stood, then walked the room's length for the fifty-first then fifty-second times that night, the room entirely dark save for the single bulb hanging in the shitter. Every passage past this cone of light allowed his muddled thoughts to further clarify until they'd finally settled again, and he walked to the window and took in the hotel's courtyard view.

He pulled it open, lit a cigarette, and exhaled outside with force enough that it escaped like puffs from a train engine's chimney. He saw movements in the hotel's opposite wing—just some nobody at a window. Still, he didn't like the exposure.

He took one last drag, stubbed in on the windowsill, shut the window, and pulled tight the curtains. He grabbed his gun and went to the can, lifted the lid, dropped trou, and sat his wide ass down.

"Tried to shit, but merely farted," he said with a smile.

Then, beyond the bathroom's threshold, he saw shadows moving in the thin strip of hallway light that shone underneath the room's front door.

He pinched it off and crouched, pants still around his ankles, and quietly pulled the light's chain. The bulb blinked out.

He aimed his gun with an eye closed.

After a minute of playing the moves of the approaching shootout in his head, he remembered the hinges.

They were closer to him, so when the front door opened there'd be a barrier between him and them. Not ideal to pop whoever was coming in. In the bathroom, he'd be trapped.

He lifted his pants back up quietly while doing his best to keep his muzzle trained on the door. When they were secure around his waist, he took a gamble and tiptoed on the tile, then out of the bathroom and across the way, into the cramped closet.

Now, at least he'd be able to see who he was shooting.

Half an hour later, still tucked in position, his legs finally fell asleep. He stretched them out and felt tingling pain rush through them as the blood flowed again. When he regained sensation, he stood up and stepped back into the room proper to examine his options again.

There was a spot under the desk, but he was too big for it. He could maybe kneel in that tiny gap between bed and wall, but staying in a crouch all night would be excruitiating. Then he saw the strip of darkness underneath the bed.

He dropped to a crawl and situated himself so he faced the front door then slid back into position. He squinted down the sights and, from that angle, mentally prepped for the entry of two or three men—never more, three would be the max for a job like this. They'd shove open the door and spray light in from the hallway illuminating everything except, he hoped, this space under the bed.

The first gunman might see a muzzle flash, but if Lloyd aimed right, that unlucky guy wouldn't be able tip off anything to the trailers, who'd then go down next, one at a time.

Another hour under the bed and the adrenaline was gone.

Lloyd allowed himself to lay his head on the carpet, and suddenly he was sitting in a rocking chair on a porch in Missouri.

The sun was setting on the horizon, past the farmhouse that'd been in the family for generations, where the fields swayed like a purple ocean. Someone behind called his name and he knew right away it was Brian, back home from school. But when he sat up in his rocker and turned to look, no one was there.

He spun back to the field, but now the wheat stalks had become men with tommy guns. An army with blank eyes and scarred faces.

Advancing toward him.

Step by step.

Lloyd snapped awake under the bed, and saw twin vertical shadows that soon materialized into legs. The legs wore brown wool trousers and faced the door, as if waiting.

Lloyd felt pressure on his back; weight from the man as he sat down on the bed. He tried to stay silent as the squeeze of the bedsprings compressed his lungs. Then he heard breathing coming from this man.

Loud, wheezing breaths.

A painful noise.

Lloyd tried to grip his gun, then realized that his hand was empty.

He groped around, desperately searching for where he'd dropped it, then suddenly came a booming concussion.

He felt the blast rattle his teeth and had time enough to think, "well, that's it for poor ol' Lloyd."

It took him a moment to realize that thinking it at all was proof that it wasn't, at least not yet. Then it took him another moment to realize he wasn't hit at all.

His fingers continued searching and found gunmetal. He collected it and aimed at the trouser-clad legs still in front of him.

All at once these legs shifted and slumped to the side, then fell over to the floor. The rest of the body followed, and the man landed facedown on the carpet.

The side of his head held slick black hair where a bullet hole had entered, and the man's white t-shirt was stained. Lloyd smelled fresh blood.

A sudden splash of light as the hotel room door burst open.

Lloyd aimed at the glow and pulled the trigger three times. The blasts rang out in his ears, and he saw three holes appear in the wood of the door on the other side of the hallway.

"Shit!" a red-haired kid with a trimmed beard screamed in the hallway among the clattering of falling silverware. "Wrong fucking room! Wrong fucking room"

When Lloyd's eyes adjusted to the brightness of the hallway, he saw a tray of spaghetti and meatballs bathed in thin watery red sauce scattered near the door.

Then Lloyd realized that the man in trousers, who'd lain dead with a bullet in his head, had disappeared.

He pulled himself out from under the bed, frantically crawling to where the man had just been, but only found a deep red stain in the carpet. He watched as it lightened, faded, then vanished entirely.

He heard screaming for help in the hallway, that damn whiny red-head baby who didn't even get a scratch, which meant that it was time for Lloyd to go.

He collected his belongings as a loud ruckus of footfalls came from the hall. He'd have to seek out another exit.

He opened the window and climbed onto the fire escape, then turned back once more just to check for any witnesses he may need to dispatch in the future.

There he was again.

The man in the brown wool trousers and bloody white t-shirt.

He stared back at Lloyd.

Half of his face was mangled red gristle, but he still managed to stretch out a partial, squishy smile.

Lloyd blinked and he was gone, revealing stark shadows in the hallway heading to his room.

He pocketed his gun, descended to the ground floor, and escaped into the city night, hoping to stay safely hidden away until tomorrow morning's train. Hoping to stay alive long enough to see Brian again.

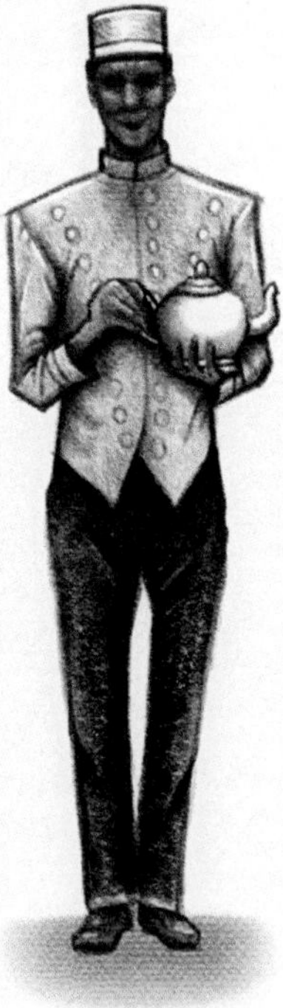

3. Mrs. Abernathy Waits.
Room 204

MRS. ABERNATHY ran her fingers through the deep groves in the chair's wooden arms as she watched the Palmer's revolving front door shudder in the strong wind from outside.

Through the glass, she saw a large blue banner that hung from the awning. Across its top read "Welcome Home," along the bottom, "We Are Proud." In between was an image of a smiling Uncle Sam with his arms outstretched.

She'd watched the hotel staff hoist the massive sign into place weeks back, but by now, its corners had begun to fray in the gusts, and Uncle Sam's face was darkened with soot, dusted by plumes of exhaust from the cars wobbled by.

She daintily sipped the last of her tea as a figure came into view outside.

A giddiness crept into her throat as it always did whenever someone new arrived. It could be anyone at that point.

It could even be him.

She shifted to rise, but then the door spun to reveal that it was just another businessman, so she slumped again back into her seat.

"Another round, Mrs. Abernathy?" said that kind voice behind her.

Hoight, trusty Hoight.

The Palmer's young bellhop, only ten years old despite his shocking height, and always there with a silver pot of steaming tea.

"You're always just here when I need you," she said, holding up her cup.

Hoight flashed his blinding white teeth as he carefully poured. Then, as had become their custom, he pulled a cloth from his pocket, set it on the table, and placed the hot pot on top before he too, slumped into a nearby chair.

"What a day," he said.

He let out a steamboat whistle, then shifted his bellhop's hat over his eyes to mime taking a nap.

Mrs. Abernathy had met Hoight on her first day at the Palmer as she struggled to pull her suitcase through those damn revolving doors. This young man in his adorable bellhop's outfit, four decades her junior, had found her stuck, her bag somehow jamming her inside.

He'd shook his head in mock disappointment.

"This simply won't do," he'd said.

Hoight had pressed some secret catch above the door which opened a plate of glass, allowing for her exit. He grabbed her suitcase, brought her back outside, and took her around to the metal door on the side of the building, the one he called "our V.I.P. door."

"It's reserved for our most special clientele," he'd stage-whispered as he held the door for a delivery man pushing a cart filled with toilet paper. "Think I'm joking," he said to Mrs. Abernathy, nodding to the cart, "but you try managing a hotel of guests who can't wipe themselves clean."

Right away, Hoight was a godsend for Mrs. Abernathy. When Red at the front desk gave her a fifth-floor room, Hoight saw the fret in her eyes and the balk in her knees, and had her squared away on the second floor instead. Without her permission, he'd made her standing reservations in the dining hall at 9:45 p.m. every night for the rest of her stay, however long that was. He explained that was the best time of night, "after the rush had died down."

Most importantly, he was always there when she needed more tea.

"Oh, you're too young to be tired," Mrs. Abernathy said to the slumped-over bellhop.

Hoight raised his cap off one eye and lifted a skeptical brow.

"Is that right, Mrs. Abernathy?" he grinned.

He spoke in the high-pitched register of boys that age. It reminded her of the summer when Johnny's voice had cracked and changed. One of his older cousins had called him McCrackin', and it became an in-joke between the two of them that stuck for years.

Never would've known he'd be Johnny McCrackin until the day he died, Mrs. Abernathy suddenly thought.

The notion shot through then departed, mercifully, before it had a chance to settle.

"Who am I to argue with a V.I.P.?" Hoight said.

He hopped from the chair, planted his feet in a cross-step, and unwound his legs so that he spun a full twirl back to her. He fell to one knee with arms opened and, suddenly, held a rose.

"A little gift," he said. "Happy Mother's Day."

She blushed and offered him a few nickels as a tip, but he shook them off.

"On me," he said.

Hoight doffed his hat as he retreated back into the hallways of the Palmer, back to work.

Mrs. Abernathy smelled her rose and watched the front door some more.

A woman in a flowery dress came in with a man twice her age. Next walked in five besuited men all chomping cigars, bellowing with mockery at the expense of some poor chap named Jacobson. Then came a stout older Polish woman who led a little girl, probably three years old, tethered to a rope.

"Ran off one too many times," the old woman said to Mrs. Abernathy's inquisitive glare, before she erupted in loud, wet laughter.

Still, no Johnny.

She waited some more, always running her fingers through the chair's wooden grooves as she glared out.

When half past nine struck on the lobby's grandfather clock, Hoight strolled in again and sat down. He pulled out his cloth again, dabbing theatrically at his forehead.

"Got to give them the impression they're getting their money's worth," Hoight confided, then tucked the cloth back into his pocket. "Got a surprise for you tonight, Mrs. Abernathy."

Rather than simply kissing Mrs. Abernathy's hand and wishing her goodnight, Hoight stood up and elegantly offered her an arm. She took it and used his youthful leverage to counter the stiffness from her long day at the lookout post. She promised him she'd take more breaks tomorrow, the same promise she'd made yesterday, same one as the day before.

"No need to worry about tomorrow, that's when he'll be here," Hoight said, giving her hand a squeeze. "Got a good feeling."

He escorted her past the front desk into the grand hallway.

It split into three directions—to the left and right, each with a bank of elevators, six cars apiece, that rose into the hotel's north and south wings; and straight ahead, to a short stairway leading into the hotel's courtyard dining hall.

The hallway was littered with tall rolling carts tagged with destination room numbers. Hoight shook the hands of a half-dozen night porters like a politician making rounds, whispered into their ears, and they all wished Mrs. Abernathy a "Happy Mother's Day" before the odd pair took the stairs into the dining hall.

It was a tall, open space formed entirely of glass panels, allowing the red, hazy light from the hotel's rooftop sign to filter in. In the room's center, the panels converged in a small pyramid. A few conversations still echoed from round tables covered in white cloth.

Hoight led Mrs. Abernathy to her usual table in the north end corner. She liked looking up through the glass and watching the show as the guests above turned off their room lights one by one. As they approached the table, she noticed it held three place settings rather than the regular two—hers and Johnny's. She looked inquisitively at Hoight.

"How about some company tonight?" he asked.

"I'd be enchanted," she said.

They took their seats and the waiter came over. She ordered a martini and the precocious Hoight said, "Make it two." The waiter mocked out a, "Yes of course, sir" and returned with a sparkling water and lime.

"We'll see what kind of tip he gets," Hoight scoffed.

The meal was steaks well-done and a side of mashed potatoes, studded with garlic and a parsley garnish. Mrs. Abernathy followed her martini with a red wine then another tea.

They spoke of Hoight's own history at the hotel. He'd been there for years, since birth really, and loved every second of it. But most of that night's conversation was about Johnny.

"When he was your age, I tried to get him a job at a mechanic's shop," Mrs. Abernathy said. "Thought it'd be good to get him some training. Boy didn't last a day."

She laughed, until her laughter turned to tears—not of sadness, but of reminiscence.

Hoight unfolded the napkin from the unused table setting and offered it to her. She dabbed the outside corners of her eyes, leaving behind streaks of grey mascara.

"The next day, when it was time for him to go back, I found him in the backyard taking aim at a rabbit with a wooden gun that he'd carved out of a log," she said. "There were no bullets or anything, no moving parts, it was just a carving."

She sipped.

"He was always sharp at whittling," she said. "Guns, toy cars, tiny spoons. Kid had a talent."

"Has," Hoight corrected. "He *has* it."

Mrs. Abernathy nodded and sipped her tea again.

They finished and crumpled their napkins, Mrs. Abernathy's stained with blotches of mascara. Hoight offered his arm and she gently picked up her gifted rose. They walked out of the hall, turned right to the elevators, and rode up to the second floor. Outside of her room, as he wished her a good night, she reached into her purse and fished out three dollar bills—the kind of score boys Hoight's age could only dream about. He thanked her, pocketed the money, and said he'd see her tomorrow.

Mrs. Abernathy crossed her room to the window and looked across the courtyard. Above were windows were washed by the rooftop's red, below the dining hall ceiling glowed white from within.

From her vantage, she saw the dining tables, all of them empty save one: "her" table in the north end corner.

At one of the seats was a man. Older, in his late fifties or so, streaks of grey running along his temples. She absentmindedly smelled her rose as she watched.

The man brought the fork to his mouth, finishing a last bite, then set it back down in the puddle of brown grease on his plate.

The waiter came over—a different waiter, one that she'd never seen before—and opened a small menu for the man to look over. As he pointed to his preference, Mrs. Abernathy noticed that the diner was without a left arm. Nothing but a loose sleeve safety-pinned near his shoulder.

The waiter returned with a small bowl of ice cream and a new metal spoon, but the man picked up the spoon and offered it back. He wouldn't need it. Instead, he reached into his front pocket and pulled out a rolled napkin that he set on the table and unfurled. Inside was a small wooden spoon.

The man leaned over his bowl, and Mrs. Abernathy made out a dark brown military coat draped over the back of his chair. It was adorned with medals.

Perhaps this man knew about the war, Mrs. Abernathy thought. Perhaps he knew Johnny.

Still clutching her rose she slipped into her shoes and took the elevator back down to the ground floor. She walked the hallway, now lined with different stacks of luggage, suitcases of strange design, maybe from foreign countries, ones she'd never encountered before.

She poked her head into the lobby and was struck by the silence. Not even the grandfather clock was ticking out its stark metronome anymore.

She turned and walked into the dining hall.

The one-armed man was still at the far end, licking the last bit from his wooden spoon. Mrs. Abernathy took a long deep breath to calm her nerves, then walked to meet him.

Halfway there, he looked up with sad, knowing eyes, and that's when she decided to gift him her rose.

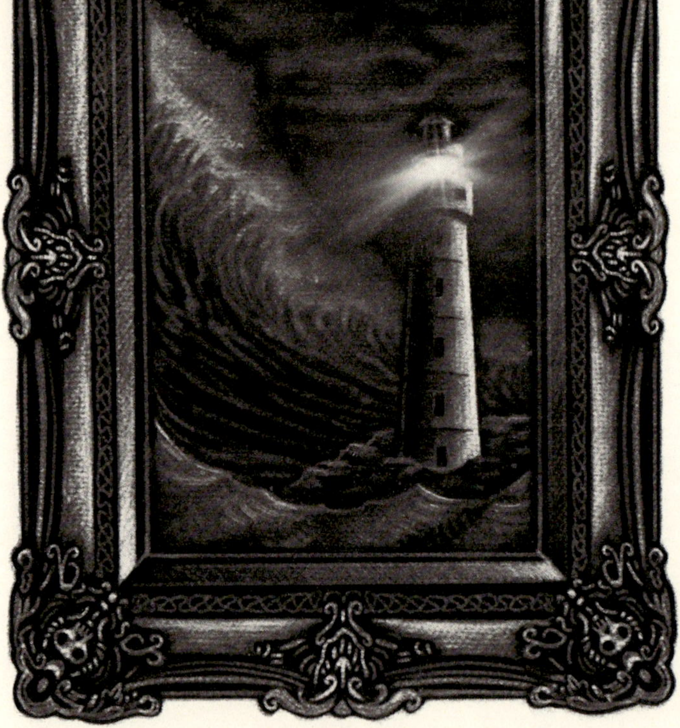

4. Kimberly Finds a Fake.
The Penthouse Suite

KIMBERLY GRACE sat on the window ledge and faced the expansive space of the penthouse suite.

The wind gusted in from the open window, but her short-cropped blonde hair remained plastered in place, the hairspray doing its job. She stretched her legs out from beneath her high-waisted black skirt while her white blouse, tucked into her belt, billowed out.

Behind her, the city lights twinkled.

People said the Palmer's top floor was the best view in town, but Kimberly was ignoring all of that now. Her only concern was framed and leaning against the suite's opposite wall.

It was a seven-foot-tall canvas set in a baroque frame that bore the title Midnight Cabaret. It depicted a tall lighthouse on a lonesome island, its lamp frozen in mid-spin, glaring harshly into the viewer's line of sight. This gleam partially obscured a pressing concern: a giant dark wave three or four times the height of the lighthouse approaching in the distance.

Without taking her eyes off the canvas, she dipped to her side and reached into her purse, and grabbed her lighter and a soft pack of Marlboro menthols. She plucked one out, let the pack fall to the hardwood floor, and slightly bent forward to rest her elbows on her knees. She lit the cigarette, inhaled, and let the smoke escape from her lips without any concern for where it wafted, indoors or out.

Over the years, Kimberly had been in enough penthouses to know that the penthouse's smoke alarm probably wasn't even connected to the main network, more likely hooked into a more private system that'd send someone up to discreetly examine a situation before triggering any building-wide alarms. Hotel managements knew better than to mess with the partying of big shot clientele.

Kimberly took one last drag and reached back to stub it out amongst several other fallen soldiers in the silver ashtray on the ledge. She stood and crossed the room, her attention now on a small section of the painting that'd caught her intrigue, a part of the looming wave that she couldn't figure ou—

"Whatcha think, hun?" a gruff voice shouted from the penthouse's next room.

It took everything in Kimberly's willpower to not shout back at him to shut the fuck up.

The voice belonged to Harold Doyle, also known about town as The General.

An oil magnate in his late 50s, Doyle had paid $25 million for the painting, in addition to the sum he'd earmarked for Kimberly to verify if it was, in fact, a legitimate Gertie.

But to make that determination, as she had told The General twice before, she needed absolute silence.

"One more warning," Kimberly said.

"Okay, okay, I'm sorry," The General said playfully. "I'm sorry, hun."

Kimberly closed her eyes to recenter her focus.

In her mind she conjured up the image of a lion. First only an outline, then she filled in its complexity, its details. Tail, eyes, color and thickness of its mane and coat, those giant white teeth. When a satisfactory lion had been summoned, she reopened her eyes to again examine the wave threatening the lighthouse.

Most untrained consumers of art, of which The General was surely one, believed that painting forgeries are uncovered in their smallest details. The discovery of a type of brush fiber that hadn't yet been invented, or paint layered onto the canvas years after the artist died. But that type of analysis was for the nerds with their costly machines. By that point, someone like Kimberly had already sown enough skepticism to warrant that kind of technological investment.

It usually never got to that point, though. If she found "the appearance of potential dubiousness" as she'd put it to the painting's owner, the auction house usually settled quietly, everyone then getting to keep their reps intact—one sin you couldn't come back from in today's art market was being duped into passing off a fraud as the real deal, and that went triple for a Gertie.

Kimberly had read bits and pieces of the artist's story over the years.

Gertrude Wagner, born in 1890 to the servant class of Pasadena. She'd forewent school to take an apprenticeship at the architectural firm of Greene and Greene, and then her past grew blurry around 1908, when she left the firm amidst rumors that necessitated some unknown amount of hush money. With the new cash, Gertrude went out to see the world and simply never stopped, living from city hotel to city hotel, an ever-expanding collection of boxes and supplies in tow.

One story went that she rented out an entire train car for her trip from Berlin to Munich, the only proof being an old sulphide print that showed her broadly smiling from the window, a thin white-gloved hand waving to the photographer as her blonde hair billowed in the breeze. The train's movement had blurred the photo, but somehow, her face remained perfectly in focus.

She died in 1954 in Saint Petersburg, and it was only then that her crates were opened, her paintings discovered. A limited portfolio and a compelling story drove up her work's valuation in the collector industry. A new market was born.

Kimberly didn't care much about that right now. She'd seen enough of Gertie's work that she knew she'd only ever used a specific combination of bristle and hair from a Kolinsky sable, a weasel from Siberia. These fibers had a certain absorbency that allowed for a particular type of paint application. But while any expert forger could access this type of brush, Kimberly was alert to a particular shibboleth: the rhythm to her strokes.

Gertie had a staccato flinch as she painted, as if she wasn't sure which direction she'd end up, always second-guessing herself.

This is why Kimberly focused on the wave.

It was violet with a spray of white moonlight delicately caressing each liquid flutter, giving it an extra depth that—

"Anything?"

That damn voice again.

"You have been warned," she said, softly and calm. "Please leave."

"You said I had one more warning," said The General.

Kimberly remained silent, waiting him out. Soon enough she heard the springs in his chair rebound as he lifted his hefty frame, then out came a soft mutter and loud huff. She continued to wait.

She'd handled these types often enough to know that all they needed was time to come up with an excuse to convince themselves that they were actually the ones making the decision.

"I have calls to make anyway," The General said to no one in particular. "Closing a big deal tonight."

He waited for a response, and with none forthcoming, Kimberly heard his fat footfalls cross the room, then the door slam shut behind him. She waited until she heard the penthouse elevator ding in the foyer, then the sound of its slow descent, before she closed her eyes to re-imagine the lion.

When it was to her satisfaction, she examined the waves again.

Dark violet in the moonlight. White foam at the crest like the mouth of a rabid dog. There was anger in this painting. Violence. Something Kimberly hadn't seen from Gertie before. It was enough to give her a moment of hesitation.

Until—yes, she now saw—there was Gertie after all.

She leaned close enough to the canvas that she felt it graze against the fine hairs on the tip of her nose. There were those squiggles of Gertie's hesitation she'd been looking for.

She leaned back and relaxed her shoulders.

While it was always fun to break it to some rich swine they'd been had, it was difficult to know how they'd react. One pig in Baltimore had thrown a chair against the wall next to her head and it shattered; a wooden shard had nicked her neck and drawn blood. They gave her a quarter-million for the trouble, as if she had any choice but to take it and keep her mouth shut.

When a person gets to that kind of wealth, their idea of another human becomes warped. Or maybe that's how they attained that wealth in the first place.

An unknowable puzzle.

Chicken and Faberge egg.

So, informing the rich that their investment had passed her test was always preferable.

Kimberly tore her eyes from the painting and walked back to the window. She picked up her soft pack of Marlboros, retrieved another menthol, and sat back on the ledge. The General would want to know immediately that his purchase was the real deal, but she still needed to get herself back to seeing the world as it was again, to blink out the microscopic specificity she'd been living in.

"Unwind on the company dime," she said, and lit the cigarette.

She let a puff billow as she relaxed her eyes. As the cloud dissipated, she noticed something else in the painting. Something within the wave itself.

Shadows.

She took another drag, stubbed it dead in the ashtray, then crossed the room again.

How could she have missed this?

The shadows were within the sheet of water and lit from behind by the moonlight, their features intricately chiseled. Sea creatures of some sort, that's all she could guess. No coherent shape, simply blobs with tentacles, maybe arms. Seeming to emerge through the wave.

She blinked.

Yes, in fact, the scaled skin of a creature was coming through the wave, lit by unobstructed moonlight.

She blinked again, and now could make out the creature's head, a bulbous monstrosity with eyes like waxed buttons.

She blinked, and its mouth was open, exposing rows of jagged teeth.

Kimberly stepped back, forcing open her eyes so as not to miss one second of whatever mental break she must be experiencing. She reached behind and felt the ledge, plucked the half-cigarette she'd stubbed, twisted off the burnt top with a thumbnail, and stuck it in her mouth to re-light.

Smoke got in her eyes, so she blinked, then blinked again, and again.

Each blink was accompanied by a sopping wet slapping sound on the wooden floor somewhere in front of her.

Kimberly forced her eyes open, they reddened in the smoke.

The lighthouse had disappeared now. So had the wave. The canvas was all aqua and green, tiled by thin lines.

She was looking at the scales of some creature's skin.

A reflection appeared on the floor in front of her. Two wide, wet circles, one afront the other, like steps stalking to her. They leaked outward at a steady rate, as if water was being poured into them from an invisible spout.

She blinked again and heard another sopping sound. There it was—another wet print on the floor, closer.

Then—the soothing sound of a wave crashing. Calming, tranquil. Leaving her without a worry in the world. For a moment she felt weightless, as if floating in the sea.

She took another inhale, blinked again. Another sloshing slap, another puddle, only feet away from her now.

She smiled and laughed and pulled a drag from her cigarette.

Maybe this wasn't a real Gertie after all.

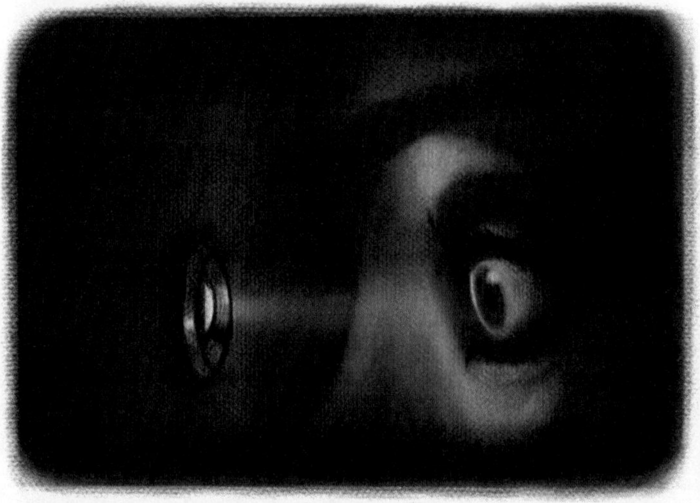

5. Jacklyn Has Birthday Drinks. Apt. 8L

JACKLYN FELT THE MOUTHSWEATS beginning to gush from inside the folds of her cheeks.

She woozily lifted her head off the thin wooden table she'd found last week on the street, the one she'd cashed in a few months' worth of flirting with Zed the Doorman to help her lug it upstairs. She closed her laptop, still playing that Snowden documentary she'd passed out in front of, and hustled into the kitchen, where she grabbed a can of beer from the fridge before stumble-jogging into the bathroom.

She carefully knelt on the pink rug facing her toilet then set the ice cold can on the floor beside her, cracking it open with a swift single motion from her thumb and forefinger like she was snapping off the back of a bra. The spritzing sound of the opening tab reverberated against the tiled walls, and on cue, she unleashed a violent torrent of puke into the bowl.

She squinted through her tear-filled eyes at the disgorge—by that point in the night, it was mostly all liquid with a faint amber hue. The rougher stuff from the birthday meal she'd made for herself—same as every year, spaghetti and meatballs—had thankfully exited a few hurls back.

One more exorcism, maybe two, and that'd close the books on another year for Jacklyn, her 40th trip around the sun.

For the past decade-plus, as friends became acquaintances and family gatherings spun off into their own satellite affairs, Jacklyn's birthday ritual had pared down to simply this. She'd turn off her phone, log out of Facebook—recently, she'd taken to giving her password to a friend who'd reset it for the night—and sit quietly alone with her own thoughts, perhaps a book or a movie. Oh yeah, and either a gallon of wine or a 12-pack of beer or a fifth of vodka or whiskey, depending on that year's drinking whims.

She flushed the toilet and washed out the bile taste with a long swig from the full can, then breathed in deeply through her nose, a meditative reset, before rising into a wobbly stance.

She looked at herself in the mirror. It was flanked by the pair of skeletons that hung on the wall, decorations for the holiday she shared her birthday with. She allowed herself another moment of self-pity before another swig, then Jacklyn noticed something on the wall.

A small divot.

She slightly pushed the mirror aside so it hung askew on its nail, and saw that there was a faint engraving behind it.

A small, hard-carved spiral.

Strange she hadn't noticed this before.

"Ding, dong," interrupted a woman's soft voice.

It was the apartment's front doorbell, pre-programmed with 45 different voice greetings, one of the advertised "perks" that came with the place. She never figured out how to turn it off, and it was obnoxious as hell.

She let the mirror settle back in place and looked at her watch. It was 10:27, way too late for trick-or-treaters, according to the book-length thread of emails on the listserv for The Palmer Arms.

It had been a fierce debate among the two classes of occupants: those with kids, those without. Jacklyn was in the latter camp, but she didn't really give a shit about any of this, so she didn't even chime in. Eventually, after intense negotiations and threatening legalse, it was decided that trick-or-treating would stop abruptly at 8 p.m.

Whatever, she thought.

Jacklyn twisted on the faucet and sucked down water straight from the spigot, sipped from a tiny bottle of mouthwash, and spit the faint green mixture out before leaving the bathroom. She grabbed a werewolf mask that she'd set on top of her shoe cubby for the evening's festivities and put it on before opening the door.

"Roar!" she screamed to the trick-or-treating kids.

No one was there.

She wobbled past her apartment's threshold and examined the hallway in a sweeping arc from left to right through the mask's eyeholes. Empty. Only a single piece of torn plastic lying in the middle of the bright red carpeting.

"Fuckers," she said, pulling the mask off her face.

The loose plastic was another indication of the disgusting tenants that lived in this place. They'd track mud into the building's lobby downstairs, and leave their trash outside of their doors, drawing rats and cockroaches. Now and then, she even came across actual dog dumps spiraled on the hallway carpet! Forget vampires and werewolves, these were our world's true monsters.

She walked to collect the plastic and do her neighborly civic duty, but halfway there, as she heard her front door slam shut behind her, she remembered that she didn't have her keys on her. She ran back to twist the knob, hoping she'd disengaged the door's auto-lock, but knew that was wishful thinking.

She was locked out. Again.

"Fuck," she said.

Jacklyn pressed her forehead against the door and counted. This would be the fifth time she'd pulled this idiotic boner since moving into The Palmer Arms last summer.

Thinking back on it, she'd justified it to herself at the time by saying she'd needed a new experience, and there were jobs in her field in the city, and the rent was getting bad everywhere else too so why not. Plus, this "converted luxury high rise in a historic space" promised a gym, outdoor movies next to a rooftop cocktail bar, a laundry room, and nightly group functions. She'd hoped that she'd finally be able to meet some new people, her old friend circles having felt more like a noose for years.

But since the move, the cocktail bar had stayed empty, the outdoor movie schedule had lapsed to once every few months, and there were no real group activities to speak of. In retrospect, she shouldn't have been surprised. Who wants to hang around with their neighbors anyway? Who wants people nearby knowing all their business?

It didn't help that the building always seemed empty. Of the twenty or so units on her floor, she only knew for sure that four were occupied. The others sat in cold silence.

To be frank, she hated it here and she couldn't wait to get out as soon as her two-year lease was over.

Jacklyn rocked her forehead across the door as if rolling dough with a pin and closed her eyes. Her wooziness was incredible, and her mouthsweats soon returned.

She opened her eyes to relieve her dizziness. Eye-level to her door's peephole, she saw the blurry fisheye'd view of the inside of her apartment.

And then a figure walked past on the other side.

She pulled back her head and made a meek squeak of fear, dropping her mask to the ground. She unblurred her vision before returning to the peephole, but the walking figure was gone.

Suddenly, she heard a loud knocking rap on the door and felt the metal vibrate against her forehead.

She backed away as the shadowy figure returned in the peephole view, then she heard the lock on her door disengage.

The door slowly crept opened.

An old woman was on the other side. Deep brown skin, a sharp nose, three pronounced wrinkles running across her sweat-drenched forehead, her hair pulled tightly back into a ponytail.

"Hello, doctor," she said, gesturing for Jacklyn to come inside.

"Show me," came a voice.

It was deep and booming, resonating around Jacklyn but also through her as well, almost like she was hearing someone speak while she was underwater. It throbbed against her skull and tickled the insides of her eardrums.

"This way," said the old woman, and turned into the room.

Everything had changed.

White track ceiling lighting was replaced by scattered lamps with dim bulbs. The kitchen area was now a drab bathroom. There was a wooden desk where Jacklyn's bed had been. Even the geometry of the space had changed—it was now smaller, more cramped.

She followed the old woman around the corner past the closet where a bed sat in an iron frame. Atop it was a white sheet that seemed to squirm from within.

From it protruded a pair of brown feet, toes curled in agony. A wet cloth obscured the person's face.

The old woman went to the bed and slowly lifted back the covers and reveleard the patient—young, thin, her flesh coated in a sheen of sweat. She thrashed her legs back and forth, and the motion tore aside the bedsheets, disclosing her full, distended belly.

"How far along?" the disembodied doctor's voice said, now hovering somewhere in the space near the bed.

"We think seven months," the old woman said.

"What's her name?"

"Alice."

"Okay, Alice," the voice said to the woman in bed. "Let's see how you're doing."

The wet cloth was suddenly lifted from Alice's face as if held by some invisible force—blotchy skin, pursed lips, fluttering eyes searching the room in pain and confusion.

"We're going to help you out," the doctor's voice said.

The pregnant woman's arm raised and Jacklyn heard a series of taps against her flesh, then watched a vein rise. A moment later, she made out a small crease that soon became a puncture wound, and the arm slowly lowered back down onto the bed, the writhing ceased.

Jacklyn walked to the bed for a better look. The pregnant woman's eyes had steadied into a blissful gaze, one that now seemed partially aware of her medical condition, or at the very least where she was.

As Jacklyn walked, she realized that the woman's eyes were now tracking her movements as she approached.

"Let's begin," the doctor's voice said.

The metallic clack of a briefcase lock opening sounded somewhere near the foot of the bed. The sheet was yanked up with a flutter, and Jacklyn looked into Alice's dark eyes. They stared back with urgency, as if she was trying to say something.

The old woman held her down, so Jacklyn bent forward, but still couldn't make out whatever the young expectant mother was whispering over the room's growing commotion. Instead of communicating, they simply stared at one another—examining the other's iris, speaking silent mysteries from one moment in time to another—for a period that seemed limitless but also gone in an instant.

At some point Jacklyn realized a new being had entered the room. Its cries echoed through the room and the young mother broke eyes with Jacklyn to greet her new child.

Jacklyn woke up sometime the next morning, her face pressed against the carpet in the corner of her living room, now officially forty years old and incredibly hungover.

Later, when she left her apartment and found her werewolf mask still lying in the hallway, she simply picked it up, brought it back inside, and tossed it on the bed, choosing not to think how she'd ended up getting back inside.

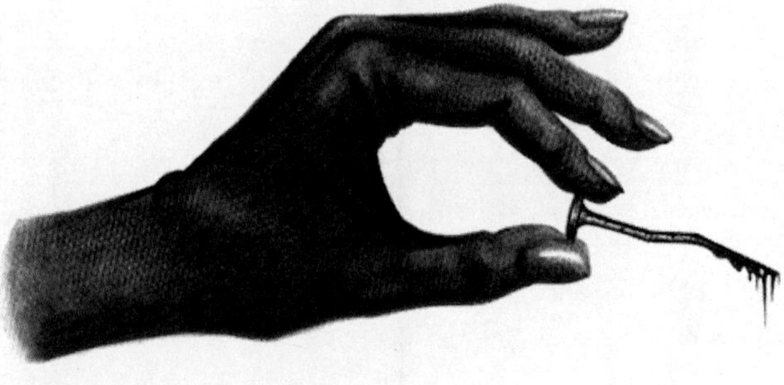

6. Gus Goes Home.
Room 207

"**A**NYTHING YOU WANT is on us," the handlers had told Gus when they dropped him off, so as soon as they scooted their asses out the door, he ran to the mini-fridge and cracked open a Bud.

He downed it in half a minute, crushed the aluminum in his bare hand, and banked it off the wall into the trash can. Then, he went back for number two, "his first real beer," as Gus had grown to think of it, the last one being more an aperitif.

He sat at the desk and unbuckled an end of his denim coveralls, letting his gut expand to its naturally curvaceous state. He'd just taken another sip when a powerful knock boomed against the door, so he set his beer down. It perspired a dark ring on the desk's wood.

He opened the door without peeping, and on the other side were his two lawyers. He'd forgotten their names already.

They wore dark suits and silence. The tall one carried a briefcase, the pudgier one only a grin and a handshake. They stepped past him into the room.

Tall pulled the desk away from the wall with a shoove, negligent of the can still resting on top, which Gus snatched before it tipped over. He sipped as the suits sat side-by-side on the bed, creaking the springs beneath them, Gus soon taking their cue that he was supposed to sit in the desk chair across. Tall opened his case and pulled out a stack of papers.

"This is what we're dealing with," Pudge said.

Tall fanned the papers like a deck of cards.

"This is all sworn testimony from others who've been fucked over like yourself," Pudge said, "people who've also had their hard-earned money taken for these union dues without say in the matter."

Gus drank and used his opposing hand to mimic a chin rub, trying to give off the impression that he was deep in thought.

"I'm just the husk," Gus said, then waving his hand over the stack. "Representing them."

"Well, not exactly," Pudge said. "You're part of this group. But for the lawsuit, we need one of you to physically be present, which is why you're here, living large in this lavish hotel."

Gus hacked phlegm into his open hand, wiped it on his jeans.

"So, I'm kinda like the boss," Gus nodded in understanding. "I'm in charge of all these folks here."

"No, not at al—," Pudge caught himself. "Actually, yeah, sure whatever."

Gus smiled proudly, but he was just fucking with them.

He knew the gist by now, he just didn't want to roll over for a tummy-scratch because these hacks said so. He wanted to make them sweat a little in their thousand-dollar suits, their polished shoes, their salaries that could afford actual city real estate.

It felt nice to be on the dominant end for once.

They'd approached him months back in a Des Moines diner while he was on a break en route to Indianapolis to drop off a shipment. Pudge had set three creased $20s on the table and said all they wanted was time to chat. He could even eat as they did.

Halfway through his burger, they told him that a settlement would grant him five years pay all at once, but as he dipped his last fry into the pool of leftover beef grease, they hinted that if he were willing to go even further, they could get even more together.

They said he could change the world.

"Why should hardworking Americans be forced to give their money away with no say?" Pudge had said, pounding the diner table in an act of frustration that Gus immediately read as performance. "So some union head can collect a six-figure salary for sitting on his ass all week?"

"I sit on my ass all week," Gus countered. "Doing it right now, in fact."

But Gus would be lying if he didn't admit the argument resonated some. Then, they promised Gus even more money down the line, and the argument resonated with him even further.

They'd traded information and told him they'd be in contact soon. A few more phone calls, then a verbal agreement, then the paperwork and the train ticket into the city for tomorrow's initial court hearing.

"Any questions?" Pudge asked.

"Don't see what they'd be," Gus said. "Show up tomorrow, shut up, look pretty."

Gus opened his mouth and flashed his yellowed chompers, their gaps filled with crud from his last meal, some rotten fish sandwich he got from the diner across the way. Not too shabby.

"Maybe not as pretty as that," Pudge said.

He stood from the bed while Tall stacked the papers back into the briefcase. They bid farewell for the day, but after a few steps, Tall spun around and glared at Gus.

"Six a.m.," Tall said, his first words all meeting. "On the fucking dot."

He turned his back and they continued down the hall.

Gus let the door close and crushed the beer can in his fist. He swished it into the trash can and retraced his steps to the mini-fridge, opened another Bud with a satisfying ker-chick, sat back on the bed, and sipped. He reached to the nightstand for the alarm clock, twisted its knobs for a 5:30 a.m. wake-up, and set it back down.

"On the fucking dot," Gus mocked out in a high-pitched voice. "Don't worry about me. I actually work for a living."

He sipped some more in front of the TV, and eventually the new episode of The Jeffersons came on. He reached for one last bedtime beer before turning it of, but made it only halfway through before passing out on top of the covers in his work clothes, same as usual.

Gus dreamt that dream he always did. He was floating above the highway in a seated position, watching the hot, black asphalt blur beneath his feet. He was still pressing the gas and manning the clutch, but the rig itself was gone. He just hovered in the air while cornfields on either side swayed in the breeze.

He passed under a highway sign that was painted the standard forest green, but the lettering was all scrambled into gibberish.

Then, in an instant, he was seated atop the sign itself, his workboots dangling over its edge, watching his truck as it approached over a distant hill. But as it came closer, he saw that it was being piloted by someone other than himself.

A new driver.

A stranger.

He was blurry at that distance, but still looked a lot like Gus. Broad-chested and wide-gutted, but freshly shaven. Sweat poured down his brow from under his red-and-white Local #90 hat. Gus could tell he was nervous about something—the stranger's knuckles, covered with red scratches and purple bruises, gripped the wheel.

Gus sat motionless as the truck passed below his feet. Suddenly he was behind the wheel. Not the invisible mass of his recurrent dreams, but his actual rig.

When he looked down at his hands, he saw they were now marred with cuts, like he'd just been in a brawl. Gus could feel that he wasn't in his own body anymore, and began to nervously tap his left hand against the wheel.

tap. tap. tap.
tap. tap. tap.

Ahead on the highway was an off-ramp. His hands or whoever's they were gripped the steering wheel and swerved to the right. Over the horizon, Gus saw that the ramp led only to open, empty space.

He tried to swing back onto the highway, but his hands or whoever's they were didn't respond. They held firm, aiming straight ahead into nothingness. He felt his foot depress the pedal, then the rumble of the engine below rattling his balls with faint pleasure as it picked up speed and shot up the ramp into—

Gus was in a rocking chair on a porch, watching the sun set beyond fields of corn. Someone behind yelled out "Lloyd!" so he naturally stood up and walked inside.

The screen door shut with a thwap behind him. Halfway down the hall, he felt a sharp pain, and looked down to see a long, rusty nail lodged in his left foot. He fell to the ground in agony.

A young boy with frizzy hair and a worried look on his brow came running up, a towel draped over his shoulder.

"Look what you've done now," the kid said.

He pulled the nail out from Gus's foot, and two drops bled onto the hardwood floor. The wound started to coagulate, and it itched something awful, then Gus tried to stand back up.

"Don't you dare," the kid said, holding him down.

Gus lay back, and he was now on a bed, looking up at the ceiling in his room at the Palmer.

He tried to move his toes, then his fingers, but no response. He stood up; his or whoever's body did, at least.

A tremendous sharp pain throbbed in his foot as he was guided to the bathroom. His hand flicked on the light, and he looked in the mirror.

Staring back was the stranger from the truck. Cold blue eyes, his brow full of nervous sweat, and now Gus noticed a fresh scratch running down the side of his face, crusting over into a scab. It looked ripe. Desperate to be plucked.

Gus felt his fingers run over the scab and they made a dry rustling sound, like flipping through an old book, like leaves raked into a pile. Then his thumb and forefinger circled into a tweezing shape and, after a few false starts, the nails got a hold.

His hand pulled downward and each new separation of scab and skin brought new pain in his face, fresh blood in the sink. He felt himself looking down and saw the entire basin stained with red and quickly filling, as if a spout had opened up.

It filled and filled, then went over the sink's brim and spilled onto the floor, first following the tracks between tiles before those canals overflowed and begin to run smoothly across instead.

The alarm clock went off.

Gus groggily sat up and cracked his head on the bottom of the bathroom sink. He pulled his hands from the cold tile and felt the first signs of a goose-egg forming on his head.

He stood up in a light-headed daze, and staggered back toward the alarm into a waft of stagnant beer from the unwashed and half-emptied cans scattered about.

"Fuck this," he said.

He grabbed his overnight bag, slung it over his shoulder, and went downstairs, leaving the alarm clock buzzing behind him.

The lobby was empty at this early hour. Gus passed through the revolving doors into the street and saw his breath in the cool morning air.

As he walked, he heard a few huffs from the ground to his left. There were three men resting against the building's brick exterior. One held a homemade poster calling for "Fair Wages Now!" tucked under his armpits and using it as a blanket. Next to them was a deflated balloon, folded and dimpled. Gus pried it open with his foot and saw the beady eyes of Scabby the Rat staring back.

Gus doffed an imaginary hat to the sleeping men, walked to the train station, and took the first express back home.

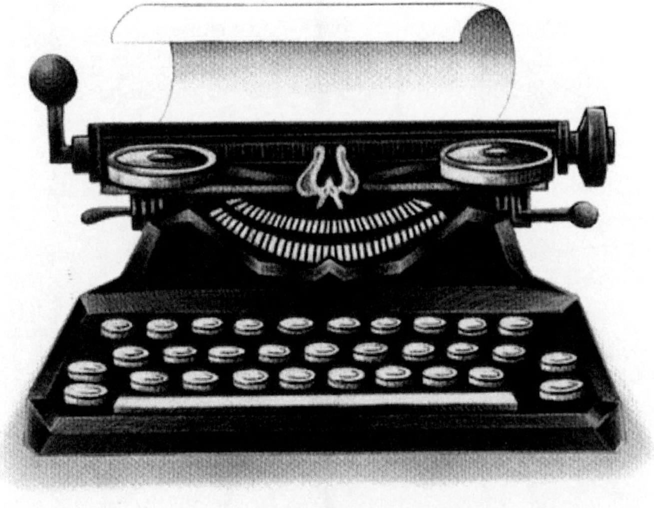

7. Henry Finds Out Where to Begin. Room 460

"**T**HE OLD MAN," as Henry liked to be called—even though he wasn't really, not quite yet—lugged the black fiberboard case up to his hotel room and set it on the desk.

He unbuckled the latches and lifted out his typewriter, licked his fingers, pulled out the first sheet of paper, and fed it through the rollers. He closed an eye to perfectly align the edge, then he began to type.

Then he began to type.

"Then he began to type," Henry said.

He plucked his fingers from the keys and took a sip of the scotch he'd poured twenty minutes ago, stroked his goatee, and looked at that empty page. After fraught contemplation, Henry decided that it was the desk's location blocking his inspiration.

He dragged the desk so it faced out the fourth-floor window then opened the curtains to reveal the courtyard, lit now in the evening light. And he began to type.

He began to type.

"He began to type," he said again, then sipped some more scotch.

Henry had booked the room at the Palmer Hotel for two weeks, loudly proclaiming to the front desk clerk upon check-in he was there to write his memoirs.

"A lot of interesting stuff to get through," he'd told the disinterested man with the pockmarked face and the long, broad nose, who'd simply mumbled something before handing over a key.

Henry stood up from the desk, picked up his scotch, and paced the room, still muttering to himself—"He began to type, he began to type, he began to type"— until he sat down again, gulped the remaining scotch, and began to type.

He began to type.

"Damn it," he said.

The problem with trying to do this memoir writing at his home was all the interruptions.

Sure, his daughter Janice had married and moved away over a year ago. And sure, he'd retired with enough money in the bank to keep him and Molly, now empty-nesters, financially secure into the foreseeable future. And maybe Charlie the dog didn't need as many walks these days after they'd had the fencing put in around the backyard.

But still, so many interruptions back at home. No way to concentrate.

These memoirs were something Henry had had on his mind for years now. Decades, even. Finally, he could tell it like it is, or like it was. Whatever the proper tense was in this case, he wasn't quite sure.

He'd blow the lid off of so many scandals that he'd witnessed during his time in advertising. So many stories about how he got extra press just because he'd gotten the right person drunk at the right time at the right party. Or how he'd finagled a rider for a top star to ensure she got a giant bowl of Cool Ranch Doritos in her trailer. And how about that afternoon he spent with Dolph Lundgren—very nice guy! And similarly intriguing stories that would surely render any reader rapt.

Surely.

"Fuck," he said.

All 55 years of Henry's slim build stood and paced. He looked at the phone sitting on the desk and realized that he hadn't eaten in some time, at least a few hours. Maybe that was the problem. He called the front desk to order a cheeseburger and fries, and then he began to type.

He began to type.

"I just ordered a cheeseburger and fries," he typed with a loud clatter. "I haven't eaten one in months, and I am looking forward to it. Because," he hesitated. "Because I am a dumb piece of shit."

Henry groaned and stuck his thumbs on either side of his nose to relieve the growing pressure building in his forehead. He gave them one last squeeze and, his eyes now blurry, looked straight ahead through the window overlooking the hotel's courtyard.

"I am sitting at a desk in Room 460 of the Palmer Hotel," he typed. "I am looking out of a window that faces into the courtyard."

He leaned forward.

"In the center is a glass structure with a small triangle in the middle of its roof," he typed. "This is the hotel's dining room. It's about six in the evening and I can see the shadowy blurs of people inside. One is wearing a red coat. It may be that older woman I saw earlier in the lobby, but it's difficult to know for sure."

His eyes drifted across the courtyard to the hotel's other wing.

"I'm in the North wing, which faces the South wing," he typed. "In the South there are a handful of windows lit from inside. One floor above me, I see a man eating a sandwich as he watches TV. Half the sandwich is resting on his bare stomach, and his feet are resting on the edge of the television set. It looks like he's watching Night Court."

He looked higher along the wall of windows.

"In what appears to be the penthouse," Henry typed, "I see a group of men in suits standing on the balcony. They're looking down on the courtyard with glasses of wine in their hands and cigars in their mouths. One of them spits off the balcony, and it hits the dining hall roof. He gives another man a high-five."

Henry lowered his gaze to the window directly opposite his own.

"I see a flutter in the white curtains across from me," he typed. "A small hand pulls them open, and now I see that it's connected to a young woman. She's in what looks to be a costume. Long skirt, grey blouse with frills. In her other hand she's holding a red rose. Its vibrancy contrasts with her paleness. She scans the courtyard windows, and now she's looking right at me."

Henry froze.

He shifted in his seat to hide behind the curtains, clumsily.

When he poked his head out again, the pale woman gave him a look of confusion and offered the faintest of waves. Henry waved back.

A dark silhouette in the shape of a man appeared behind her.

He wore a dark cloak that fluttered at the sides as he gracefully crossed the room which, from Henry's view, looked significantly larger than his own. Slowly the man approached. Hesitantly. As if sneaking up to surprise her.

The man reached into his cloak and pulled out a shiny object. As he stepped closer, Henry saw that it was a knife.

"Um," Henry said out loud to no one. "Lady?"

The woman tilted her head in a questioning glance and then turned her neck slightly as if hearing something. Her smile washed away, then the woman disappeared, the white curtains pressing against the window.

"Help," Henry said.

The curtains bunched and thrashed with chaotic movement.

"Help!" Henry screamed, alone in his room.

He dialed the front desk. Busy. He ran to the window and opened it, yelling "Help!" The only response was laughter and a mocking "Help me pwease!" from the jerks in the penthouse.

He slipped on his shoes and ran out of his room to the bank of elevators, pressed the call button one, two, three, four times, and finally gave it up for the stairwell. He took steps three at a time down four flights, exiting on the ground floor and catching his breath as he ran to the front desk.

Behind it was the same clerk as before, tall with a receding hairline and a sharp nose rising from a pockmarked face. His nametag read Gerald, and he held a phone to his ear. As Henry approached, he whispered one last thing to whoever was on the other end, then hung up.

"Can I help you?" the clerk said.

"A woman," Henry stuttered. "A woman's being attacked in the next..."

"Oh dear," Gerald said matter-of-factly. "Where?"

"Fourth floor," Henry said.

"Follow me," he said.

They walked to the South elevator bank and stepped into the first car. The doors slowly shut behind them before the lift's jittery ascension.

"We have to hurry," Henry said, out of breath. "We should've called the police."

"Before we go any further—" the clerk began.

But before he could finish, the elevator doors opened and Henry ran out.

There was an eeriness to this new environment. It was cold. The wallpaper was torn and hung in shreds. Stale cigarette smoke lingered in the air. Behind him, Henry heard a sparking sound and turned to see the clerk lighting up a cigarette.

"As I was saying," Gerald said, exhaling grey wisps and he walked down the hallway. "This floor hasn't been rented out in years."

"But I saw..." Henry started.

The clerk responded with a wave of his arm, inviting Henry to look around for himself.

Some of the floor's doors were cracked open, and beyond them Henry saw only the dark outlines of furniture, rooms void of any guests. At the hallway's end was a small curved alcove where an old yellow couch sat, its cushions torn and speckled with dark stains.

They reached the room directly across from his own where he'd seen the young woman. The clerk turned the knob on the unlocked door and pushed it open.

Inside were the basics: bed, TV, desk, mini-fridge. But no sign of a woman, a man, a struggle, a knife, or really anything at all.

"This used to be the old hotel's top floor, before they added skyward," the clerk said, jerking his thumb towards the ceiling, "and across."

He nodded to the courtyard.

Henry walked to the window and held the white curtains gently in his hands. They were intact, free of any blood or rips. The only sign of any occupancy was a faint spiral in the wall someone had seemingly carved decades ago.

He let the curtains fall and looked across to his room.

All at once, the courtyard was bathed in a glowing red.

Henry traced its origin to the North wing's rooftop sign. He looked again to his room and saw his typewriter glistening in the scarlet.

The small metal tag attached to its back glared as if on fire. He couldn't read it from this far away, but he knew what it said by heart.

"To the Old Man."

The typewriter had been a gift from his daughter, Janice.

She'd been premature. That was the first thing his mind always went to whenever he thought about her. The first few weeks were touch-and-go, with Molly in the hospital bed as Janice squirmed in the incubator. Whenever Janice's tiny mouth opened to cry, Henry had to keep himself from smashing through the glass just to hug her, to tell her that it would be alright.

"You ready?" the clerk said, stubbing his cigarette into the wall spiral.

"I am," Henry said.

Henry returned to his room and sat at the typewriter. He inserted a fresh page and began to type.

He knew where to begin.

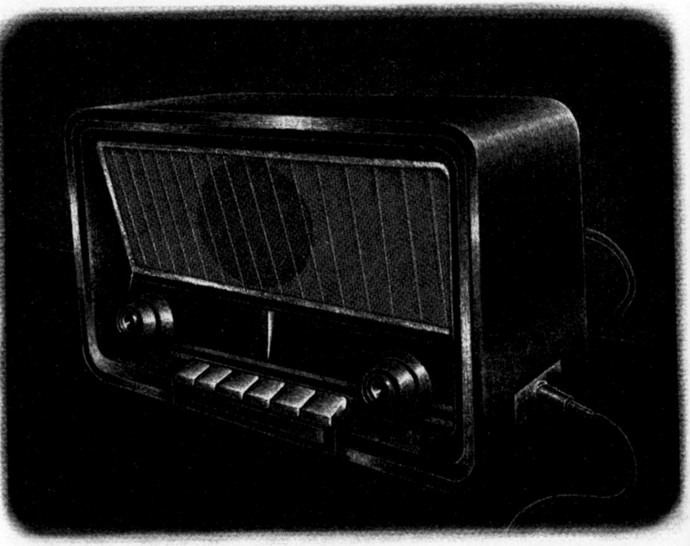

8. Vincent Retires.
Room 579

VINCENT SAT UPRIGHT in bed and stared at the clear afternoon sky through the window he had to close once the voices echoing through the courtyard had grown too loud.

He used a single finger to adjust the earpiece connected to his transistor radio. Curt Gowdy was on the call as the Orioles's Jim Gentle came up to bat.

"Muffet winds up and tosses the pitch, and Gentile swings and lofts the pitch to right field. Brooks Robinson tags up at third and Lou Clinton makes the catch, Robinson darts home, and the Orioles take a three to two lead," Gowdie said as an anticipatory murmur simmered through the crowd.

Vincent heard a muffled thud from the next room, so he yanked the earpiece out and set his radio down on the bed. He stretched his rubber gloves over his fingers, grabbed his work bag, and waited for the official signal.

It was a soft one-two-three-four knock on the door that connected Rooms 579 and 580. When that fourth beat rapped, he walked to the door and mimicked the four-count right back.

Vincent unlocked his side of the connecting door and, heard the other room's front door click shut, then the shuffle of feet in the hallway. Another gentle four-stroke knock on his own front door, which was the signal meaning that the other room—the kill room—was cleared for him.

He opened the connecting door and got to work.

The body was face down, blood from a head wound already seeping into a mushroom spread on the carpet. This was unfortunate.

Vincent knelt near the body and removed three towels from his bag to create a perimeter to stem the flow. With that accomplished, he stood and scanned the scene. The curtains were closed, the lamp was knocked over and cracked at its base, bloody brain matter and skull was stuck against the wall.

He walked to the kill room's front door, plucked the "Do Not Disturb" sign from the interior doorknob and hung it outside, then sprung the deadbolt.

The body was that of a large man with pale skin, its hair slicked back except for the sopping mass near the entry wound. It wore a tailored grey pinstriped suit, its arms lay near its head—some instinct to catch its fall perhaps, the body acting out of reflex, irrespective of the fact it wouldn't matter. Vincent had seen it before. A sour shit stench already came from the back of its pants.

Vincent reached under its jaw to inspect the exit wound, and within the red mess were splinters of bone peeking from its forehead. He set the head back on the carpet to imagine the bullet's trajectory, an exercise that took him to the wall between rooms.

The painting that hung above the desk had been pierced by the bullet, creating a small tear in the canvas. He'd return to it later.

He pulled out a plastic bag and wrapped it around the body's head to collect any blood that might leak during transport, then reached into his satchel and withdrew a nylon bag. I
nside was a bundle of pipes and screws and wheels that he laid out on the carpet, then spent forty-three seconds exactly putting together his rolling pushcart. It was only a few inches above the ground, but it made all the difference in the world. Vincent used to be able to carry them to the bathtub without fuss, but his back wasn't what it used to be.

He grabbed it by its armpits, took a deep breath, and hoisted the torso onto the cart. Next came the legs, then a cursory pass to check that nothing would drag, before pushing the cart into the bathroom. This is where the dismemberment, the big part of the job, would take place.

He maneuvered the cart parallel to the tub, sucked in another deep breath, then lifted the body over the tub's edge and dropped it inside. It could drain there while he administered to the kill room.

Paper towels and sponges took care of the brain matter that spackled the wall, a garbage bag was used to collect pieces of skull, tweezers for hairs and threads. He dropped it all into a large plastic bag then poured his bespoke mixture of cleaning ingredients onto the carpet. They fizzed the blood into a pink froth.

As the chemicals worked, Vincent unplugged the shattered lamp from the wall socket and carried its pieces back into his own adjoining room, pausing near the bed for a moment to pop his radio earpiece back in.

"And Woodling takes the pitch," Curt Gowdy said from miles and miles away. "Don Giles grabs the grounder and tosses it to Pumpsie Green coming over to cover second base. But all the action lets Ron Hansen hustle in from third base, so now it's four to two, Orioles."

He let the earpiece drop back on the bed and went to the desk, where he substituted the kill room's broken lamp for his room's intact one. It was a trick he'd used plenty of times over the years. It was always easy enough to tell the front desk that he'd knocked over his lamp accidentally and take a small extra charge to his check-out bill. He'd invoice that cost to his employers anyway.

Vincent returned to Room 580 and, the mixture having done its job, fiercely scrubbed the carpet. As it dried, he inspected it with his loupe lens and tweezed a few leftover organic fibers, then returned to the bathroom for the big job.

He pulled knives from his bag and sliced open the body's veins. Blood gurgled down the pipes. He cleaned the knives under the tub's faucet and set them on a towel to dry, then used his handsaw to carve through muscle and bone. Vincent was always pleasantly surprised at how easily a human body was dismantled.

When each piece was portioned out, he wrapped them in thin towels and slowly built a pyramid out of the long rolls. The head always came last, placed on top like a Christmas tree angel.

One by one he bunched the wrapped limbs into another plastic bag, an extra safeguard against leakage, and brought them back into his room next door, where he placed them in the empty luggage he'd brought along. When the transfer was complete, he returned to the kill room for one final cleanup.

He watched the last of the blood circle the drain, then scrubbed down the tub. He flipped off the bathroom light, retrieved his tweezers, and went to work on the bullet hole in the painting.

The print that spanned the width of the desk depicted a scene of an old man on a park bench. It was twilight, and a smoldering cigar between his fat fingers as he read from a newspaper.

It seemed to Vincent that the man was peering past the top corner of the newspaper, as if spying on something in the distance, but it was tough to know for sure as the bullet had pierced the man's inquisitive eye.

Vincent stepped onto the chair to lift the painting off the wall then lean it against the desk. A hole was revealed in the wall. He turned on his flashlight and stuck it in his mouth, then began extracting the bullet with his tweezers.

But as he tried to grip, his tweezers caught nothing but air and he heard a metallic echo as the bullet rattled through some hidden space on the wall's other side.

Vincent angled his flashlight through the bullet hole and saw that a thin passageway ran between the walls of this room and his own, and placed an eye on the hole. A few feet away, he saw that the darkness was lanced by a pinhole of light.

That was odd, Vincent thought.

He stepped off the desk and walked through the connecting door, hugging the wall to locate the pinhole in his own room. When he found it, he aimed his flashlight and looked inside.

A wooden chair had been wedged in the narrow crevice between the rooms, as if someone had set it up to watch.

A hot summer breeze came in through his room's open window and made a whistle as it streamed through the peephole.

He turned to the window to examine this incongruity—hadn't he closed it?—and saw a brief flash of light in the corner of his eye, then heard a muffled pop.

Suddenly, Vincent was no longer in control of his body.

It fell to the floor. Its cheek lay on the carpet.

It couldn't move, yet still felt a warm liquid seep down past its ears. It smelled an acrid smoke in the air, and heard the shuffle of feet on the carpet. It saw a pair of black shoes walk into view.

"—getting too expensive," it heard a deep voice mutter somewhere above.

Then it heard the tinny narration from the radio earpiece that still hung off the side of the bed.

"Everybody quiet now here at Fenway Park, after they gave him a standing ovation of two minutes, knowing that this is probably his last time at bat," the radio said.

It no longer remembered the announcer's name, nor what was even being broadcast.

"One out, nobody on, last of the eighth inning," the announcer spoke, "Jack Fisher into his windup, here's the pitch—"

The radio clicked off as the man in the black shoes stuffed the radio into a plastic bag that had already been filled with the rest of its belongings. The man then dropped to a knee and started to assemble his own rolling pushcart.

Motionless on the floor, it began to fear what next was to come.

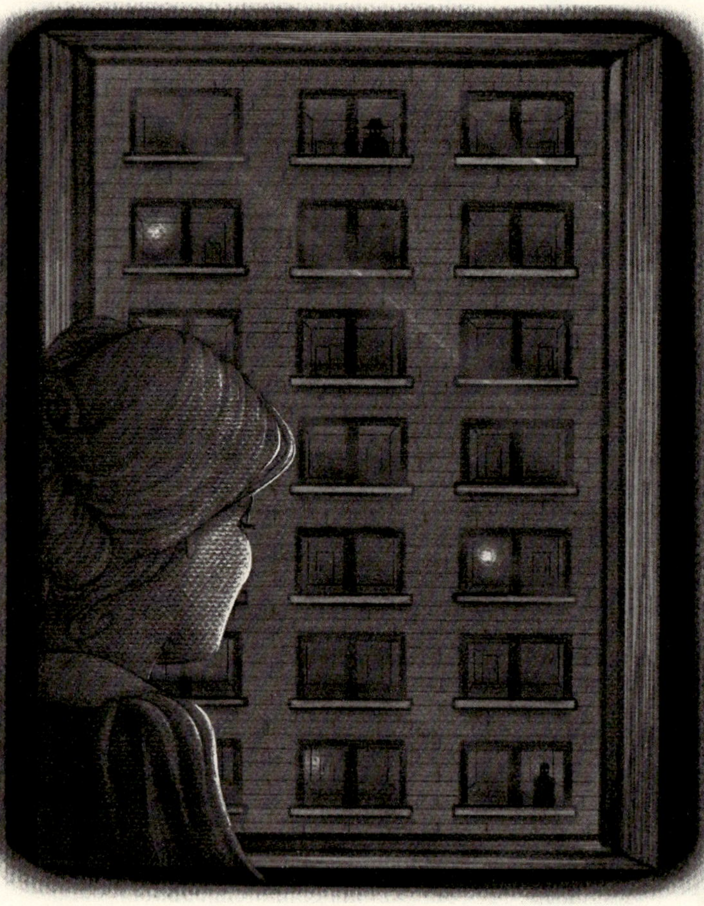

9. Lydia Meets a Bird.
Room 680

As THE DOOR CLOSED BEHIND LYDIA, the light from the hallway that had illuminated her path narrowed down to a sliver, then nothing at all, so she had to navigate the rest of the dark room's length from memory and feel.

When she finally got to the desk, she carefully removed her bowler-bag purse from her shoulder and set it down, making soft kissing sounds the entire time. She pulled the chain on the desk lamp and cast the room in an orange haze, then opened her purse.

Out burst a flash of white fur that leapt onto the vomit green carpet then under the bed, out of sight.

"I know, dear," Lydia said. "I know. I'm sorry."

She knew that it would take Phillip the Cat the Second a few moments before trusting her again, so she turned to the full-length mirror and ran a hand through her stark white hair, her fingers finding a tight curl.

She pulled it taut for a moment, then let it free to rebound, and there in the mirror behind her as if summoned by a spell was that regal white head poking out from below the bed.

"Been a long day for me, too," Lydia said, and slumped in a chair.

Phillip The Cat The Second crept out one paw at a time, looked up curiously at Lydia, then dug his claws into the carpet for a stretch and a purr. Lydia reached into her purse and found a small metal tin; this caught Phillip's interest. He strode closer.

Lydia opened the top, poured a few morsels into her hand, and tossed one into a far corner of the room. Phillip sprung, snatched the treat, and returned back for more.

Lydia threw another into the bathroom, and he vaulted and slid across the tiles, his nails tapping in the dark. He choked it down and came back for a third round. Lydia threw this one into the closet.

"Long day," was all Lydia said.

That was for sure.

They'd begun it in what felt like years ago in her apartment before taking the subway ride into downtown's Central Station, Phillip nestled in the crack of her curled arm. They still had an hour to kill before the train would arrive to take them halfway across the country, and only then, as she sat on a station bench, did she discover the train line's new transit policy—if Phillip was coming with, he'd have to be kept in the baggage compartment beneath the cars.

This obviously wouldn't do.

So, Lydia hustled across the street to the discount store and bought a cheap bowler-bag to smuggle Phillip in. She dubbed these accommodations "Purrst Class," and was proud of the name, but she didn't have the chance to tell anyone yet.

After an hour delay at the train station, then another, then one more for good measure, it'd become clear that the mechanical failure was more serious than the crew was letting on. A few hours more and they began distributing to all the passengers a ticket for the first train tomorrow and a voucher for a free night's stay nearby. She set out for the hotel rather than navigating the subway back home as it was really the only way the timing would work for her trip out of the city.

She needed to be on tomorrow's first train if she was going to make her sister's funeral.

Lydia hadn't seen Patricia in years. Last time was at the lake, after Dad had negotiated the terms to "the great Powell reunion" as he'd put it. It was an extended weekend with just him and his gals. Before that, Lydia hadn't seen Patricia for an even longer stretch, the last being when they'd met at that same lake to toss Mom's ashes off the back deck of the boat.

"The poop deck," Patricia had pointed out.

"What do you think she's up to now?" Lydia had asked, ignoring her joke.

"Cooking up a feast for the ranch hands, I imagine," Pat shrugged.

That's what they'd always called it—the "Old Ranch in the Sky." It was a remnant from grandpa and grandma, coined in that unique time of their lives when it seemed they had to face another friend's funeral every week.

"Time to send 'em to the Old Ranch in the Sky," grandma would tell Pat and Lydia as they were getting dressed.

"But before they go, one last hoedown," grandpa would say with a wink and slight shuffle of his feet.

The sisters had had their big falling out a year after the lake reunion, right after Dad died. It all happened over the phone.

It'd been brewing for a while, based mostly on Patricia's simmering resentment that Lydia had chosen to move away from their small town. It intensified when Mom had died, then boiled over when Dad joined her. Pat felt she was left with all the dirty work—the wake, the funeral, figuring out what to do with all the stuff they'd left behind. There was probably some truth to that, Lydia admitted, but really only to herself.

She'd thought they'd patch things up eventually, but that clock ran out, so here she was at the Palmer, the night before Pat's last hoedown.

She grabbed another treat from her purse and flung it listlessly at the wall, where Phillip the Cat the Second retrieved it with relish.

Lydia walked to the window and lifted it open to the sounds of the city night, a magical symphony she never grew tired of. The honks and shouts, the rattle of the elevated train, all swirling within the brick walls of the courtyard. It somehow comforted her, being surrounded by constant activity, human ingenuity, the quaint chaos of happenstance. It was something she never could get Pat to understand, and now it was too late to try one more time.

She felt Phillip's weight spring onto her lap.

"Okay, okay," Lydia relented.

She flung a treat hard against the front door, and Phillip scurried to get it.

She returned to the window and looked across to the Palmer's other building. Most windows were darkened, but two held backlit silhouettes. One a few floors above hers, one a few floors down, both figures appearing to stare out into the night, just as she was. It was hard to tell in this light—moonless, only the hazy red from the rooftop sign—but Lydia swore they were both staring directly back at her.

A loud knock on the door. She jumped at the sound.

She waited for a moment.

Another knock.

She crossed the room and peered into the peephole, but there was only empty hallway.

"Hello?" she offered.

No response.

She waited for her heartbeat to settle, then opened the door.

She stepped into the hallway, looked left then right. It was indeed empty, so she retreated back.

"Just the building settling," she said to Phillip.

But when she looked down, she realized she was only speaking to herself.

She ran to the bed and ached down on her hands and knees to check. A previous guest had carved some jagged graffiti into the bedframe—the shape of a spiral—but there was no sign of Phillip.

She hustled into the bathroom and flicked on the light. The white halogen bulb flickered once, twice, then caught. She made kissing sounds searching between the wall and sink, behind the toilet, then she pulled back the shower curtain to expose the filth-ringed bathtub.

Empty.

She opened the closet and pulled the hanging light inside.

Bare.

She returned to the bed and checked under one more time. Nothing except that spiral.

For an instant, a memory of Pat flashed in her head. Pat was in third grade, in some argument with Mom and Dad about whatever silly thing one disputes at that age, but this time she'd gotten so upset that she'd written out a note saying she was gonna go run away and live on her own. She'd left it on her desk and had opened the window, but instead of leaving, she'd hid under the bed. Lydia found her and decided to hide with.

"No, this is my thing," Pat pled, but Lydia wouldn't budge.

They waited for what seemed like hours in silence, quietly breathing as they stared into the bottom of that box spring, now and then elbowing each other for extra space, until Mom and Dad finally showed.

"Guess she went out the window and somehow put the screen back in," Dad had said loudly. "Ah well, better give all her stuff to Lydia then."

Lydia awoke to a car's blaring horn outside. She had somehow fallen asleep on the hotel room's carpet.

From the foot of the bed, she felt a soft breeze flow through her white hair, then saw the open window. There was Phillip, meowing from the other side of the swaying curtains, sitting placidly on the iron fire escape.

She jumped to her feet and grabbed a treat.

"C'mon, fella," she said, holding one out.

He didn't budge.

"C'mon, Phillip," she said.

He lightly stirred, and suddenly bounded up the fire escape stairs.

"Phillip!" she called out, then took the chair from the desk and used it as a step-stool to climb onto the iron grating.

The wind hit her like a cyclone and rustled her mop of hair into a puff of cotton. She pulled it back out of her way and waited for her eyes to adjust in the red of the rooftop sign.

Above, she heard another meow. She looked up.

Phillip had climbed up to the next platform and curled back into his tight ball.

"Come on, now," she said.

Phillip saw her, spooked, and leapt up another floor.

"Goddamnit," Lydia muttered.

Her bare feet felt the chill of the metal as she gripped the railing and pulled herself up the thin stairs to the next level, then the next, then the next, Phillip always one floor ahead, luring her higher and higher.

She kept calling out his name, feeling increasingly helpless and afraid as she ascended, but knowing even that wouldn't get her to stop.

On the tenth, the final floor of the hotel's North wing, she watched Phillip bound up the steep stairs onto the rooftop. She slowly followed behind.

The roof was a flat surface with scattered exhaust pipes jutting skyward. A single doorway—presumably hiding the access staircase—protruded from its center.

The dominant feature on the rooftop was the two-story-tall sign that announced

PALMER HOTEL

to the city in electric red. But from its rear side, behind the wooden beams of its massive truss, where Lydia crouched as she called for Phillip, it was just a mist of rouged haze and stark shadows.

Lydia scanned the roof—there on the distant edge was Phillip, curled in a ball. She reached into her pocket for the last treat she had and waved it in front of her like a lure.

"C'mon," she said, more out of exhaustion than anything. "It's cold."

Phillip didn't budge, so she began to cross the rooftop. As she walked, Lydia saw the city's ambient glow cast high against the clouds above, and heard the wind bring with it sounds of a faraway train whistle, then conversations from somewhere below, too faint to make out beyond scattered laughter and shouts.

When she got to Phillip, he was facing away from her, looking out into the night. She followed his gaze to a small cardinal perched on a wire running between the buildings. Lydia slowly approached Phillip, but then all at once, the cardinal fluttered its wings and Phillip crouched into a squat and leapt off the rooftop.

Lydia stretched her hands into the air over the edge and grabbed nothing.

But then she grabbed the air again—out of desperation, out of fear—and felt fur, then claw.

Excruciating pain lanced through her thumb and forefinger, as if they'd been torn down to muscle and sinews. Her body wanted to let go, to rid itself of this torture, but she knew if she did it'd mean the splattered end of Phillip the Cat the Second.

She sucked in a deep breath and felt cold air gather in the bottom of her lungs, then let out a loud wail.

Her fingers got a firm grip on the writhing ball of fur and, as she heard her own shout echo into the night, she pulled Phillip back into her cradling arms, soothing him until he stopped squirming.

She held him close and felt his warmth against her face, and she began to cry.

The tears came like icicles down her cheeks as they sat on the roof long enough for her arms to redden in the cold, for her bare feet to lose feeling.

Eventually, she said a little prayer and stumbled to the door in the rooftop's center, hoping it was unlocked. It opened easily and she walked down the interior staircase to the sixth floor, then into her room.

She shut the window and latched the lock, only then letting Phillip slip from her arms. She pulled back the covers, crawled inside, and the disobedient cat soon jumped in too and curled next to her affectionately.

She slept in well past the next day's first train, then the second and the third.

As she stroked Phillip's fur on the subway ride back to her apartment, she thought that was probably for the best. There wasn't much left for her in that small town anyway.

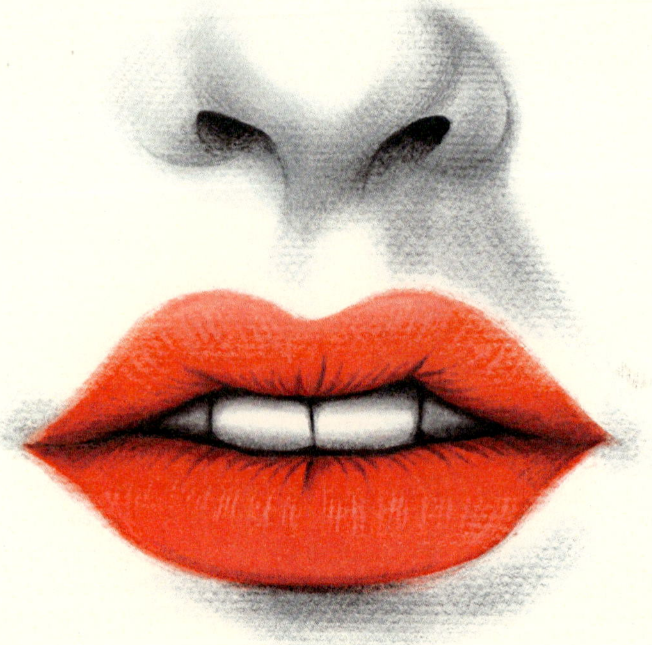

10. Graham Goes Through His Motions. The Fourth Floor

WITH THE TIP OF HIS FINGER, Graham traced a streak through the grime that'd coated the window on The Winthrop's top floor. Disgusted, he made a mental note to fire the young man in charge of this duty, but that anger all but disappeared the moment he saw her through the sliver of glass he'd cleared.

She was standing in the street below, her long, dark coat lit by the flickering flames of the gas streetlamps that lined the cobblestone street.

She looked as if waiting for the right time to pass between the carriages clattering down the avenue. At regular intervals, she'd step onto the cobblestones, then seem to feign a cramp in her leg, and turn back. She was trying, he reasoned, to lure new clients with her apparent helplessness and that faint purse in her deep red lips, the only color in her pale face.

Graham thought she almost looked like an angel.

He retrieved his vest from the closet, buttoned it up, and put on his long black cloak and black leather gloves. He grabbed his top hat off the nearby hook and left the room.

The sharp heels of his tanned leather shoes clacked and echoed down the hallway. He paused at the iron gate that separated this, his private floor, from the stairwell leading to the living refuse below.

Outside of the gate was young Isaac, alert in his chair. He inserted a key into the lock and pulled it open for the boss.

"Need a hand, sir?" Isaac asked.

"I won't be long," Graham said, descending the stairs. "You can retire for the evening."

"Yes, sir," Isaac said.

Graham walked down The Winthrop's four dusty flights, at this late hour lit only by gas lamps. The wooden banister was chipped and scuffed, loosened from its bolts. He'd have Isaac fix that later.

When he'd purchased this rickety structure years back, Graham had named it "The Winthrop" without any particular rationale. It wasn't a family name, nor an homage to something from his past, it simply sounded illustrious and vaguely continental. Something to sucker in the city's new entrants who were seeking "opportunity."

And sucker the suckers it did.

As he crossed the landings, Graham heard their dreadful symphony crescendo down the thin walls of the hallways. The bedframe creaks and fleshy, sweaty slaps. The night phlegm and drunken moans. The screams and shouts and open-mouthed slurps as the guests guzzled their slop.

Graham put these appalling sounds and ghastly smells out of his mind, choosing to instead preoccupy himself with the thoughts of what he'd be doing shortly with his prospective angel.

He reached the ground floor lobby and heard the grandfather clock ticking time away in the sepulchral room. He walked over to it, examined his reflection in the glass clockface, and used the aid of candlelight to smooth his mustache hairs, then made his way into the chilled October night.

Outside, a vendor was selling roses. He snatched one and paid with the flick of a coin that the vendor bit to judge its accuracy before sticking it into his pocket and handing over a rose in the trade. Graham snatched it, checked its smell, and crossed between the horse-drawn carriages to the lovely young woman.

"Lovely night," Graham said.

"Lovely," the woman said softly, her breath making grey wisps in the cool air.

"Got a gift for you," he said, extending the rose.

She took it in her small, spindly hand, inhaled deeply from its petals, and fluttered her eyes in such a way that gave away its choreography.

"A gentleman," she said. "And how might I repay you?"

Graham stepped to his side and with a flourish of his arm gestured to The Winthrop.

"That'll do," she said, taking his elbow.

They stepped between the carriages and into the hotel. Upon crossing the building's threshold, he removed his top hat, and led her to the staircase.

"How far?" she managed.

"To the top," he said.

"A true gentlemen, then," she smirked.

Another minute and they reached the gated entry to the fourth floor. Graham unlocked it and they passed through, letting the gate shut and lock behind them.

"Can't take too many chances in this flophouse," he said, pocketing the key.

She ignored his comment, taking in the floor's layout.

The hallway had eight doors, four to a side, each with a flickering gas lamp that cast stark shadows against the wallpaper, twin displays of miniature phantoms dancing to their own peculiar rhythms.

"Quite a lovely space, sir," she said.

Her host remained quiet.

The woman started hesitantly down the hall and noticed that, mounted in the spaces between the doors, were oil paintings nestled in ornate wooden frames. Each depicted a natural scene augmented by the progress of man. Forests felled to make way for a wide road, a rail line carved around a mountain rim, a dam strangling the passage of a river.

"Been to some of the lower floors before," the woman said, "never seen anything like these down there."

"You wouldn't," Graham said. "This is my personal collection. I paint when the mood strikes me. I would rather tailor the decor to my own specificities then be left to the whims of others."

"Smart, sir," the woman said. "Classy, too. Well, where we off to then?"

"That is up to the lady," he said. "Which room do you prefer?"

She unshouldered her long coat and let it fall to her ankles, exposing a long skirt and a grey, frilly blouse. She crossed the hallway with a flirtatious skip and grabbed the nearest door handle, then turned back to Graham, who licked his lips in anticipation.

She giggled as she withdrew her hand and continued on.

"I like this game," she said, letting her nails run across the vinyl wallpaper, making a prickly sound in their wake. "Any room, eh?"

She skipped across the hall again and reached for another door, put an ear against it, then pulled away, shaking her head with a mock look of fright.

"Tiger behind that one," she said.

Suddenly, she crossed to the opposite door, twisted the handle, opened it, and jumped inside, disappearing from view.

Graham leaned against the wall and with a smile on his face pictured the room she'd walked into.

It was his favorite, larger than the rest. There was a small rotunda in the ceiling's center, and along one side was a row of windows adorned with embroidered white curtains that rippled in the breeze.

On its walls hung his proudest works: the paintings he'd made of his angels—she would soon be one as well.

Graham closed his eyes and imagined these depictions. There was the tall woman with the green eyes swimming in an ocean, the short, brown woman floating on stage as if a magician's assistant, the meaty woman with that deep, hoarse laugh that he'd set on a horseback. The trembling light from the brass lanterns he'd set on iron hooks nearby made it appear as though the paintings were alive, as though the angels were still breathing.

He wasn't quite sure in what setting he'd place his newest one quite yet. Like the others, it would all be revealed in the moment and not a second before.

He considered tonight's moon, clear and rising above the patch of trees along the river. He considered how its light would shine upon her fair skin. How her eyes would be illuminated in pale moonlight and lantern orange as the life behind them faded away.

Graham began to count. When he'd reached ninety, he strolled to the door, and at one hundred, he stepped inside.

She was standing at the window, looking out onto the young city.

"It's quite lovely from up here, isn't it," he said.

As he approached, Graham watched her eyes in the glass reflection to see if they were tracking him, but her attention had been fully appropriated by the view. She continued staring out the window, silently.

With her attention diverted, Graham reached into his cloak, withdrew his knife, and lowered the blade to his side to conceal it—but only clumsily, halfheartedly. It was always safer when they were taken by surprise. That shock in recognition, their immediate resignation as the act commenced. But another part of him rather enjoyed it when they caught on early enough to steel themselves—to put up a fight.

He looked into the mirrored window; the woman now completely ignored him, focused intently at some strange point in the night sky.

Graham watched her raise her hand and offer a gentle wave, but he couldn't make out where it was directed. Then he watched the wave slow down as her eyes shifted and locked onto Graham behind her, then onto his knife.

She twisted as he lunged forward.

The hunt was on.

Graham's blade carved into the flesh of her side, piercing through and rending the curtain, but despite taking the blow, she'd spun free, and Graham's momentum carried him forward, pressing him against the window.

The impact jammed his wrist, and he winced as he turned to face her, but as he did, he sensed a flash of movement to his left—and felt the concussive impact crash down upon his skull.

Sometime later, Graham awoke with a huffing gasp. The back of his head throbbed. He traced his teeth with his tongue and tasted blood.

He twisted into a lurching crawl before pulling himself, grimacing, into a seated position.

The room was empty. The quivering gas lamps provided only dim amber, but in that faint light he caught a metallic glint on the floorboards.

He crawled to collect his blade.

She just had to choose this room, Graham thought.

While it was his favorite in decor, The Knife had its own challenges.

The Noose and The Broadsword gave enough distance from his prey, while The Revolver and The Crossbow turned marksmanship into a joyful exercise. But The Knife and The Poison were tied for the most difficult. And then, of course, the remaining two doors for freedom.

The odds were fair, he felt. Sporting.

Graham seized the knife and slowly stood back up. He steadied himself against the doorframe, then crept into the hallway, and saw that the iron gate to his private floor was still locked. He reached into his pocket and felt the metal of his key.

She was still here somewhere.

"My lady?" he said.

He began to open the remaining doors, one by one.

"Just a misunderstanding is all," he offered, before loudly admitting. "Forget that line. I don't disrespect you enough to imagine you'd believe that."

He finally opened The Revolver and saw her right away.

This room had a flat ceiling, a small bed in the corner, a row of windows facing the brick wall of the building next door. In the corner was an easel, placed here so he might capitalize on his regular fits of inspiration. The painting it held was now covered in a white cloth, and beneath it were the young woman's legs, quaking in fear.

"This doesn't need to be all that difficult, my love—" Graham said.

His words, however, were interrupted by a loud boom as a smoking hole appeared on the canvas.

It was all so very confusing to Graham. He heard the pitter-patter of her dainty footsteps running behind him—how? Stranger still was the smoke, in the air yet somehow also coming from inside his body. But the oddest thing of all was this new feeling in his chest, as if it was collapsing inward.

He sat down to consider all of this for a moment and his eyes turned back to his easel. The white sheet had blown away, revealing his work.

It was a piece he'd been tinkering with for months—a lonely lighthouse at the end of a cove, a wall of cresting waves approaching behind. The bullet had gone right through the largest wave.

Graham put a hand to his chest and pulled it back to examine his palm, now slick with blood.

He heard the screams of the woman echo down the hallway, then the clattering of the iron gate as she threw herself against it over and over again. But that was no longer any of his concern. Graham was transfixed by the painting.

The tableau of the lighthouse had come in a dream, but his rendition was not yet complete, he knew that. Something was still amiss. It lacked an essential element, leaving his vision as-yet unrealized.

He lay on his back, now more tired than ever, drowsing off to the shouts of the woman, crying for someone to unlock this gate. To let her through. To let her back outside, to her place under the street lamps.

Her wails died down as another voice came from the other side of the bars.

Isaac, his young study.

A key rattled in the lock, and he told her she had nothing to worry about, that he'd help her, that he'd get her to safety.

Graham sat back up, newly energized, and gripped his blade again. As he waited for his assistant to return with his clay, he considered again what his painting was missing, hoping it would come shortly as he created tonight's angel.

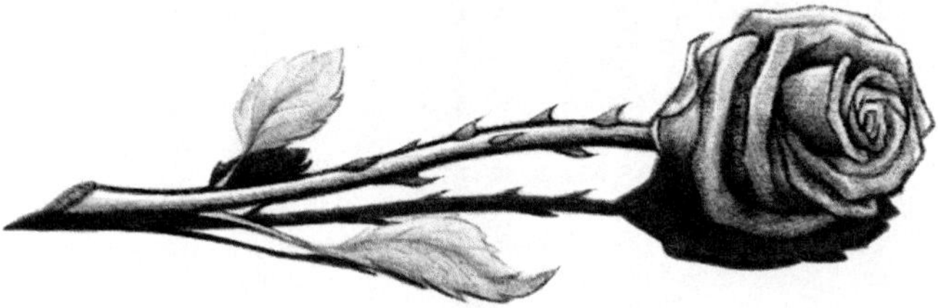

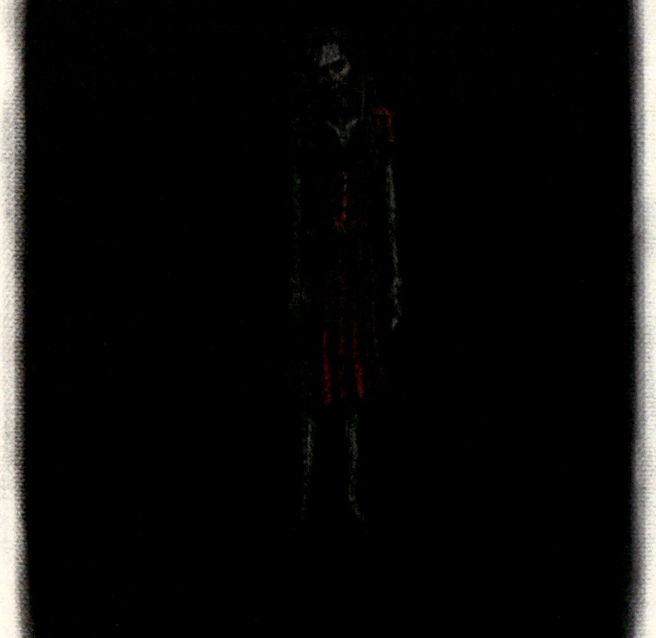

11. Leo Makes a Hit.
Room 708

LEO ZANN WAS A GROTESQUE LITTLE MAN with a scowl permanently etched into his face and thinning black hair that hung like a horse's mane down his hunched shoulders. He plucked a cube from the metal ice bucket that was emblazoned with a ₽ and plunked it into his glass of scotch. He retrieved a second then a third and dropped them in as well, and they settled with the satisfying sounds of fresh clinks.

He hummed to himself and dipped his raw, sinewy pinkie into the scotch and swirled the cubes for a moment before he retrieved and licked it, tasting the faint traces of alcohol as it stung the micro-cuts on the side of his tongue. He winced with delight.

Soft violin music floated into his room, and he stood from the desk and walked to the open window. He peered out to examine the courtyard, and while he couldn't locate the musician, he picked out the direction where it was coming. Northwest, into the setting sun.

He inhaled in preparation, then spoke his mind.

"Shut up!" he shrieked into the courtyard. "Shut the fuck up! You fucking loser! You piece of shit!"

The violin screeched to a halt. After a moment, it began again with a hesitant strum.

"Yes, I mean you!" Leo screamed. "What gives you the right to subject us to your bullshit! You louse! You incompetent bore!"

The strings scratched again and never came back.

Leo toasted to his own reflection in the window, then downed the rest of his scotch.

It was time for him to get back to work.

Leo had checked into the Palmer three weeks previous because he needed to make a hit, and he didn't have much time to lose.

He was at the tail end of his contract with Victory Records, the label that signed him after the success of Foggy Forest, his debut. Before the major label took an interest, he'd been tinkering on the album in fits and starts for a full decade. He'd jot down an idea here, befriend an underpaid talent who'd play for their dinner there, all the while putting away a few dimes at a time into his production fund. When all of those pieces were finally in place, he recorded it all in about a week.

It became an unlikely hit, and soon all the record labels were ringing him up. Most wanted a deal to re-release Foggy and then produce his next couple albums, but Victory wanted Foggy and upped their offer to his next *five*, so that was the end of negotiations.

The first two records post-Foggy sold fine, but failed to live up to the breakout buzz that had preceded them. The two after that were met with accusations that Leo had phoned them in, and they weren't necessarily wrong, but the more pressing issue was that sales numbers had reflected a lack of enthusiasm by the listening public as well.

This fifth album, then, was Leo's last guaranteed

paycheck before he became a free agent again. And who knew if anyone would want to take the risk.

Over the weeks at the Palmer, Leo's routine had cohered into a regular schedule. He'd wake up with a nasty hangover, down a pint of orange juice, and then, barring regular pauses for thrice-daily room service, he'd work. Unfortunately, "work" for Leo had come to mean "staring at the wall" or "writing random notes and then spending the night burning them up in his trash can" or "yelling out the window at annoying strangers."

Leo sipped from his glass in the quiet simmer of the city twilight, and after the sun fell completely into moonlit evening he finally walked over to the piano that he'd convinced Victory to cover the cost of installation. He hadn't played it once yet.

He rested his fingers on the keys but didn't dare press them. No, not yet.

He closed his eyes and a strange calm washed over him, as if a condensation was dissipating from his clouded view, as if now he could see the rows of pines in the forest behind the house where he grew up, swaying in a gentle breeze, making that rustling dulcet.

A baby began to cry.

Leo Zann's eyes shot open.

He examined the building façade across from him and soon found the silhouette of a young woman, a scarf draped over her head. She held a baby swaddled in cloth that had frayed at the ends, and Leo heard her cooing sweet nothings as she gently rocked her wailing baby.

Leo leaned out the window into the hotel courtyard.

"Shut up!" he shouted. "Some people are trying to work! It's not my problem you can't take care of your whining, sniveling little brat!"

The woman looked up, but didn't seem to see Leo in the darkened wall of windows. The baby's cry hesitated, then stopped entirely.

"You're welcome!" Leo screamed, slamming the window shut.

He went back to the piano and rested his fingers on the keys for another hour. Then another. Then one more.

He thought about his father, an organ grinder who would spend hours on the street corner, twisting the crank handle for tips as the children danced and cheered him on.

The trick, his dad had told him, was watching these kids. They were the audience, his tiny bosses, the ones directing how quickly or slowly he should be cranking.

Leo stood from the piano bench, left his room, and took the elevator downstairs.

The old grandfather clock ticked in concert with loud snores coming from behind the desk of the empty lobby. These belonged to Red, a thin man with a freckled complexion and trimmed auburn hair parted down the middle.

Leo lightly coughed into his fist, and Red twitched and nearly fell back off his chair before righting himself.

"Uh," Red said.

"Do you have a large room or something here?" Leo asked. "Something that holds a lot of people?"

"We have the Tabor Hall, sir," Red said, groggily standing up. "Best ballroom in the city, at least that's what management told me to say."

"Splendid," Leo said.

Red yawned and led him from the lobby into the hallway. They turned left and passed the bank of elevators leading up to the hotel's South tower before coming upon a set of double doors.

Red pulled one open to reveal a cavernous room with a ceiling that rose two stories high. It was completely dark, lit only by a single bulb off in the distance toward the bottom of what looked like a stage.

"This work?" Red asked.

Leo's brightening face told him that it would.

Red flipped on a light switch and the new brightness revealed the entire room—a second-floor balcony with rows of velvet-lined theater seats wrapped around and loomed over the dance floor. In the room's center hung a massive, sparkling chandelier. Leo was overjoyed.

But then, in this new harsh light, he also saw the faded colors of the walls, the dust and grime that had accumulated over the years. There were even specks of confetti still littering the floor's corners from some previous celebration.

He shut his eyes and grimaced.

"Off!" he shouted. "Turn them off!"

Red flipped the lights off, pitching the room into darkness except for the single bulb at the bottom of the stage.

"You can now leave," Leo said, and Red went back to doze in the lobby.

Leo placed one hand to his chest and curved the other out in front of him as if cradling a dance partner, then began to sway awkwardly and his footsteps rapped on the slatted hardwood and echoed through the spacious room.

His knees didn't work like they used to, his muscles growing more constricted with every passing year. He began to hum, out of tune.

"And we danced," he mumbled, trying to force the syllables into a melody. "We can never stop dancing. We can never stop. Dancy dance dance."

He nearly retched at the atrocious sounds he was making.

"You piece of shit!" he yelled to no one, to himself. "Get it together you talentless hack!"

He took a breath, shut his eyes, and began to sway again. Smoother now, finding some sort of vague rhythm.

Leo Zann imagined that he was moving through a crowd of people spinning around him in a loose sequence. These would be the dancers, the ones he was really writing the music for.

His audience, his bosses.

Leo's knees loosened and his heels tapped out a staccato rhythm.

"And we danced, we danced," he quietly sang.

He pictured the dancers again, and he swore he could actually feel their body heat as they surrounded him. He imagined the women in their long dresses with pearl strands clasped around their necks, and the men in suits and slicked-back hair who held their partners close. He thought about those populating the ballroom's upper balcony, the darkened spaces where secrets were told, where gossip was spread, where couples were made and rivalries born.

This, Leo thought, is what the job was. Not making money for Victory Records, but creating the right atmosphere for where these moments could take place.

His eyes still shut, Leo picked up his pace, and suddenly felt a new presence nearby.

She was a few inches shorter than him with long brown hair, and she wore a red dress in a style he couldn't quite place. She danced alone, her steps in perfect rhythm, her arms swaying around her body. As she moved, the crowd parted to give her more space, almost as if she was in command of their movements as well.

Somehow, Leo Zann knew that if he opened his eyes, this woman would disappear from him forever.

Now, as he moved, he was certain that the crowd around him was real—that they were all really there. Not just fictions he'd conjured up, but presences with flesh and bones and sweat.

They encircled him, swaying to the music he

hummed. Their conversations sounded near and far all at once, like his ears were popping. One fretted about a conflict with a neighbor, another was happy about a raise at work.

And there in the crowd was that woman in the red dress again. She turned to Leo and he saw her eyes, an alluring aqua blue.

She took his hands in hers and he felt their warmth.

The two began to dance in sync, but she was decidedly in control. Any discomfort he'd had in his joints was now gone. His hunched shoulders had straightened up, even his scowl had smoothed.

She leaned forward to whisper in his ear, but he couldn't hear—the music was too loud.

"What!" Leo shouted.

She spoke again, but her voice was again drowned out by the music. It was a four-on-the-floor beat with a crescendo that peaked around the third note.

"I can't hear you!" he shouted. "Because of the damn music!"

The music.

His eyes shot open.

The woman in red stood there with a faint smile—but only for a moment before she faded away.

Leo was left all alone in the ballroom, darkened save the lone light near the stage.

He searched his pockets for paper and a pen to capture what he'd heard in his head, the tune that he'd been humming, but when he came up empty, he sprinted through the double doors and took the elevator back into his room, where he ran to the piano and began to play.

Meanwhile back downstairs in the hotel ballroom, the souls continued their anticipatory linger, waiting for Leo's music to return.

Interlude I.

I SINK BELOW TO THE GRAND DANCE and twirl for awhile, then I float away and open my eyes.

I hear the clock's pendulum ticking in the dark corridor, and through the half-circle of its glass face can see the lobby. Between the hour and second hands of the clock, there is the one who killed me.

He taps a finger against the front desk to the pendulum's rhythm, and he stares at the clock, but not into it, not at me, here on the other side.

I hear the squirming, squishing coterie approach from behind, and I'm again enveloped within its tendrils, warm and slick. They steer my arms and legs, my head, fingers and eyes. I can feel them inside me too, controlling what's left in there.

They spin me from the lobby back into the hidden corridors, then through their predestined pathway, their camino real, up to the eighth floor. Through another portal I see the courtyard, bathed in moonlight and flickering red, and the limbs move me again.

I'm in a corridor dotted with pinholes of light on all sides, like a night full of stars. They bring me to one and push my head to look inside, but then I hear a shuffling behind me. The coterie twists me around to face my assassin's faded outline.

It has a dark aura with fuzzy outlines, a jittering interior. Its movements blur on approach, then I feel the sharp pain in my guts, fresh like the first time.

The arms waltz me back down the corridor and force me against the ground, force me to tap.

tap. tap. tap.

They hoist me up again to leer through the portal into the courtyard's glow, almost as a taunt before the limbs squeeze my insides, making me scream.

She falls away.

I sink below to the grand dance and twirl for awhile again.

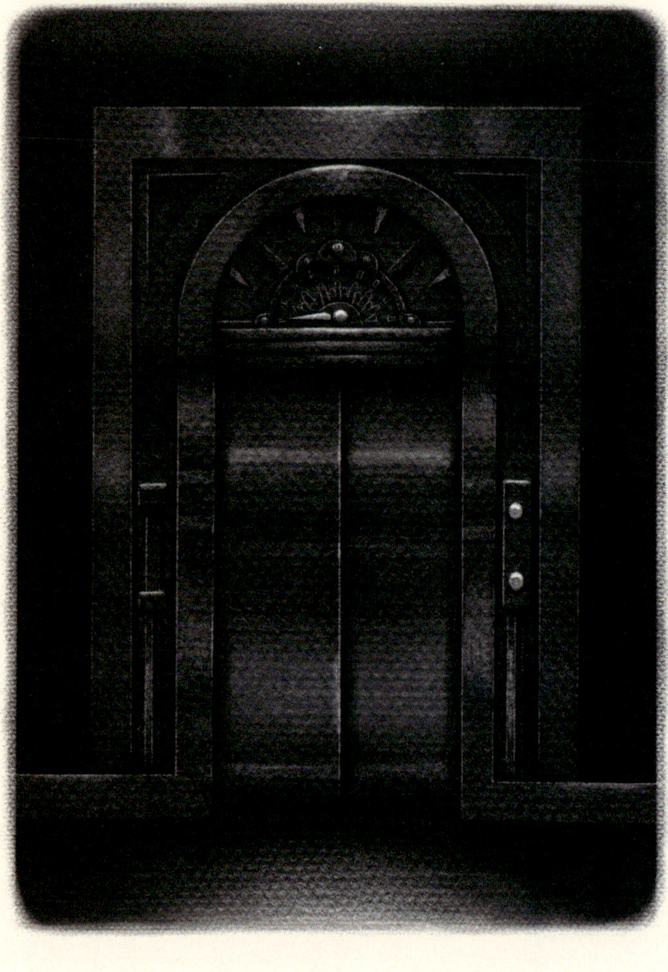

12. Laurie and Fred Catch Up.
The Anchor

LAURIE TOOK ONE LAST DRAG outside and exhaled into the night, and the smoke blossomed into a cloud of glowing red, courtesy the Palmer's historic sign high above.

She squibbed the cigarette under her sneakers and peered through the glass brick into the hotel's ground floor dive, The Anchor. She could make out only blurry silhouettes, so she pulled open the dented brass door and walked inside.

Blinded at first by the harsh glare from the old cigarette machine, she looked deeper into the bar to let her eyes adjust to the darkness. Once they did, she saw velvet-lined booths to her left that were half-populated by couples, their limbs desperately intertwined.

Fred wasn't among them.

She walked to the bar, a wooden half-circle with

a wall of dimly-lit bottles behind it, took a stool at the far end, and examined the two drunks at the bar's other end.

Both were in their 50s wearing collared shirts with loosened ties and clean-shaven, pasty faces with above-lip dampness that reminded Laurie of her dad. Judging by the empties on the counter, they were each at least half-a-dozen beers deep.

She ordered a tequila sunrise from the hefty, smiling bartender, then listened to the drunks rant about the approach of Y2K.

"Been storing up cans of beans!" one shouted to the other, even though they were seated adjacent and the bar was quiet. "We're gonna eat 'til our farts blow down the doors!"

They laughed with great volume and wetness, and complete disregard for social niceties and their own self-consciousness, the stuff that comes when happy drunks are deep into their cups.

"What do you think's gonna happen?" the other yelled back. "How do broken computers mean you can't get beans?"

"It's all supply lines, Joe!" the first shouted back. "All the supply lines are on computers! No computers, no bean supply, and no beans!"

They laughed some more.

Laurie suddenly felt a presence behind her, then a meek tap on her shoulder.

"Sorry I'm late," she heard, and there was Fred alright. "It was a longer drive than I'd remembered."

"Fred. Fred. Freddie," she said, going in for a hug. "It has been some time," she whispered in his ear.

The last time they'd seen each other was nearly a decade ago during that frantic summer.

They'd been friendly in their high school years, overlapping in each others' social circles but never on a daily-phone-call level of connection. That changed the summer before college, when everyone was playing makeout musical chairs in the hopes of staving off future regret.

They'd first made eyes at the Watson twins' graduation pool party. The week after that, they kissed at Gary Yurtz's BBQ, and were essentially inseparable over the next month of last hurrahs. Then, their respective paths simply diverged—he stayed in the suburbs for a community college track while she moved across the country to get her Bachelor's, then a Master's.

A few months ago, alone in her studio apartment one night—and, admittedly, after a few drinks—she'd sent him a catch-up email that concluded with her AOL Instant Messenger screenname, CrookedRain_69. The next day, her desktop computer dinged with a new message from FryedChyken00. They traded messages, and when she mentioned a trip back home, he'd suggested this joint for a catch-up drink.

"What are you having?" he said, sitting on the stool.

The years had been kind to Fred, Laurie thought. His skin was clear, the new beard suited him well, and his nerdy wire-framed glasses were gone. His frame was fuller than the twig she remembered, but not out of shape. Just more like a man.

"One more tequila sunrise, por favor," Laurie said to the bartender.

Fred held up two fingers and the bartender got to mixing.

"So, what brings you back?" he said. "Been keeping the town nice and warm for you."

"I can see that," she said. "Haven't seen my family in a while."

"Of course," he said.

As the bartender returned with their orange-tinged drinks, Laurie began to breathlessly relate to Fred all the facets of her new life. She was handling accounts for a production company out west, but didn't love it.

Working in Hollywood wasn't as glamorous as one would expect, but she did meet Robin Williams once.

"Very nice guy," she said, before dipping into her wallet for a photo of her cat Snickers. Fred made the requisite "aww," and she put it away.

"God, these are such sad bullet points," she said. "What about you?"

Fred turned to the bar and glanced at the mirror behind it as he took another sip.

She noticed a strange weariness in his eyes, and it was then she put together there was something different about Fred. That old casual ease she'd remembered, that had shown itself once again in their IM conversations—it had all but disappeared.

Fred finished his sip and turned back. He told her how his parents had taken a gamble on a city apartment as an investment, but after a few years, decided to kick out the tenants and take it for themselves. So now he lived on his own in their old three-bedroom back in the suburbs. Hank and Jessie came by almost every night.

"Remember those clowns?" he asked.

"I haven't heard those names in forever," Laurie said, a broad smile forming on her face. "How are they?"

"Same as ever," Fred said, finishing the drink and tap-tap-tapping his fingernail on the bartop for a second. "Same as ever."

He told some stories of their recent exploits, but his voice was joyless, monotonous. As if he'd rehearsed the tales. As if he'd repeated them to himself over and over and over again.

"The end of the world I say!" one the Y2K drunks shouted. "The end of the world!"

"Wanna bet?" yelled the other and reached into his wallet.

"You know, I think about you a lot," Fred quietly said.

The voices of the drunken wagerers faded into the background.

"And what do you think about?" she said.

"How things could've been different if you'd stuck around," Fred said.

"Oh, I was out of here no matter what," she said. "You know this place couldn't contain me."

She placed an arm around him and gave his bicep a squeeze, and she felt him tense up so she unraveled her half-hug.

"Anyway," she tried.

Fred excused himself to the bathroom and back walked the bartender, who introduced herself as Barbs.

"You two doing alright?" Barbs asked.

Laurie held up two more fingers and Barbs spun around to make another set of concoctions. Laurie looked around for anything worth seeing and noticed the wall next to the bar. It was covered in dollar bills.

She leaned forward and saw names scrawled in black market on each one.

"What's that?" she asked.

"War deposits," Barbs said. "This place goes back to long before the war, one of the last stops before the boys were sent overseas. They'd have a few last drinks in here, something to fog up their nerves before what was to come, and spend the night upstairs before shipping off in the morning."

Barbs poured the shots of tequila onto some ice and stirred in the orange juice as she nodded to the dollars.

"Some made down payments on their next drinks, so they'd have something to celebrate with when they came back," Barbs said. "Which is to say, what you're seeing here are the dollars left behind by the boys who never did come home."

She set the drinks on the bar and told Laurie that these were on the house.

Laurie sipped.

This round was a lot stronger than the last.

She turned towards the bathroom and was startled to find Fred already standing next to her, only a foot away, a strained smile on his face.

"Sorry," he said. "Seeing you again brought back memories, but now they're gone. Can we start over?"

They spent the next hour forgoing mentions of the past in an attempt to find some contemporary overlap.

She chatted some more about her celebrity sightings, a few of the new movies she liked, the anthropological eccentricities of California culture. He brought up the local sports team, how his parents were loving their life in the city, and a few more recent exploits with those clowns Hank and Jessie that sounded remarkably similar to ones she vaguely remembered from their high school days.

Nearing midnight, a few drinks deeper, Laurie put another arm around Fred.

His tension had dissolved.

After midnight, he reached into his pocket and withdrew a hotel key that he set on top the bar.

"Interested in a nightcap upstairs?" he asked.

She said that sounded nice and closed out their tabs, giving Barbs an extra hefty tip.

They exited The Anchor's back door into the Palmer's lobby. The ceiling was a dim grey from cigarette smoke, and a few guests—or maybe loiterers?—were slumped on couches that were in dire need of new upholstery.

Fred placed a hand on the small of Laurie's back and led her past the front desk, where a tall man with a pockmarked face ignored them as he stared at time ticking away on the grandfather clock.

They walked into the hallway and turned right towards the bank of elevators. When one opened, an old man in a scarlet bellhop uniform was already inside.

"Going on up, so come on in," he said with a smile.

"Hoight's my name and elevatin's my game."

Laurie giggled, but Fred remained stone-faced as he pressed the number seven.

The doors closed.

"Ask me how my job is?" Hoight said, breaking the silence.

"How's your job?" Laurie asked.

"Oh, it has its ups and down," Hoight said.

His loud chuckle clanged through the car, and the old elevator rattled to life and began to rise.

The bellhop faced the elevator doors, but in the reflective silver, he made eye contact with Laurie.

"You two coming from The Anchor?" Hoight asked.

"Indeed," Laurie said.

"Best bar left in the city," Hoight said. "Happen to see those dollar bills?"

"Barbs told me all about them," Laurie said.

"As she does," Hoight said.

Her eyes shifted to Fred, who stood silent, almost brooding.

In the reflection, she saw his jaw clenched, his brow strained and stretched, a vein on his forehead visibly throbbing. She glanced down and saw that his hand was tensed into a tight fist, his nails gripped deep into his palm, as if ready for a fight.

"Know what I think about those dollars?" Hoight said, then answered his own question. "You can't know if those men died in the war, or if the experience of war just changed them enough they didn't want to go back to their old lives."

The elevator slowed to a creep as it neared the seventh floor.

Laurie snuck another glimpse at Fred's balled fist, now gripping so tight that his hand shook. His knuckles blared white and the rest of his curled fingers flushed bright red as his hand trembled.

The elevator stopped.

"You know what they say, they say a man can never step in the same river twice," Hoight said. "And it's not only because the river has changed, what with the water flowing and shifting and moving this whole time—but that the man has changed as well."

And then Laurie saw a single drop of blood fall from Fred's strained fist onto the elevator floor. It left a small dot of red and slowly spread away as it soaked into the carpeting.

The elevator dinged, the door opened.

Fred nodded, forced a strained smile at the bellhop, stepped out, and started down the hall, the keys to the room rattling in his hand that, to Laurie, sounded like a jailer walking through the cell block.

"Well, goodnight," Laurie said to Hoight on her way out.

He said it back.

She turned around for one last look, and she saw something sad in the bellhop's eyes.

There was a certain weariness, like he'd seen all of these same cycles repeated over and over in his life, and even though he did he was always helpless to change them.

"Oh shoot," she called out to Fred from inside of the elevator. "I left my wallet at the bar."

Fred spun around in the hallway but Hoight was already tapping the door-close button.

"Wait!" Fred screamed through the hallway. "Don't fucking go! Don't leave me again!"

"Be right back," Laurie offered, and the doors slammed shut.

As they rode down in silence Laurie saw the bellhop's face flush with a hint of some strange joy. He straightened his back and smoothed out the wrinkles in the arms of his red coat with a sense of earned pride. His nostrils flared and she saw his eyes begin to water as if he was about to cry.

When they reached the ground floor, Hoight wished her a good night and she responded in kind. And then Laurie hustled through the empty lobby past the thunderous sound of the ticking grandfather clock, out through the front revolving doors and off to anywhere else as fast as she could.

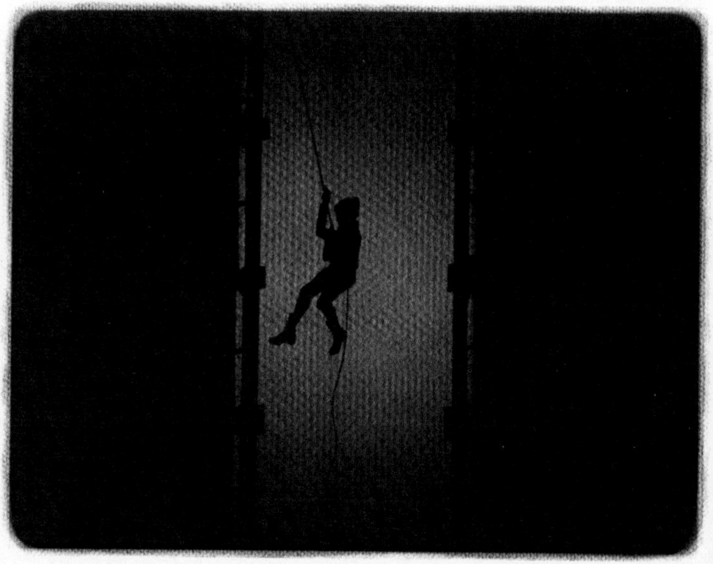

13. Edie Debates a Score.
The Penthouse Suite

The second hand on Edie's wrist watch dragged itself to 3:57 a.m. and triggered the lever that released the pent-up hammer. The alarm buzzed.

Like an automaton she sat up in bed, twirled her feet to the carpet, and walked to the window to examine the night sky. Through the scarlet haze from the rooftop sign she saw it was clear save a lone black cloud, with the moonlight bright enough so she wouldn't need a flashlight.

She closed the curtains and turned on the desk lamp, illuminating the suitcase she'd prepped last night on the room's luggage rack. She cycled through its combination lock, it popped open.

She unfolded, then stepped into her outfit: custom-fit black wool pants that kept a tight contour around her legs; a long-sleeved black turtleneck she tucked into her pants; black socks; black high-tops;

leather gloves; black ski mask.

She unrolled a small hand towel with her single-shot pistol and stuck it in her pocket.

She hoisted her gig-bag over her shoulder, flipped off the lamp, crawled out the window onto the fire escape, and began to climb.

Over her career, Edie had learned that the trick to a rapid ascent wasn't trying for speed, but simply maintaining a rhythm. When feet and hands were perfectly in sync, quickness was a side effect.

In less than a minute, she'd climbed seven flights and was outside of the Palmer's penthouse suite. She pressed a gloved hand against the window to jar it from its frame, but after a millimeter of movement, it caught the interior lock.

It was worth a shot.

She climbed the ladder to the rooftop and poked her head above the ridge to make sure there wasn't some graveyard shift worker up there on a smoke break. With the coast clear, she ascended and removed the thirty-foot length of rope from her bag, tied a slipknot, and hung it around a pipe. She tested its strength and, satisfied, rappelled down the bricks of the building's side.

Edie hated exterior entries.

She'd last pulled a job like this way back in '49, when she was in her mid-20s and in better shape, or at least more confident of her invincibility. But purses in the tens of thousands, like the one waiting only a few walls away, didn't come around too often.

The current occupant of the Palmer's penthouse was one Gregory Hurst, a gangster from Kansas City who'd come into the city last week to put the finishing touches on his relatively simple boxing scam, the classic kind where the heavy favorite took a dive in a predetermined round.

The only unique bent to Hurst's plan was spreading

the bets across twenty accomplices, each of whom walked away with a cut.

This plan was meant to accomplish two goals.

First, the number of people would mitigate the stink of the fix before it took place. Second, and primarily, it would send a message to the city bosses when they inevitably got wind of it. For Hurst, this wasn't just a way to snatch dough for his operations back in Kansas City, it was an advertisement that there was a new man coming into town, one they'd have to get used to dealing with.

It was a taunt: a show of power, a display of resources, a demonstration that he could get so many local bookies and bettors to play along. This is what other bosses feared the most—a new boss with a cohesive and bonded gang coming into town all at once. And that fear, warranted or not, would be needed by Hurst to stake his claim on the city's take.

But Edie had gotten wind of the scheme, too.

The nature of the plan meant that all twenty bettors had to show up at the hotel after the fight was over and they'd collected their winnings. They'd take their cut, give the rest to Hurst, then scurry off back into the shadows and wait for the next plan.

Earlier on, right after midnight, Edie had sat in the lobby to watch the procession from behind a newspaper, seeing each and every one come in, go upstairs, and quickly leave again through those front rotating doors with a fresh spring to their step. A few faces looked familiar, but they wouldn't notice her in the dowdy outfit she was wearing. Women that were dressed like her blended into the background for guys like these.

After the twenty showed and left, she returned to her room for a few hours of sleep until her alarm buzzed, and then it was time to climb.

On the rooftop, Edie pulled the rope taut, wrapped it over her shoulder and under her leg to form a kind of pulley chair, then clambered along the wall to the penthouse's next window. She pressed and it slightly shifted in its frame, just like it had two nights ago when she'd cased the spot.

She reached into her pocket and removed a metal tool, slipped it under the frame, and flicked open the lock with a tweak of her wrist. She pried open the window, snuck a foot inside then a knee, and limbo'd the rest of her body through.

She left the rope dangling behind for her egress.

As soon as Edie hit the hardwood floor, she heard loud bassy snores coming through the door leading into the next room. That's where the slumbering Hurst and his money would be.

The wall of curtainless windows allowed her to guide herself by the moonlight through the array of furniture, which had been dragged around the expansive room into a haphazard array, almost like intentional barriers. After a stressful minute, she was through the maze without making a sound.

Edie grabbed the bedroom doorknob and began to twist it gently, but just before it was nearly free of the catch, she heard a faint ding behind her.

She spun around.

It came from beyond the door leading into the foyer for the penthouse's private elevator. The ding was followed by the sound of the elevator doors whooshing opn, then a pair of muffled gunshots and a concussive thud as someone, likely Hurst's guard, hit the ground. Edie then heard the soft metallic screech of a lightbulb being loosened, and the sliver of soft yellow from under the door blinked out.

Edie let go of the doorknob and walked briskly to the piano in the corner next to the bedroom wall. She gracefully stepped onto the wooden bench, grabbed the piano's top, and slowly lowered herself into the cramped space behind.

She squatted down and reached into her pocket for her pistol.

This new development hadn't shaken Edie, not too much at least. These kinds of things, she found, were largely out of one's hands. She'd do her best, and that would have to be good enough, because that's all it could be. Nothing else for anything to do but prepare in advance for situations like these, and that time had long passed.

The door into the penthouse opened.

Sharp footsteps rapped the wooden floor as the shooter approached the piano on their way toward the bedroom, where the loud snoring still sounded uninterrupted. Edie gripped the pistol and aimed it where she imagined the shooter's head would appear. She heard the bedroom doorknob twist, then the door itself creak open.

A booming blast rattled the window panes as a spatter of buckshot splintered the door.

The shooter had triggered a trap.

Edie heard a grunt nearby, then two rapid muffled gunshots in the bedroom and the sound of bedsprings that had been stretched to their capacity. A strained, painful bubbling wheezed for a moment until another muffled pop silenced it.

It seemed like the assassin had taken care of Hurst for good, but the loud snore still continued. Edie was confused until she heard the sound of a tape being stopped, and the snoring silenced.

Hurst's gambit had failed.

In her crouch, Edie heard movement in the bedroom—clothes being thrashed aside on their hangers, luggage unzipped then zipped up again. In a moment, sharp footsteps rapped again, out of the bedroom and past Edie toward the elevator foyer.

There goes the score, Edie thought.

It was worth a shot.

Suddenly the footsteps stopped.

Edie remembered her exit rope, still dangling in the courtyard, catching the moonlight and the rooftop sign's red. She clutched her pistol and aimed again.

A few seconds went by, then a minute, then another, but she remained still in the room's looming heaviness. She heard only her own heartbeat pulsing through her temples.

Edie then heard a sound—a quiet, wet gurgling.

With her pistol leading her way, Edie poked her head up from behind the piano. Halfway between her position and the foyer door she saw a grey figure standing in the middle of the expansive room.

The assassin, his back to her.

His hands were at his sides. One gripped the silenced gun, the other held a duffel bag.

Edie rose and took aim.

Bright moonlight streaming in from the row of windows cast the assassin's long shadow onto the wooden floor, and that's when Edie noticed something peculiar.

The man's toes were pointed down to the floor, but they weren't touching—there was a two-inch gap between shadow and shoes.

He was floating in the air.

The night sky's lone black cloud floated in front of the moon and cast the room into darkness. Edie heard the bag drop from the assassin's hand with a weighty thud, then the gun clanged to the floor. A moment later, the assassin's body slumped with a sickening snap.

The cloud cleared and moonlight revealed the assassin sprawled on the ground. His legs were akimbo, his elbows were both bent backwards, and his neck had been completely swiveled around so that the skin had rippled, tightened, and split.

His head now faced her, his eyes staring back with a glossy focus. She wasn't sure if there was consciousness somewhere behind them.

Edie waited for her heartbeat to settle, then lifted herself over the piano, never lowering her pistol, never taking her eyes from the shape. As she crested the piano's top, her foot caught the ridge and she fell forward, her knees striking the keys, making a cacophonous discord in the room as she faceplanted onto the ground.

Her gun spun out in front of her.

She frantically crawled to retrieve it, snatched it up and trained it again on the dark shape. But as the piano's dissonance evaporated into silence, the assassin never moved.

Edie slowly stood and took a hard swallow. To her left, the open window and her dangling exit rope. Straight ahead, the fallen assassin, the duffel bag filled with the dough, and whatever else was still hiding over there.

She tucked her pistol back into her pocket, and considered.

Maybe the score was worth a shot.

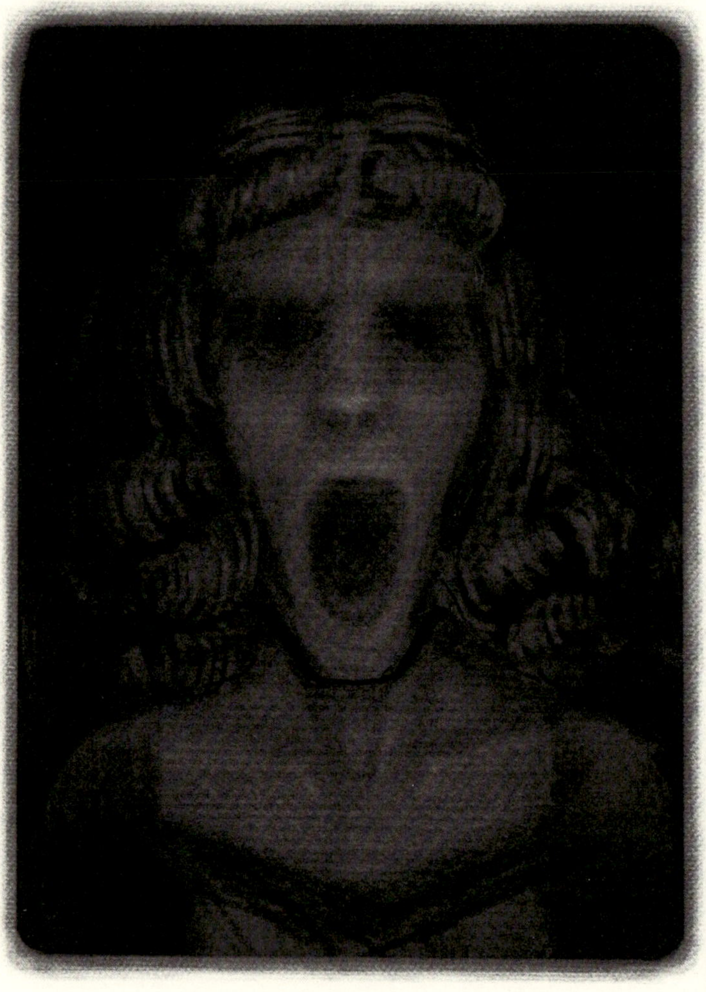

14. Eli Makes Believe.
Room 489

ELI DID AS HE WAS TOLD and made himself busy.

His dad had important calls to make, as he had over their past two nights at the Palmer, and one of the biggest lessons Eli had learned during his seven years was that when Dad said to keep himself busy, well, he'd better keep himself busy.

Or else.

Eli walked to the window and tucked his short, thin frame behind the white curtains so that from the bed it looked like someone had clumsily tried to hide a barstool. His straight brown hair drooped down over his forehead as he pressed his nose against the glass and felt the cool of the night against its tip. The sun had just set and the windows across the courtyard were slowly lighting up as the guests inside gave in to the day's death.

Eli's show had begun.

He'd come to enjoy watching the rooms come to life like this. It was comforting, like the windows of that Christmas advent calendar he used to get excited about. The first December week was joyous, the second week even more wonderful, but nothing matched the anticipation of Christmas spoils over those final days.

But that was before his dad stopped that tradition a few years ago. He said that kind of calendar was for babies, and Eli wasn't a baby, right?

Eli saw movement across the way, a few floors down. Inside was the old woman who he'd named Grannie Jo.

Eli had a grandma himself, his mom's mom who was named Ruth, but to Eli this stranger seemed like a Jo, and so that was the name she got.

Grannie Jo was all alone tonight, again. Her hair had a sheen like snow, but the kind that'd been plowed into the gutters, speckled with dirt and grime. She continued to knit something Eli couldn't see, but he thought it simply must have been a sweater for her grandson or granddaughter. The TV flickered blue light against her face, and now and then she'd pause to watch the screen before returning to her knitting rhythm.

"You have to get rid of him," Eli heard his dad say into the phone. "This isn't the plan that we'd worked out."

Dad made phone calls every night since they had left home a month ago. They'd spent a few nights in some motel here, another few somewhere else, on their trip. Dad always had important business to do, especially at night. When the sun set, it was "business time," he'd told Eli.

"Time to punch the clock," he would say with a wink, then shoo him away with his hands.

Eli liked the Palmer the most of all the places they'd been to. The others had smelled like cleaning solution, their furniture was sharp and weird. But the Palmer reminded him of nights he had spent at Grannie Ruth's.

Comfortable and tended to.

Familiar.

Plus, at the Palmer he had his view.

Grannie Jo was the first person in the window that Eli had noticed. When he'd first seen her, she was talking to herself, as if trying to work out some puzzle. Eli imagined she was deciding which of her grandkids she liked the most, and therefore, who'd get the best Christmas present that year. And then she walked over to the window and lit a cigarette.

"Pee-ew," Eli had whispered to himself, but he'd gotten used to her bad habit since.

"I already got the passports, and they cost me everything I had," Dad said into the phone. "What we're talking about now is something where there's no going back."

Dad's voice began to rise. This was Eli's cue to put his fingers into his ears.

He didn't like hearing Dad on business calls. He wished Mom was around so they could go to the playground while he was working, but she didn't come on this trip. It was "a father-son vacation," Dad had kept saying. "Something special, only for the boys. A secret getaway."

Another window across the courtyard lit up, the curtains parted.

Inside was a thin woman with short brown hair and a pale face. She scanned the courtyard breezily, like she was getting a lay of the land. She saw something in another window near Eli, and she quickly backed away. But then Eli saw a crack open in her curtains again. It looked like she was giggling.

"I can see you," Eli whispered so softly he couldn't even hear himself.

Eli thought this new woman looked like a school teacher. Named Mrs. Brown. Yeah, Eli thought, that name fit just right.

She'd probably get her students to name all the dinosaurs, list off what kind of food they ate, then get them to name some of their famous features, like spikes or tiny arms or lightning-quick speed. But whenever the students would get it wrong, she wouldn't yell at them, she wouldn't make them feel bad, like they'd never be smart enough.

No, not like Mrs. Turner.

Not like her.

Instead, Mrs. Brown would give the class a few hints, and if that didn't work, she'd tell them the dinosaur's name then give them a few tips to remember it all by.

"You can't do this to me!"

Dad screamed loud enough that Eli's ear-plugging didn't work anymore, so he started humming instead. Quietly. Just enough to block out the sounds, but definitely not enough to disturb Dad's work.

No, never that.

He looked across the courtyard again. This time he saw a window that was blurry from the layer of condensation on the inside. Still, he could make out the shape of man in a chair.

The man sat still, staring.

Eli thought maybe he was watching TV, but there was no light shining onto him. Maybe he's just thinking to himself, Eli thought, and then the man's arm moved and Eli saw a metal object in his hand. Something small, shiny and silver. The man brought it to the side of his head.

Eli thought it best to close his eyes then.

He made believe that the man was a toymaker named Eugene, and the metal object was just some tool he was going to use to make an amazing toy. Probably for his son back home, Eugene Junior.

"You bitch!" Dad said.

Eli realized that he'd stopped humming, so he

started again.

A loud boom erupted.

Eli kept his eyes slammed shut and his fingers in his ears, but then his curiosity got the better of him so he squinted one eye open.

Eugene the toymaker was now at the window, staring out through an arc of glass that he'd cleared of the vapor inside with a swipe of his hand. He had short brown hair and thick eyebrows like Dad.

"You'll get 'em one day too," Dad had once told him.

The toymaker's curious metal object was now down at his side, still grasped in his hand. He was searching the courtyard below and the hotel windows across for the origin of that booming sound, and when he saw Eli, he offered a faint wave.

Eli waved back.

As he did, Eli took his finger out from his ear and heard the sounds of a struggle—coming from behind him.

In the hotel room.

Dad was yelling at someone, telling them to let him go.

A mean new voice said "Shut up!" Another said "Where is he?" before a bunch of bad words that Eli knew he wasn't allowed to say, then loud footsteps as Dad's shouts got further and further away, out of the room and down the hallway.

Eli closed his eyes and he put his fingers into his ears again.

He waited for what seemed like forever. When all seemed quiet behind him, he delicately took one finger out, then the other, and there was no noise in the room at all anymore.

Eli opened his eyes.

On the courtyard's other side, on the floor across from theirs, each window was now filled by a figure staring back at him.

They were all women, and all young, but looked old-fashioned. Like actresses in a play. Chalky with black lips and quivering eyes.

None of them smiled as they looked at Eli.

The one directly across looked kind of like Mom, but her eyes were different. Sunken but alert. Wide-open. Like she was past being tired, now into a form of lunacy. Like she hadn't slept in months, maybe even years.

Eli tried to make up a story about her, but couldn't think of one that made sense, so he just waved. As he did, the woman who looked like Mom opened her mouth—her lips, a bright red, brighter than Eli had ever seen before—and Eli noticed that the entire row of women in the windows all mimicked her movements, as if they were one person.

They opened their mouths in synchronicity, as if trying to scream, but nothing came out.

Suddenly, the windowpane in front of Eli's face rattled with tremendous force. Like a sonic boom.

He heard their screams, all at once.

They were in pain. They needed help.

Eli yelped and shut his eyes and crammed his fingers back into his ears and began to hum, louder than ever, but their screams still came through, rattling the insides of his head.

He felt a hand on his shoulder, and Eli yelped again.

The hand gave a light squeeze of comfort and pulled away.

Eli turned around and opened his eyes, and there was that old man in a bellhop's uniform, funny hat on top of his head and all.

Eli had seen him earlier downstairs during their comings and goings. He had seemed nice. Eli started to make up a story about him—the hotel was his home, and everyone inside was his family—but didn't get very far.

"We've been looking for you, little buddy," the bellhop said. "It's going to be alright."

The bellhop took Eli's hand, and Eli let himself be guided out from his curtain sanctuary. And then Eli turned back over his shoulder for one last glimpse into the courtyard.

The women were still there in the row of rooms. Eli saw that while their mouths were now shut and their screaming had stopped, their eyes remained angry.

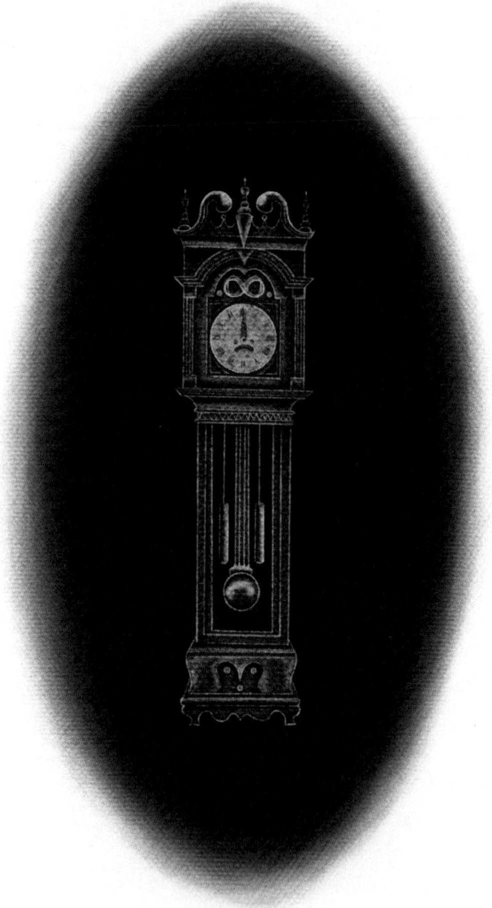

15. Joseph Palmer Jumps.
Room 1150

JOSEPH PALMER WAS EXAMINING his mustache in the mirrored face of the lobby's grandfather clock when, in the reflection, he saw a streak of scarlet flash behind him.

He slowly turned around and saw a young brunette woman in a red dress pass through the lobby. She was in the middle of a costumed group, all giggling and rambunctious, looking to be in their late 20s or so, heading into the Tabor Hall for another big Halloween party.

Just like old times, Joseph thought.

The woman in red glanced at Joseph with eyes so aqua blue he thought it must be some trick of the light, and then she did a double take as a smile formed on her face.

She pulled urgently at the air in front of her lips, a motion Joseph took it as a signal for him to mimic. His fingers found the mass of hair and glue that was drooping off the side of his fake mustache. It had already come loose, despite the promises on the package of skin glue he'd bought for this particular caper.

He nodded a thank you in her direction, but she'd already moved on past the front desk and down the hallway, so he turned back to the grandfather clock.

It was seven feet tall and made of ashen oak that, family rumors percolated, predated even the Palmers' own possession of the building.

It was supposedly a leave-behind from previous ownership, back before the turn of the new century when it was still called The Winthrop. Joseph's mom, Jacqueline, had always called it "the albatross," but never said anything else about it. Just that "it came with the place, and here it will stay, ticking away long after we've moved on."

As a precocious kid running around the business that would one day be his own, Joseph would lounge in the lobby and let the ticks of the clock lull him to sleep. Whenever it began to sound a little funny, he'd tell his mom and she'd invariably send down Hoight with his box of tools, who'd perform some magic with his screwdrivers and wrenches and would get it sounding right again in no time at all.

"Just know how she works is all," Hoight would say with a wink. "Know all her secret spots."

Joseph looked in the clock's reflection, saw how silly the fake mustache looked, and pulled it right off. By the looks of things, it wasn't going to be the sort of visit that necessitated one of his disguises anyway.

Back when his family owned the joint, back when his mom was still in charge, she taught him to wear costumes whenever he was lurking around. At first, it was to help her keep track of the staff—see who was slacking, and who was putting in the elbow grease and could be leaned on to take over more duties. But after a while, that felt like an actual job to Joseph, so he stopped keeping a strict ledger of who was adding value and who was subtracting, and instead just spent his time watching, not spying.

He'd get pretty intricate with these disguises, too. Fake mustaches and eyelashes, pillows taped on his sides to make him appear weightier, accents and prosthetics. That became part of the fun, pretending to be someone else.

All of that ended when his mom dead, thrusting Joseph into a position of real responsibility. There wasn't time for watching and playacting when you were the boss.

His employees saw his reign as mostly benign, especially after his mother's strong fist. More than a few employees even came to her funeral, and that meant a lot to Joseph, especially after the nasty feelings from the long strike.

And when Joseph eventually did take charge, he rewarded his most trusted employees by delegating more responsibility to them. Most of all, that meant Hoight.

It was vital for Joseph to have him around all those years, walking the hallways always in those curious bellhop uniforms. He was the only one who knew how it all ran, how the circuitry was designed, the one who could pick up the slack whenever Joseph was on one of his mental safaris, which got more frequent with each passing year.

The only other one Joseph ever considered putting in charge was Stroud, but there was something about his demeanor, something vaguely sinister that Joseph couldn't put his finger on, but that always worried him.

Not with Hought, though. Hoight always took care of the place like it was his own.

It had been over a decade since Joseph saw him, since he saw any of them, or any of this.

The last time was the big announcement after the deal had closed with Lathan, that investment firm. Joseph hadn't heard of them before they showed one day with lawyers and an offer—the kind of money that'd let his sons and at least three generations after get by without needing to work.

Legacy kind of money.

It had felt like the right time too, business-wise. The industry was changing, Joseph could tell, what with the rise of the internet and all that new booking technology. "Disruption" they called it, and no one was questioning it yet, it was just wide open space to do whatever you wanted.

It meant that the offer would only get worse with time, and so, Joseph sold.

The first years after the sale included an extended trip around the world with Annie and the boys. The best hotels in the poshest cities, private museum tours, dining on the most exquisite cuisines prepared by Michelin-starred chefs. But after a few years of that, Annie started getting worried that the boys lacked a stable setting to grow up in, so the Palmers came back to their estate across the river.

Joseph spent a few years involved with local politics, but without an ownership stake in the city, he was always kept at arm's length. He was invited to the parties when the old guard retired, but was kept on the sidelines when the new guard was introduced. Hobbies bubbled up, but nothing took. The only one that stuck was having his driver take him past this old joint whenever he happened to be nearby.

And all of that's the long way of answering why Joseph Palmer ended up here on the last day of his life.

Now free of his fake mustache, Joseph strolled to the front desk and was greeted by a young woman. Maybe greeting wasn't the right word, as she largely ignored his presence entirely. It took three rings of the desk's bell to rouse her from behind the cover of her paperback novel.

"Sorry, sorry, it's really fucking good," she said, closing the book while keeping her finger as a bookmark.

Things sure had changed around here, Joseph thought.

He'd already noticed that the desk without its Jack-o-Lantern, something Hoight would never let slide on today of all days, but this casual cursing from the front desk clerk was an entirely new style of service.

"Anyway, can I help you?" she finally said.

"I'd like a room," Joseph said. "Something on the 11th floor, if you got it."

"Here's the deal," she said, leaning forward with a key card, another new quirk. "We told this party of techies they got the whole place to themselves. But no one's paying attention, and we could use the dough, so just go along with it if anything weird happens, okay?"

He nodded with a heavy wink.

"Say, is there someone named Hoight who works here?" Joseph asked.

"Who?" she responded.

"What about a fella named Gerald Stroud?" he asked.

"Sure, Gerry," the clerk said. "He's around somewhere, but who knows where. Haven't seen him in a few hours, but I could send him up if he shows."

"No, no, that's okay," Joseph said, and tapped his fingers on the desk as he went through his mental Rolodex. "What about Barbs?"

The clerk nodded, made a mock gun with her fingers, and aimed at the wooden door with the anchor carved into it on the lobby's other end.

"Thanks," Joseph said, and walked into the bar.

A few hugs and many bourbons later, and Barbs was dishing all the gossip again. The place across the way got a sleek new coffee shop. They found another dead guest last week, up in Room 916—he'd suffocated on a damn hot sandwich. And, not surprising or anything, but Stroud was still the same old suck-up to management he'd always been.

"Whatever do you mean, suck-up to management?" Joseph said, feigning amazement with a twinkle in his eye.

Joseph asked about Hoight as the TV in the corner loudly spit analysis about the upcoming presidential election between Obama and McCain.

"A graphic that is surely on everyone's mind—" the commentator got out before Barbs hit the mute button.

"Hoight just disappeared one day," Barbs told him. "One day he was there, one day he wasn't. Not upstairs in his room or anything, and strangest of all, he left everything behind. We never did figure it out."

Joseph sipped his bourbon, considering this strange news.

"People blame new management," Barbs said with a raised eyebrow, taking the rag from her shoulder and wiping down the bartop. "But honestly, I never heard him complain, even though he had plenty of reasons to, like any of us have."

Barbs said she had to get to her other drunks, so Joseph said goodnight and how good it was to see her and he'd stop in tomorrow, even though he knew better, and walked back into the lobby.

He took one more pass around to see if he was missing any old faces, but none showed so he stood there and breathed it all in, remembering how he walked that space as a kid.

It felt so giant back then, its ceilings so tall, the crowds waiting to check in like a whirling hurricane of black coats.

But those days were over now.

The revolving door out front squeaked as the wind battered it from outside. The lobby furniture was not in need of repair as much as full replacement. The grandfather clock ticked, but its time felt off, like it was missing a second or two every hour.

He walked past the front desk and said goodnight

to the clerk, who mumbled back something incoherent. He saw that the dining hall was closed, even at this relatively early hour, then heard the raucous noise from the Halloween party in the Tabor. He took the elevator up to 11, and after the rusty gears finally pulled him up, the doors opened onto his favorite floor.

Joseph didn't love this floor because its décor or layout were anything special—it was merely because of its height.

It was one floor below the penthouse, which was always off limits to him when he was growing up, but through the courtyard-facing windows on the 11th you still got the city views augmented by that red rooftop sign he loved so much.

It was the proper place for what he had in mind. No other place would do, really.

Halfway down the hall, a storage closet door stood open. As he approached, Joseph saw that standing inside was a woman in a maid's outfit.

He subtly coughed into his hands and she leaned back to investigate the noise. She was Latina and past middle age, with black hair pulled tightly back into a ponytail, emphasizing her forehead. She held a lit cigarette in her mouth, which she quickly stubbed then tried to dissipate the smoke with frantic waves.

"Sorry, sorry," she said.

Her name tag read Amber.

"Didn't think we were renting out this floor tonight," she said. "Can I help you?"

"Depends?" Joseph asked. "Can I have one of those?"

She reached into her front pocket and took out the pack then held it out. He took one and they lit up.

"You new here?" he said as he exhaled.

"Not too long," she said, then began shaking her head. "Wait, that's not right. Half a decade now. Time kind of runs into itself here."

"You're telling me," Joseph said. "Do you like it?"

She opened her mouth to say something but then suddenly thought better and instead took another drag. The orange amber glowed to life as she shrugged off the question and blew smoke into the hallway.

"Hey, do you mind if I see something?" he asked.

Before she could answer, he moved past her to pull on the closet light. She stepped to the side, and he reached towards a metal shelf stacked with clean white towels. He collected them and handed them to her, then leaned forward to examine the wall.

There it was: His spiral.

Faint, but still there.

He tapped it with his finger and turned to Amber with a broad smile.

"I carved that," he said. "Back when I was a kid."

Amber didn't know how to react, so she just said "okay."

A silence simmered around them.

Joseph replaced the towels back in their proper place and thanked her for sharing her break with him before walking down the hall and entering his room.

He didn't know why he'd settled on those spirals.

The first one was on the underside of a table in the lobby. He'd been bored one day, and when he heard his mom's voice in the lobby he realized what he was actually doing—defacing hotel property—and finished carving it before he got caught.

He completed it just in time. It was a rush.

There was always a strong "fuck you, mom" element to them all, a rebellious streak that, now in retrospect, was likely just a cry for attention. He liked the look anyhow, so ended up carving them throughout the hotel whenever he had the chance.

Those were fun times, he thought, standing in his last room.

Joseph took his prewritten note out from his pocket and set it on the desk. He picked up the chair and moved it to the window, watching the red light of the rooftop sign flicker every few seconds, putting him into a sort of trance.

He thought about Annie and the boys, then once more about what his diagnosis portended in order to steel himself, then, as he traced spirals on the wood of the windowsill, he thought about his time here in the hotel.

At some point, Joseph felt it was the proper time, so he boosted himself up to the window ledge, walked onto the fire escape, peered one last time at the windows of the hotel's other wing, then stepped off the ledge.

The gravity drop turned his stomach into a fluttering quiver and the wind hustling past made his eyes tear up.

Suddenly, he saw a figure a few stories below him. It was falling too.

It was a woman, that woman in red he'd seen earlier in the lobby. She fell with her back to the ground, facing up, facing him.

It felt almost like they were dancing.

Joseph mustered a wave and thought of how strange of a world it had been, then he slammed shut his eyes so as not to see how the woman's landing would preview his own, hoping that the rushing wind would obscure the sound as well.

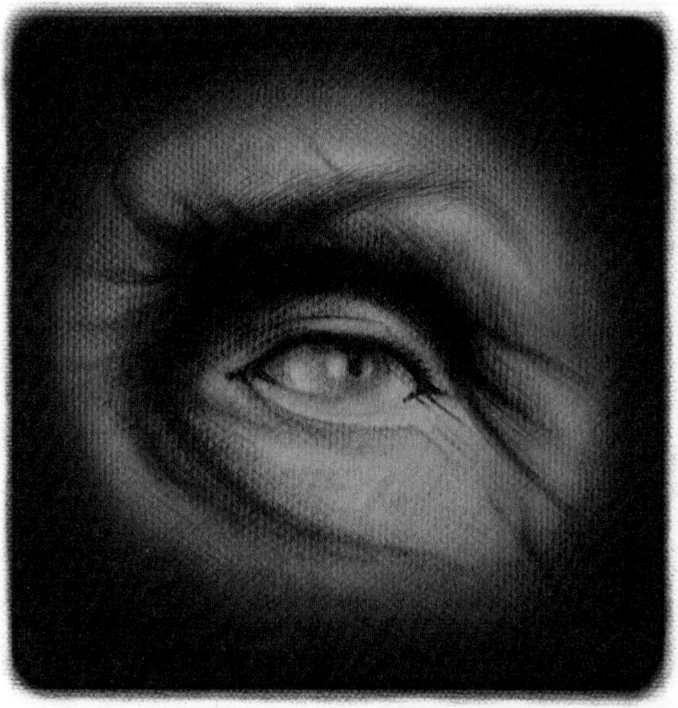

16. Natalie Cleans Up.
Room 584

NATALIE CLOSED HER EYES and retreated into her own thoughts as she always did at this point in the date. Facing away made it easier.

In her head, she calculated how many more dates she'd have to go on before hitting her goal. There was the tuition fee, but also those heavy books at marked-up prices that, sure, you could sell them back at the end of the semester, but for like a tenth of the cost.

What a great scam, she thought.

And then of course there were the expenses of moving across the country, and rent and food for the four years that she wouldn't be working doing this gig. At least not as much as she was now.

"Maybe once or twice a week, just for walking around money," she thought, before Mr. Opal dragged her out of her mental cocoon by digging his sharp fingernails deep enough into the fat of her hips that it felt like they'd bruise from the stress.

She slowed her grinding down for a moment to give him the benefit of the doubt.

Mr. Opal didn't seem like one to get rough, let alone do something that would leave a mark. She had him figured more the older, gentler type with a nice slow, steady rhythm before his tiny little pop at the end. She hadn't been wrong yet when it came to judging her clients, but she also knew that her first mistake was always looming just around the corner—she just hoped it wouldn't be her last one.

He was silent except for a slight wheeze in his breath, and his nails kept digging into her hip, like he was trying to pierce her skin, to draw blood.

"Stop it," she said, and grabbed both his wrists.

He kept squeezing, even harder now, and his wheezing was now accompanied by gargling rattles from the back of his throat.

Natalie shifted her weight and adjusted her knees so they dug directly into his shins. It was a self-defense move that a friend had taught her months back.

She twisted into a spin and out of his grasp with such force that she fell off the bed onto the hotel room carpet. She quickly stood up in a defensive stance, naked and still on the clock.

"What the fuck, man?" she said.

Then she saw the strange look in his wide brown eyes.

They were ignoring her completely, focused on the darkness outside of the window.

His lip was quivering, his eyes wide and filled with tears. His hips still thrust the air, as if he was stuck in some lustful loop—his condom-wrapped dick flopped against his thigh like a fish dying on the deck of a boat.

"Woman falling," he whispered. "Across courtyard."

Natalie walked to the window and, remembering that she was naked, draped the white curtain across her body as she scanned the Palmer Hotel's courtyard.

Only a few lit windows across the way, the haze of the red light coming down from the rooftop sign.

No woman, no body lying on the ground. Nothing out of the ordinary.

"I don't know what you're talking about," she turned back to her customer.

Mr. Opal's face had a new look to it now. A contorted, tightened smile. A strange clarity.

She'd seen this look once before, and with that as her only frame of reference, a hot flash shot up through her chest and into her face as she ran over to him.

"Fuck!" she said. "Are you fucking dying on me!"

"Woman," he hissed.

A deep breath.

"Falling," he rasped.

He grabbed the side of his neck and tipped off the bed, and she heard the crack of his skull against the sharp corner of the bedside table. Jolted by his weight, it toppled over and the lamp fell to the ground. Its shade twisted off and the exposed white bulb cast stark, strange shadows onto the ceiling.

"Fuck!" she said. "Fuck, fuck, fuck."

Natalie ran around the bed and he was face down on the carpet. She grabbed Mr. Opal's black trousers from the floor and crumpled them into a ball. She went to her knees and spun him over, prepared to apply pressure to the surely gaping wound.

When she flipped him over, his eyes were closed, but it didn't seem bad other than the odd indentation in the center of his forehead.

Then it was like someone had ruptured a rusted over sewage pipe.

"Fuck!" she said, her tone reaching a new register as blood poured down his face in a slick red sheen, forcing his eyes to flutter as they avoided the stream.

She bunched the trousers onto the gash to fight the gusher.

"You're going to be fine, Mr. Opal," she said for some reason.

She waited a moment then slowly peeled back the soaked clump. The hemorrhage was now at a manageable trickle, but beyond that, there was no response from him. Only the heavy, soggy limpness of flesh and bone.

"Mr. Opal?" she asked.

She slapped his cheek and the cut on his forehead gushed another spurt down his right eye, but still, no response.

She slapped him again, harder this time, and his left eye popped open.

There was awareness in the eye, and frustration. It said that despite all of those years of preparation and organization, none of them ended up mattering to him at all. It said that this was actually how it was all going to end, and that there was an awe in knowing that truth.

"Chloe," he managed.

It was the name she gave anyone who was roughly twice her age. Something unique, but more than that, a name that wasn't likely to ruin the mood by being the same as their mother or daughter.

Mr. Opal's open left eye shifted from Natalie's face and looked again out the window, then shut for good. She felt his wrist, and his pulse slowed and stopped.

Natalie exhaled and reclined against the edge of the bed. She stretched her foot out and used her toes to retrieve her black dress, the one she wore whenever she worked The Anchor. She used to think it was good luck.

She wrapped it around her shoulders and sat at the desk to consider the angles. There was plenty of evidence that wouldn't put her on the hook for any kind of manslaughter charge. Still, she'd be interrogated, and with that would come the inevitable questions.

How she knew Mr. Opal, or whatever his real name ended up being? What was she doing in The Anchor? What was this wad of bills in her purse? And, hey anyway, what was it specifically that she did for a living?

Natalie thought about who'd seen them together. Barbs the bartender—she was always good to keep her mouth shut—as was Hoight, the bellhop. Beyond that, just a few random strangers in the lobby. That clinched the decision for her.

She put on her dress and took a moment in front of the mirror to press an errant strand of hair back into place. She wiped off her smeared lipstick, strapped on her high heels, shouldered her purse, and went to the door. She gave Mr. Opal's body one last look, made the sign of the cross for his journey to the other side and for her own good luck, then walked out.

Two steps down the hallway, she remembered the conversation she'd had with Mr. Opal in The Anchor's corner booth.

"Our family tradition was always that you handed the old car off to the new generation on their sweet sixteenth," he'd told the woman he knew as Chloe. "What Sally doesn't know is that I got a special one all picked out for her. My old baby."

He had reached into his back pocket and pulled out an old washed-out photo of a yellow Mustang. A kid with the faint beginnings of a mustache was sitting inside with a grin, waving at the photographer.

"That's me as a teenager," Mr. Opal had told her. "It took me forever to track it down, but I finally found it here in the city. Made an offer, and when they hesitated, I tripled it. Having it looked over now. New tires, new steering, the works. Just in time for Sally's birthday on Sunday."

She had seen a little twinge in his eye, the kind that precedes teardrops, before he blinked it away and stuffed the photo back into his pocket.

Natalie spun around, ran back to the door, and jammed it open with her high heel just before it shut and locked her out.

Inside, she slipped off her heels and walked to the bathroom sink, where she turned on the faucet, waited a moment for the water to warm up to what she'd consider a pleasant temperature, and soaked a towel all the way through.

She returned to Mr. Opal's body and, with the warm towel, unstuck the still-slick condom and rolled it off, then wiped down the rest of that area to remove any traces of her presence. She wrapped up the discards, stuffed them into her purse to be exposed in some random trash can on her way home, and examined the room again.

She saw gold glinting from the carpet—Mr. Opal had set his wedding ring on the bedside table before they began, it must had fallen when he'd knocked it over.

She picked it up and squeezed it back onto his clammy ring finger, and that's when she noticed the metal grate on the wall behind where the bedside table had been.

She crawled over to it and noticed that there was a faint mark on the top-right corner of the grate. A small rust-colored shape.

A spiral.

It looked old, like someone must have etched the symbol years and years ago.

She extended a finger to trace it, and when she touched it, the grate shifted off the bolts that had held it in place and, with a loud screech, swung down freely against the wall.

Natalie peered into the dark opening.

There was a bag inside. Bulging and brown. Covered in cobwebs.

It looked like it had been there for decades.

Natalie reached inside, pulled it out, and slowly unzipped it.

When she looked inside, her eyes glowed at the find, and she instantly realized that Mr. Opal was going to be her last date for a nice long while.

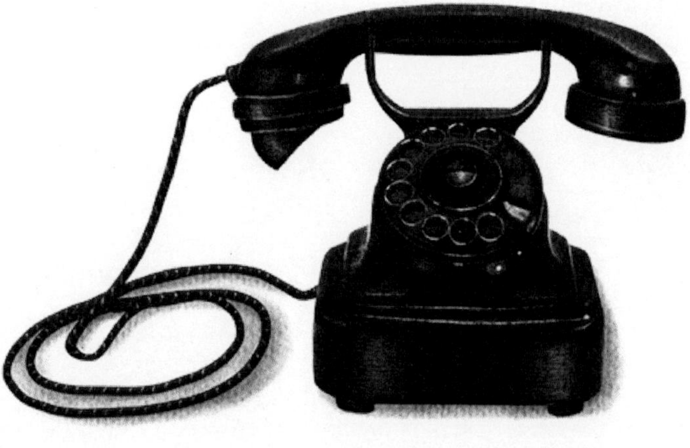

17. Baldwin Rearranges the Furniture. Room 352

BALDWIN HARVEY WAS SO HOPPING MAD that his hands were shaking.

He twisted his room key in the lock to open the door, but as he did, the key jammed and the metal bent sideways in his strained grip.

"Dang!" Baldwin shouted in the hallway. Conscious of not disturbing the other guests, he caught himself and repeated bashfully under his breath, "Dang."

He jimmied the key out of the lock, held it up to the light and closed an eye. It was bent into a soft J that wouldn't fit back in easily.

"Dang," he said again.

He set the key flush against the hallway wall and began to press it with his sweaty palm to straighten it out, carving a slight tear into the wallpaper that turned into a small rip then a divot as he thought about Susie.

Dang Susie.

"Dang, dang, dang," he muttered.

His latest fight with his wife of over a decade had been brewing for the past week before it found its footing and dug in its heels earlier that afternoon.

This time, she'd been on his ass for not keeping his promise to get rid of the old crap he'd tucked away in the garage, and in that moment, he began thinking about all of her crap she'd kept around the house.

Dozens of shoes by the door. Shampoos and conditioners and creams and whatever else claiming the valuable real estate near the sink. Clothes that took up way more than half the closet. Not to mention all those kitchen appliances, good lord. So, he returned her complaints by lobbing back a few of his own resentments.

The tone of the argument kept rising until he finally got her to gash the wall with a frying pan out of frustration. He responded with a slam of his fist against the TV dinner tray, knocking the steak that she'd cooked for him—medium-rare, like usual—onto the carpet. After he silently, fumingly wiped up the splatters of brown sauce from the floor, he packed his "time-out bag" and left, concluding this fight with another extremely satisfying slam of the front door on his way out.

On the sunset train into the city, he guessed that he'd stayed at the Palmer every six months or so. Same reason, every time.

Susie and him loved each other, but they ran hot, they always had. And whenever the tension hit that point of physicality, he needed a release valve that meant being away from her. He didn't drink, didn't run around the pool halls, had no real interest in seeing a late-night flick, he just needed a night on his own now and then to regroup and reset before returning to that combustible world he'd helped create.

When he departed the elevated train into the swampy air of the city summer night, sweat immediately formed on his brow. He huffed the block to the Palmer's front entrance, and as he approached, saw that it was surrounded by a group of ten or so people milling around in a circle. They held placards reading "Fair Wages Now!" and "On Strike For My Family," and were glumly chanting something that Baldwin couldn't make out until he got closer.

"Jacqueline Palmer! Pay Us Now!" they said. "Jacqueline Palmer! Pay Us Now!"

He stood on the sidelines waving his hand in front of his face to cool the sweat dripping into his eyes, and he recognized at least one person in the circle—that curious guy who was always in the bellhop's uniform. This was the first time he saw him in something approaching civilian clothes—jeans and a t-shirt.

Hart or Heck or Harold maybe? Nice guy, anyway.

Beyond the strikers, through the hotel's revolving glass front door, Baldwin saw a flash of movement. He peered on his tip-toes and recognized it as a hand waving in his direction, so he subtly waved back. The hand stuck a thumb out, signaling for him to go around to the side.

Baldwin went back the way he came, and as he turned the corner of the building, he saw a metal door on the hotel's side spring open. It was being held by a man with a pockmarked face, slicked-back hair, and a thin mustache. He looked familiar to Baldwin, too, but couldn't place his name.

"Please, sir," the man said with a luring smile. "Step inside and let's get you a room."

For a moment Baldwin considered if he had anywhere else to stay in the city, but then the cool interior air conditioning hit him in the stifling heat and he told himself that one single customer couldn't hurt the cause of the strikers, whatever it was—negotiation power like that didn't rely on his sole consumer discretion. So, he stepped into the hotel's side door and checked in.

Thirty minutes later, he was in the third-floor hallway, still trying to straighten out that crooked key.

"Dang," he whispered.

In the quiet, he heard the chants coming from the strikers outside. He put them out of his head and worked on the key some more until his hand grew tired.

He closed his eyes and took a deep steadying breath as he worked the metal against the wall, noticing that his frustration with Susie had settled into a simmer. When he opened his eyes, he saw the key was mostly straightened out, so he tried it again.

It fit.

Baldwin unlocked the door, walked in, and let it slam shut behind.

In his previous Palmer stays, Baldwin would've entered, walked over to the bed, straddled it, and begun wailing and clawing and biting the pillows until he'd gotten the rage out of his system. But the key mishap had taken that furious wind out of his sails. This time, he just wanted some rest.

He slipped off his shoes and sat on the bed, then laid down—but only for a moment, as the wind billowed the curtains and blew hot air into his eyes.

He pulled them shut and scanned the room. He knew he'd be going through his ritual soon enough, so why not start now?

"Dang," he relented.

He slumped to the desk, unplugged the phone, and stuffed it into the drawer. He set the nightstand lamp on the ground—still plugged, casting white light into the room—then carried the bulky nightstand into the bathroom, Gideon Bible thumping around inside. He lifted the desk chair and similarly set it on the bathroom tile. He peed, flushed it down, and shut the door on his way out, quarantining the excess furniture that'd ruin the mood.

Baldwin went to the foot of the bed, lifted the frame, and swung it flush against the wall. Not ideal, but there really wasn't another way to hide the bed, so it had to do. He removed the pillows and set them up in the corner where the wall met carpet, then pounded them into a chair of sorts before he eased his hefty body down into a seated position. He unzipped his "time-out bag."

Inside was his old alarm clock that he set up for his wake-up call. Next, he pulled out an orange t-shirt and draped it over the lampshade; he found this mimicked his old college dorm lighting well. He withdrew his tattered varsity letter that he'd pulled from one of his boxes in the garage, set it by his side, and stroked its fabric for a moment before reaching back into his bag for a small envelope. Inside was an old, delicate photo that he unwrapped from its protective plastic.

The color had washed out with time, but there he was, decades younger, dozens of pounds lighter, with a short beard and full head of curly hair. He was leaning against his old yellow Camaro, an easy smile squinting into the sun. He sure loved that car, but the significance of this particular totem was that Jenny had taken the photo.

Baldwin had met Jenny in freshman year science class, and they'd only been seeing each other for a little while—seven total date nights, and Baldwin remembered each moment of every one—before the accident. A car going the other way had hit black ice and spun out, crashing head-on into the Camaro. It was totaled.

Baldwin lucked out, Jenny didn't.

Wheelchair for life.

Her parents took her out of school and back home out west as the college wasn't set up for her needs anymore. Baldwin stayed behind because, well, what other choice did he have, really. They'd only known each other a few weeks. Can't alter the trajectory of one's life for that.

He called her for a bit but then he stopped, and they lost touch, going their separate ways. It ended with a slow dissipation more than any concrete finality. "Growing apart" is how folks put this kind of thing, whenever they have to put it.

Baldwin stared at the photo for an hour or so until he became drowsy. He laid back against the pillows and gazed into the orange hazy lit on the ceiling above, then finally closed his eyes and drifted off into a type of sleep.

Around midnight, just like every night that he'd stayed here at the Palmer, something stirred Baldwin awake from his liminal slumber. Some noise outside the window in the courtyard—a faint scream, then a whoosh and a thud. It was always loud enough that his eyes shot open, but not loud enough to spook him. No one else ever seemed to hear it. He didn't even bother looking out the window anymore.

But then, whenever he opened his eyes after this shock back into consciousness, there would be Jenny, lying next to him on the floor.

She'd be facing him but asleep.

She was now older, with a few more laugh wrinkles around her eyes, her blonde hair smashed into a stringy mass between her face and pillow, her mouth slightly cracked, and eyes quivering with dreams. Then her face would slow and stop, and she'd lick her lips before she'd slowly come out of her sleep.

She smiled at him, and he smiled back, and they'd get up to start their next day together.

It was always all a blur to Baldwin, what with their dogs to feed and the grandkids to call on the phone before dinner and calm conversations about the neighborhood goings-on, and the moanings and groanings about repairs they needed to make to their home. Then, it was time again to rock in their respective chairs on the porch as they watched the sun dip beyond the fields, casting everything in a magenta hue before fading to deeper blue then starry black.

The alarm clock went off at its usual time, and Jenny lingered for a moment longer then gently disappeared. He stretched and stood, packed up his bag, reset the furniture, and plugged the phone back in.

On this particular morning at the Palmer, he sat at the desk for a long as he sipped his coffee and stared at the phone. He still had Jenny's number, folded up and tucked away in the bag somewhere.

Maybe today, Baldwin thought—maybe he'd finally do it.

"Dang," he muttered to himself as he stood up to return back to Susie.

Maybe next time.

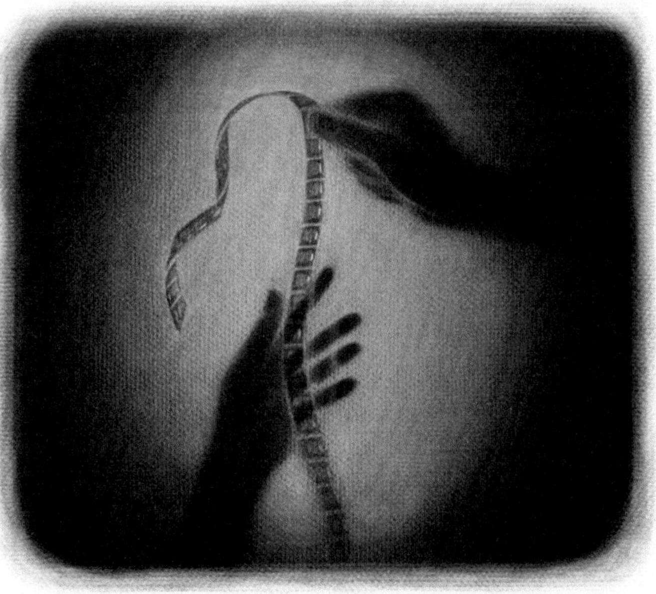

18. Franklin Pieces It Together. Room 708

THE DUCT TAPE SHRIEKED as Franklin pulled off a strip.

He tore it with his yellowed teeth and used it to hold the ends of the curtains flush against the wall, then to pinch the partition in the middle. He stood back and critiqued his work through his horn-rimmed glasses—the sunlight was diffused, but it still wasn't dark enough.

He dropped the roll of tape on the desk. It spun and settled as he hustled into the closet to pull on the hanging light bulb. He scanned the shelves and found a dark green wool blanket the hotel had provided, and brought it back to the window. He draped it over the curtain rod, straightened it out, and stepped back once again to examine the darkness.

Almost.

He spun around the room and found its source: a thin band of light coming in from the hallway through the crack under the front door. Franklin leapt to the bed, grabbed the pillows, and mashed them into the space.

He took one last look around the room for any other trickles of pesky light, and saw none.

"Perfect," Franklin said to himself in the pitch black.

He flicked on the desk lamp for momentary aid, pulled on a rubber glove, then took the cover off the film canister that sat nearby. He daintily removed the reel inside and brought it to the projector he'd set on the nightstand, then wound the reel through the projector's feed sprocket, down against the gate, and back into the takeup.

He started the mechanism rolling, sat his eyeglasses on his brow, and flicked off the lamp so that the only illumination in the room was the projector's white light cast against the room's broad, blank wall.

The film lasted about a minute, and Franklin had seen it hundreds of times by now, maybe even thousands, viewings during which he'd internalized not only every second but every frame's edge.

The reel showed a silent, grainy celebration in a large ballroom. Balloons hovered, revelers waved at the camera, a stoic man offered a subtle tip of his bowler hat. And then the man's face froze in terror as the shaking of the great earthquake began, and the ballroom collapsed before it all cut to black.

Franklin had bought it on a whim at a flea market, more for the case than anything—he didn't even know there was a reel inside until the seller asked for $20 but settled for $15.

Now, years later, he'd come across the country to sell the film to a collector for a price that meant he could finally open up that theater he'd been dreaming about—a small hundred-seater where he could screen the odd assortment of vintage reels he'd collected as a hobbyist.

The projection flickered against the wall as the tinny sound of the running motor ticked in the quiet room, and when the reel sputtered to its end it cast again nothing but white blankness.

One more look couldn't hurt, Franklin thought, so he rewound the reel through the sprockets and started it again.

One last viewing.

But on this second time through, as the man tipped his bowler hat to the filmmaker, a flash of orange came into Franklin's periphery. It was one of those things that, later in retrospect, he would wonder why he didn't jump up right away to halt it. Instead, he watched the man's face morph into fearful realization, then freeze completely as a bright hole emerged in the man's eye then expanded and blossomed across the frame.

"No, no, no!" Franklin screamed, scrambling to turn off the projector.

The strip had gotten stuck, and the heat of the light was enough to burn a hole through the reel.

Then, the projector itself caught on fire.

"Damn!"

He sprinted to the bathroom and turned on the faucet but didn't find a glass, so he cupped his hands and ran back in to splash the small flame. It sputtered for a moment, then spread again.

"Shit!"

He opened the front door, and as his eyes adjusted to the hallway light he heard a voice to his left. It was a bellhop waiting for a tip before a door slammed in his face.

"Cup!" Franklin frantically screamed. "A cup! I need a cup!"

"Excuse me?" the bellhop said.

"Fire! There's a fire!" Franklin shouted.

The bellhop skipped to an alcove that was decorated by a small, round table with a potted tulip. He grabbed it all, ran into Franklin's room, and let out a long whistle upon seeing the flame before running into the bathroom, dumping the tulip and soil into the tub, sticking the pot under the running faucet, and racing back into the room where he dumped the liquified mud all over the projector.

The fire went out in a hiss.

"Kid," Franklin exhaled, "I just set fire to ten grand."

The bellhop let out an even longer whistle.

Franklin tore open the taped-shut curtains, and sunlight flashed across the bellhop's name tag.

"Not a good feeling, Hoight," Franklin said.

"Can't imagine, sir," Hoight said, and took the pot back into the bathroom to replant the tulip as best he could.

Franklin examined the projector. The metal was mangled, but cool to the touch. He slowly disassembled it, and found that while the strip's middle chunk had burned up, the ends seemed miraculously undamaged.

He held the reel's first half up to the sunlight and saw the ballroom partiers. In the second half, he still saw that shaky view as the earthquake sent revelers scattering before the bricks began to fall.

Hoight came out of the bathroom with the tulip.

"Need anything else, sir?" he said.

The sunlight splashed on the kid's bellhop cap, that curious round design Franklin hadn't seen in decades. Something timeless about that style.

An idea came roaring into Franklin's mind.

"Maybe," Franklin said. "This is an old building right?"

"Been standing straight up for over half a century now," Hoight said with a proud grin.

"You have a big ballroom or something?"

Hoight smiled and nodded.

"How'd you like to make five dollars, kid?" Franklin asked.

The kid's nod sped up, his smile broadened.

Franklin gave Hoight a few addresses and sent

him off into the city to wrangle supplies: splicing tape, three empty pitchers, a large bucket, borax, developer, and fixer. When that was all taken care of, Franklin explained, Hoight was to find a few people who looked, well, old-timey.

"Know what I mean?" Franklin asked.

"What are we doing, sir?" Hoight asked, skeptically.

"We're making a movie," Franklin said.

He'd brought his 35mm camera on the trip with the hopes of shooting the city at night, and while it would make for a slightly different color from the original reel, and not contain the same scratches and grain that came from decades of mishandling, if he spliced the edit in just right, maybe the collector wouldn't notice. Not at first, anyway. And once the money exchanged hands and he was on the train back home, what were they going to do? The rest of the film was intact—still the only known film of the great San Francisco earthquake. That was still worth something, so why not ten grand?

An hour later, he got the phone call from Hoight to meet him downstairs. When he got to the lobby, the young bellhop was standing next to a door with an anchor emblem carved into it. Hoight opened it and yelled inside.

"Come on out, my Hollywood stars!" Hoight said.

Out of the darkness staggered a motley booze-fumed crew, squinting with confusion and annoyance at the harsh lobby lights.

Franklin winced as he looked them over. They weren't pretty, but they'd have to do.

"Said you'd give them a buck apiece," Hoight whispered.

Franklin rolled his eyes and took out a wad of bills, and handed one to each as they walked past the front desk where Red with his thick mutton chops was dozing off again. They hung a left to a set of double doors marked Tabor Hall, and Hoight held the door open for his director and extras.

Inside was an expansive ballroom with a stage in the distance and a second floor of balcony seats. As the drunks milled and swayed, Franklin shut his eyes and hummed a few bars to settle his mind.

He'd spent the last hour examining the two halved strips to figure out just what he needed to recreate the missing chunk. It was that one moment when the stone-faced man tipped his cap to the camera, then when his face turned into horrified awareness. The partygoers were thankfully out of focus behind him, so all he had to recreate was those lost few seconds.

Franklin opened his eyes and began grabbing drunks by the shoulder one by one and placing them on different spots around the dance floor. Whenever he got stuck, he'd hold the strip up to the ballroom light for consultation.

"And we danced, and we danced," he sang to himself, some tune that'd gotten stuck in his head, he wasn't sure from where.

When the drunks were all set, he walked to the camera set-up and lined the sights.

"Where do you want me?" Hoight asked.

Franklin looked him up and down.

"You're my star, kid," he said.

He grabbed Hoight by the shoulders and placed him in the frame's center, then plucked off his bellhop cap, snatched a soiled brown hat off a wobbling drunk, and plopped it onto his star's head. He told Hoight to tip his cap, then look as if a giant wave was about to come crashing down.

"What about us?" one of the drunks yelled.

"Pretend you're at a party," Franklin said.

"No problem there!" another called.

Franklin stepped behind the camera, began filming, and called out, "Action!"

He had enough film for three takes, and he ran through them as fast as he could. When he was done, he called out, "That's a wrap!" and the extras gave him a round of faint applause on their way back to the bar. Franklin slipped Hoight another few bucks, then went back upstairs to see if his plan had worked.

In his room, he filled up three pitchers with water then dissolved the borax in one, developer in another, and fixer in the third. He brought them all in the closet, turned on his portable red light, and in the ruby tint removed the film from the camera, balled it up, twisted it gently so it wouldn't kink, then stuffed it into the bucket. He poured in borax, then traded that for the developer, then finally the fixer, and used a rag to clean off chunks left on the film.

He said a little prayer and opened the door.

The sun had set so he flicked on the desk lamp and held the film in front. He began to run it through his fingers, examining what he'd made.

There was young Hoight in the drunk's hat, void of emotion. It was incredible how different he looked here compared to the happy-go-lucky bellhop that'd been bouncing through the hotel. In the film, Hought pulled the brim of his hat, preparing to tip it toward the camera, when a look of horror splashed across his face.

But then, in the next frame, he was gone.

"Damn," Franklin said.

He scrolled past a few more frames of black, thinking he'd screwed up the developing process somehow, but then a new image appeared.

It was the same ballroom, now populated by an entirely different group. They wore black suits and elegant white dresses, and they all faced away, looking at the stage. A few frames forward, a blue spotlight shone onto a silver microphone set in front of purple curtains.

Then, blackness.

Sometimes, film stock had already been exposed, and when it was exposed a second time, another image faintly appeared as a kind of double—a "ghost exposure." Franklin told himself that must be what it was, even though it didn't explain the colors—the spotlight's blue, the microphone's silver, the purple curtains.

He cycled the film forward again until he came to the second take.

There was Hoight. He began to tip his hat, then that terrified look before he disappeared, that eerie crowd of strangers taking his place.

This time however, the angle was somehow closer than before, but still only showed the backs of their heads. Slicked-back hair for the men, blond curly bobs for the women. Beyond them, Franklin watched the purple curtains onstage begin to ripple.

Blackness again.

Franklin scrolled forward to his final take.

It started fine enough, with Hoight putting a hand to his cap, his mouth opening as fear built in his eyes, but then that strange crowd appeared once more.

This angle was closer still, and it focused almost entirely on the spotlit microphone.

Scrolling through the reel rapidly, Franklin watched the curtains part.

Out walked a woman in a red dress with long brown hair and blue eyes like twin propane flames. She had a despondent look on her face, as if sick of having to go through the motions once more.

She stepped to the microphone and began to sing.

The film reel went black again, but Franklin kept winding through it, further and further, even though, by then the film should have run out.

He fed the film past the lamp light, and his motions grew frantic, almost as if his fingers were possessed, out of his own control.

He heard a faint sound in the room, like a gnat

buzzing, and he soon realized that the sound was coming from his hands. He tilted an ear toward the strip and heard what sounded like singing.

Franklin kept feeding. He couldn't stop now.

The woman in red appeared again on the film.

Her face was flushed, and her eyes were closed as the spotlight caught sweat pouring down her temples. Her forehead was contorted in a pained grimace, as if off-camera some part of her body was being branded by a scalding hot iron.

And now, Franklin thought, the noise coming out of her mouth no longer sounded like singing.

No, not at all.

It was shrieking.

The film strip suddenly caught fire with a whooshing hiss.

Flames danced in Franklin's glasses, and behind them, his eyes teared in pain then growing horror as he realized that no matter how hard he tried, his scalding hands wouldn't let go of this burning strip of film.

As a matter of fact, he thought as his blistering, reddened fingers cycled the film back to the start, one more viewing couldn't hurt.

The Palmer Hotel

An invitation.

Dearest Palmerite,

We wish we could be the bearer of better news, but alas, as we've long feared, our battle to save the historic Palmer Hotel has been lost. The loveliest twin brick buildings in the city will fall at the end of this month on, appropriately enough, October 31st, Halloween Day.

But let us not focus on that dreary day that approaches, and do instead what we do best:

Party!

As a dues-paying member of The Palmer's Preservation Society, you are hereby cordially invited to the one last great hurrah.

Where: The Palmer Hotel
When: October 30th, 2020, 10pm until... ?
Password: Joseph's Leap

The night will include:
- Musical acts throughout the building
- Hors d'oeuvres
- Magic
- Tours provided by former staff
- A special rooftop midnight séance
- Secret surprises???

Please dress accordingly. Masks preferred. As a security measure we'll also be collecting your phones upon entry, to be returned upon exit. Please keep in mind: This invitation must be treated with the utmost discretion, as what we're doing isn't entirely "legal."

Sincerely,
The Palmer Preservation Society
Mr. Patrick Jacobson, President

19. Sofia Starts A New Life.
Room 201

THREE RAPS SOUNDED SHARPLY on the door, and Sofia took a deep breath to calm herself. She stood from the desk, brushed her dress smooth, and opened the door just a tiny crack.

Past the narrow slit was a man she'd never seen before. He wore dark sunglasses and took a large white envelope from his jacket and slipped it through the crack.

Sofia snatched it, closed the door, and listened to his footsteps as they departed down the hall.

She protectively cradled the envelope against her chest, set it on the desk, and just stood, looking at it, as if it would disappear if she merely blinked. Then she closed her eyes and placed a hand against the wall, her preferred coping mechanism ever since she was a young girl in Oaxaca.

It was how she grounded herself.

There was something about the acoustic vibrations that passed within and through walls—cryptic rhythms, secret codes from strangers.

In the silence of this old building she felt a couple having a conversation, from somewhere else the metallic creaks of bed springs, then in the distance the low droning hum of a television set.

It all made her feel less alone.

Sofia pulled her hand from the wall, tore open the envelope, and poured out its contents.

Onto the desk spilled a passport and a driver's license, both with photos and personal stats matching her own. Her new birthday was now the day of Mexican independence—easy enough to remember. And her name, as far as any authorities were concerned, was now Amber Thompson.

"Thompson, Thompson," she tried out, stressing the 'th-' sound as if she was pronouncing 'throb.'

Sofia smiled through her tears of relief.

Amber Thompson would have a chance.

Unlike Sofia, Amber wouldn't have her life balancing on a knife's edge for killing Juan, her husband.

The Mexican courts didn't believe he deserved the penalty of death for the rapes he'd committed against her, then against their daughter, so she dispensed the justice herself. Amber wouldn't have to worry about being tracked by police, or hunted by Juan's violent and sprawling family, capture by either persuer resulting in a violent revenge, be it in prison or some nondescript maquiladora.

Amber would be allowed to just live.

Sofia ran to the mirror to mimic the smile that appeared in the official documents. She'd taken it back in Juarez, and the harsh halogen lights they used to make her skin look lightened. It made her pimples stand-out like welts.

"Could always say you just got over puberity," her mule, Oswaldo, had said with a laugh.

She'd heard the horror stories of mules taking advantage of their cargo during the crossing—holding them up for more money, threatening to turn them over if they didn't do what they'd asked, which could be worse than you could imagine. But Sofia had lucked out. Oswaldo was an honorable man.

Her only real fear came during that singular moment at the border. From her spot stuffed inside the rear seat cushions she'd heard the customs officer ask the standard questions—where Oswaldo was coming from, where he was going—but then after a quick rifling of paperwork, the car began to roll again and didn't stop until they reached the city late last night.

Another knock sounded on the hotel room door.

Sofia wasn't expecting anyone, so she froze as if she was back inside those car cushions, wishing whoever was on the other side would just go away.

But then came a second knock.

Louder and stronger.

The door shook on it hinges.

"Miss," she heard someone croak from the other side. "I'm with Palmer Hospitality. Here to welcome you to the hotel."

Sofia sat motionless and paced her breath, careful not to put any weight on the creaky floorboards. She closed her eyes and said a little prayer.

"Miss," the voice called. "Gift basket."

This was followed by another set of sharp knocks, then a voice that rasped close against the door.

"I know you're in there, and I know who you are."

Sofia turned to the window and saw the fire escape. She rushed to it, but when she pulled to open the window, it didn't budge.

It'd been painted shut.

"No need bothering with that," she heard through the door. "Open up and we can get this over with."

Sofia opened the bedside table and stuffed her IDs into the pages of the Gideon Bible, then walked to the door and looked through the peephole.

There was a tall man with a pockmarked face and a shiny head bracketed with hair slicked back at the sides. The side of his face had been busted long ago and held the sagging remnants of violence. He presented a toothy smile with no emotion behind his eyes.

"I have a key to your room," he said. "Don't make me use it."

She swallowed and opened the door a crack, then felt the door push inward as the man walked in uninvited. He strode past Sofia and sat in the desk chair like he owned the place.

"You can close the door, hun," he said with a pained rasp like he'd gargled broken glass. "My name's Stroud. This is my joint, in any of the ways that matter, so here's how it's going to work for you."

He rapped his long fingernails on the desk top, and it sounded like thick raindrops pounding against an umbrella.

"You need a job, we have a job," he said. "You need a place to stay, we have rooms. So, the question is straightforward—do you want to test your luck?"

"What do you mean?" Sofia asked.

Stroud took a quarter from his pocket and held it between thumb and forefinger. It caught the flickering red light coming in through the window, cast from somewhere unknown place above.

"One flip," he said. "Heads, you get a job here as a maid and can stay in one of the rooms."

"And tails?"

"Then you don't," he said, prepping the quarter on his thumb. "We get dozens like you every year, and we don't always have jobs for them. But when we do, this is the best we can offer."

Sofia felt a thick anticipation in the room, as if the walls and ceiling were closing in. He raised an eyebrow with the lingering question, and she nodded her consent.

He flipped the quarter, caught it in the air, and set it against the back of his balled fist.

"Heads," he said and slammed the quarter down on the desk, seemingly disappointed. "Congratulations. Be downstairs at 7 tomorrow morning."

He quickly walked out of the room and slammed the door shut behind him. Step one of Amber's American Dream was realized, however odd the job interview was.

She grabbed Stroud's quarter, gave it a kiss, and set it on the bedside table. She set her glasses next to them, slumped on the bed, and closed her eyes.

She thought about what her mom and dad would be doing right then. He'd be riding the rickety dust-blown bus back from work, she'd be at the stove cooking dinner. He'd greet her like always with a kiss on the cheek and a quick sample of the food, before heading to bed for his 15-minute nap. Sofia's daughter, Elena, under mom and dad's care until it was the right time for mother and daughter to reunite, would already be out with her friends at the park, walking beneath the sodium street lights, passing elotes to one another.

She stretched across the bed and set her hand on the wall, trying again to find comfort in the building's vibrations, but this time the acoustics weren't nearly as tranquil.

She heard an argument, a loud thud, the shattering of broken glass, a scream.

Then she heard the sound of heavy breathing, but this didn't feel like the others.

This was louder, closer.

In the room with her.

She opened her eyes. White moonlight came through the open curtains and shone onto a woman's face.

She looked somewhat like Sofia, and stood silently in front of a pure blankness that seemed to stretch far beyond where the room's wall should have been. The woman's mouth was closed, her lips obscured by something.

Sofia blinked to clear the fogginess in her eyes, and saw that the woman's mouth had been stitched shut. Thick yarn had been woven through her dry, swollen lips.

Leaning up for a closer look, Sofia saw something small and silvery on the woman's forehead, but too far away to make out.

In the room came a resonant hum, then all at once a loud shifting sound. Like an army marching.

The woman advanced one step closer to the bed, and the moonlight directly hit her forehead. The shiny object was a quarter, showing tails.

Another seismic sound and the woman took another step forward.

Sofia now could saw movement behind her. A row of four figures—two men, two women—appeared from the chasmic darkness. They looked similar—mouths also sewn shut, and all wearing the same quarters on their foreheads, each showing tails.

Another shuffle, and they all advanced in a synchronized motion.

Behind them was another row of silhouettes, eight bodies in all. Sofia sat higher and looked beyond, and saw these forms continuing off in the distance, their numbers multiplying with each new row, like a pyramid set on its side.

The eyes of the lead woman shifted from a vacant stare to an awareness of her condition, as if suddenly she saw Sofia lying there.

The woman mumbled through her stitched lips before seeming to recall that it would do no good, so instead she made a swift motion with her forearms, crossing them into an X in front of her.

Her eyes pled to Sofia. They wept.

The many hundreds behind her mimicked the gesture, ejecting a funnel of air towards Sofia with an eruptive sound, forcing her eyes shut.

She frantically twisted to the bedside table and turned on the lamp, and orange light sprayed through the room. The bodies dissipated then disappeared like the vision of a nightmare in the moments after you wake.

Sofia lay there silently with the lamp on all night, watching Stroud's quarter on the nightstand, still showing heads, until it was time for her first shift at the Palmer to begin.

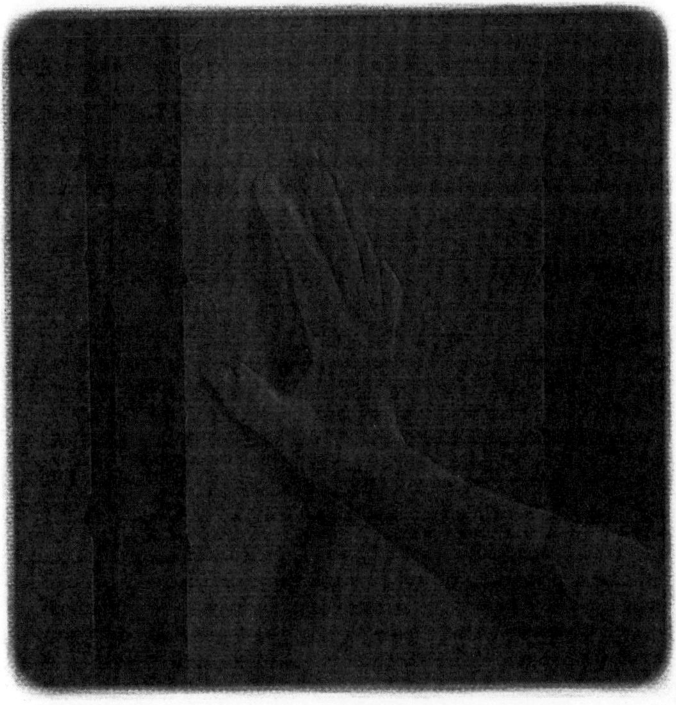

20. Stroud's Night Shift.
The Guts

WITH HIS HANDS FOLDED and resting on the lobby's front desk, Gerald Stroud glared at the grandfather clock as it ticked off the last minutes of his shift.

He heard the whoosh of the revolving door as it sucked in the outside air—another guest to waste his time. He unfolded his hands and ran his long fingers through his full head of black hair as he diverted his attention from the clock's ticks and tocks.

Through the front door walked two young kids in ghost costumes—that is, eyeholes torn out of bedsheets—and each carried a small bucket for their freeloader take. Their chaperoning mother hovered behind them, keeping a close eye. Stroud rolled his eyes at this disturbance.

"Trick or tr—"

"No candy," Stroud interrupted with a rasp, shooing them away.

The mother audibly gasped and, with a sour expression, collected the pair by their shoulders and took them out the way they came.

Good riddance.

Silly tradition for a silly holiday, Stroud thought.

As they spun out the door, they passed another fool walking in: Stroud's replacement for the night shift, Hoight.

He always worked Halloween. He loved it so much in fact that he'd always don a ridiculous costume on top of his already ridiculous bellhop uniform. Tonight, Hoight wore a cape, slicked-back hair, and plastic fangs.

"I vant to check guests in!" Hoight shouted in a Transylvanian accent through the lobby, hefting two bags of candy in his arms.

Stroud ignored this charade and retreated back into the employees' breakroom, a small space behind the desk with a table, radio, and a set of lockers.

He twisted the combination on his lock, collected his bag, and walked back out into the lobby past Hoight, who was already pouring his sweets into silver bowls for the approaching horde of precocious candy siphoners.

"Have a blast out there today," said Hoight with a fanged smile.

"Never do," Stroud croaked on his way out.

Stroud cupped his hands around his mouth and warmed them in the chilly autumn air. Wisps of cotton puffed from between his fingers and floated away. The howl of an approaching train screeched through the air and Stroud wadded his thumbs into his ears to muffle that grating sound.

When it finally departed, he turned the street corner and ran his pale, frozen hand along the building's grainy brick surface. Halfway down was the Palmer's side door—metal, handleless, flush against the wall.

Old Red had taught him the trick to get in this way. Push really hard and the door, always unlocked as per the fire code, rebounded from its frame just enough that you could fit your fingers into the gap before it closed. Then, just pull and you were back in the ground floor hallway, away from any inquisitive eyes at the front desk.

Stroud re-entered and slunk to the double doors of the Tabor ballroom, silently opened one, and slipped inside.

Stroud crossed the ballroom's wooden floor, careful to dampen the clicks of his footsteps in the cavernous space. At the right side of the stage, he loosened a panel and slid it open—just enough room for him to dangle his legs inside—then he eased himself through. His feet hit the ground in the dank, mildewed crawlspace and he slid the panel shut behind him.

He reached into his pocket and removed his flashlight. It spilt orange haze onto the concrete and caught the glint of a brass ring that was bolted into a wall.

Stroud pulled it.

The slab of concrete opened on a hinge, and Stroud stuck his flashlight into his mouth as he dropped to his hands and knees. After he passed through the small door, he stood upright again and brushed the dust and cobwebs from his knees before he began to walk down the hidden corridor.

Thus began Stroud's night shift inside of the guts of the Palmer Hotel.

He'd first happened upon this space simply by good fortune. Two weeks after Stroud had gotten the gig, years back now, he was on an overnight at the front desk when, as is the case with any job, the great expansion of his agreed-upon duties inevitably started. His boss Chet asked him to, if he could, you know, no pressure or anything, sweep up the ballroom, if nothing else was going on up front. So, around two in the morning with the lobby silent except for the grandfather clock's ticks, Stroud snagged the broom from the maintenance closet and walked into the Tabor Hall.

As luck would have it, just as he did he saw Old Red, off his shift hours ago, crawling out from some hidden space under the stage.

"Maybe it's best if you forget this," Red had said, wiping dirt from his knees and walking away. "Not for the meek of heart."

A few months after that, Stroud had enough information to make his ultimatum. He told Old Red to show him what was under the stage, and if not, perhaps Chet—hell, maybe even Jacqueline Palmer herself—would be interested in a chart detailing all of Red's unapproved smoke breaks, and how much that sum might amount to when multiplied by his hourly wage.

So, late one night after all the guests had checked in, Red gave Stroud a tour. He called it "the guts," and the name had stuck well enough.

Past the short door was a tall corridor that stretched too far for Red's flashlight to illuminate, and they walked forward through this hidden space between the walls. The old man had to shuffle sideways with his bulging stomach, but it was plenty wide for Stroud's sinewy figure.

Red paused, held up a finger to indicate silence, then clicked off his flashlight. Stroud saw pinholes of white light emerging on the walls. It looked like a clear night sky dotted with constellations.

"Quiet now," Red said. "People are sleeping but that don't mean they're dead."

Stroud stepped up to an eye-level pinhole and leaned forward to peer inside.

A room on the ground floor where a squat man was inside, wearing only a white t-shirt stained with spaghetti sauce, nodding off in a chair he'd brought in front of the TV.

Stroud remembered checking him in earlier that evening. He'd been decked out in a tailored suit and expensive tie, an attractive young woman on his arm who giggled at his bad jokes and nibbled his ear. He'd seen him before, but couldn't recall when.

As he snooped, a blast of orange light flashed in the corner of his vision. Stroud looked up and saw Red at the corridor's far end, shaking his flashlight, beckoning him on. Stroud left the fat, dozing man behind and walked to Red, who stood where the corridor dead-ended against a brick wall on which hung a steel ladder.

"Courtyard's on the other side," Red said, rapping his knuckles against the brick. "The rest of the guts are up there."

Stroud followed Red's light upward and saw that the ladder stretched up to the hotel's other floors, each illuminated by a small, oval window that faced the courtyard and allowed tunnels of faint moonlight to filter into the dusty space.

"The guts run all through it," Red said. "Nothing can hide from the guts."

On his morning shift the next day, Stroud checked out the fat man who'd been nodding off at the TV, and he remembered why he looked so familiar. He'd come to the hotel a few months back to check on a suicide on the sixth floor.

He was a police captain. Volley was his name.

All at once, Stroud was seized by a vision of what was to become his life project.

But this was years ago, before Red disappeared, before Stroud had the guts all to himself.

After entering them on this Halloween night, Stroud turned down another corridor in which glowed a wide shaft of light. At the end was the one-way mirror that Stroud had surreptitiously installed behind the face of the lobby's grandfather clock.

He walked to it, sat on a stool he'd placed there, and examined the lobby. On the front desk was the face of Hoight's Jack-o-lantern, glowing with sharp, grinning teeth.

He heard a shuffle of feet, then saw Hoight leading a group of kids to the front desk, presenting each with his bowl of candy. When they departed with their treats, Hoight returned to his station behind the desk with a broad smile on his face.

Stroud tucked the flashlight into his armpit and grabbed a notebook and pen that he'd hung in the corridor by strings. Along with the stools, he'd placed them sporadically throughout the guts to make his work easier.

He opened to a blank page and scrawled a note:

October 31st, 1968
Hoight dressed & acting like a child.
Again.

He let the notebook dangle from the string, but when he did, his flashlight came untucked and fell to the floor. It snapped on at impact and a bright white light filled the corridor.

Stroud fell to his knees and scrambled in the dust to find the light. A deep panic set in him, and when his hands finally grabbed it, he frantically switched it off.

He remained perfectly still for a moment and modulated his breath, then hesitantly stood to peek through the one-way mirror.

Hoight was still behind the desk, undisturbed.

Stroud allowed himself to let out a slight sigh of relief, left the lobby peephole, returned down the main corridor, and then climbed the steel ladder up to the fourth floor.

He walked to the stool outside Room 419 and peered through the pinhole. The guest was "Mrs. Beverly Clauson" on the registry, but he knew better. She was disguised with a grey wig and thick bifocals, but those didn't hide the dark brown mole on her left temple.

Her real name was Rita Wurtz, a senator's wife, and through the pinhole he watched her shoulder-length blonde hair thrash as she straddled some as-yet-unknown party.

Stroud took his eye from the pinhole. He never liked this part, glimpsing how grotesque and animalistic humans became when they believed no one else was watching. After he heard their grunts collapse into exhaustion, he leaned into the pinhole again.

Mrs. Wurtz and her partner reclined in bed, sharing a cigarette. Stroud noted his description.

Brown hair.
Short.
Muscular shoulders.
Tattoo on left bicep.

But when the man retrieved his glasses and put them on, it all clicked at once.

Stroud crossed out his descriptions and wrote:

Jeff Gregorian

The DA.

He let the notebook dangle from the wall and moved on.

Room 839.

Checked in here was Sam Alston, one of the city's power brokers. His exact position and credentials were unclear, but he had his hands in any number of investments.

The room's bed was empty, then suddenly Alston came into view wearing black trousers, an unbuttoned white collared shirt, and carrying a hotel towel. He folded the towel and set it on the carpet, then opened the bag on his bed and pulled out a leather cat o' nine tails.

Alston let his shirt fall from his shoulders, and Stroud saw a grouping of red, swollen slashes across his back. He fell to his knees on the towel and began lashing himself.

The third one drew blood.

Stroud scrawled a note and left.

As night drew on, Stroud continued his rounds, checking in on his known marks, peering into random pinholes to see if any strangers had something new to offer.

Perhaps his observations would come in handy someday—knowing the right person to tweak at the proper time for the right deal—but that was for later on, if ever.

The true duty he felt to his work was more than purely mercenary—in large part, it was simply about the act of collection.

One by one the pinholes began to blink away as the Palmer's guests went to sleep, so Stroud climbed down to the second floor, where Emily was staying again.

He peered into the pinhole and watched the bedsheets rise and fall with her breath, and there Stroud stayed, enraptured, until the first rays of sunlight came in through her window.

When there was light enough to see, he pulled the dangling notebook over to him, flipped to the correct page, and lost himself shading his lovingly rendered sketch of Emily's prone and distant form, getting as far as he could before it was time for his morning shift at the front desk began again.

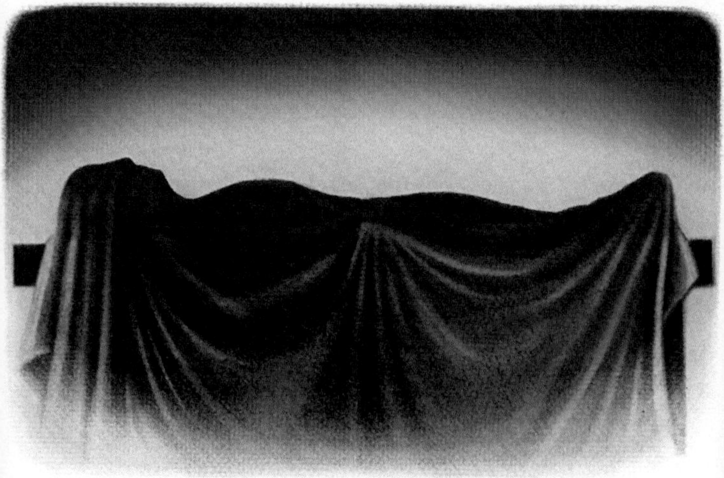

21. Lukas Opens the Case.
Room 699

LUKAS LANE, six-foot-four with a flattop crewcut that made him look like he was carved from a chunk of ice, exited the elevators onto the Palmer's sixth floor.

Every swinging dick from the 14th Precinct turned at the elevator's ding and gave Lane the once-over before going back to their job of doing nothing but taking up space, as if the city had no other pressing problems needing their attention. He saw a few familiar faces, but none that knew his, so he ducked under the flimsy strip of drooping yellow police tape and walked into the clown show.

Barreling through the ruckus came Captain Volley, a round man with a shock of white hair and a clean-shaven face that somehow always looked wet. He extended his bulbous hand.

"So you picked the short straw," Volley said.

"Something like that," Lane said, accepting the shake. It felt like a slippery eel.

Volley gave him the rundown as they walked the hallway. One of their own had offed himself.

Steven Harrison, detective from the 14th. Nineteen years on the force, one more to go before being in line for his full pension.

Unlike the commotion in the hall, the room itself was quiet and clear, save the stiff face down on the desk.

Its knuckles rested on the carpet at the end of a dangling arm. Blood and brain and other bits were spattered across the wall and TV.

"We already had them pull up tonight's Perry Mason," Volley said with a smirk at the muted TV set. "See if it was a particularly upsetting episode."

Gallows humor, even now.

Incredible.

An hour ago, the chief had called Lane at home just as he was sitting down to Adele's turkey and potatoes. He said he needed him across the river for this one. And right away too, before they all mucked up the scene.

It looked open and shut, Lane thought as he walked the scene, laid out neat and pretty. Revolver on the ground, Harrison's fingerprints no doubt on the trigger, the fatal spent casing still in the chamber.

Lane bet there was even a note left behind.

"He left a note on the nightstand," Volley said.

And there it was.

Lane opened the envelope and gave it a quick read. It was written in a hesitant scrawl, but otherwise seemed to be standard fare for this kind of thing. Getting too hard out there, no end in sight, tell my wife and my daughter Abigail that I tried, blah blah blah.

Lane had read this shit enough times before to have the beats down cold.

"Maid heard a shot around 7:30," Volley said. "We got the door down an hour later."

"Why so long?" Lane asked.

"Didn't know exactly where the shot came from,

and we couldn't just start breaking down doors," Volley said. "Process of elimination took time."

Lane glanced at the door. Splinters near the busted-open hinges, a broken chain dangling.

A few patrolmen stood outside looking in. Lane scanned their faces and found mostly curiosity, except for one of them who wore a weary face with red, swollen eyes.

"You think you're good to go here?" Volley asked.

"Getting there," Lane said. "Shouldn't be much longer."

"I'm going out for a smoke," the captain said, and walked into the hall.

Lane approached the looming patrolman with the red eyes. His name tag read Hoover.

"I'm Detective Lane."

They shook hands.

"Can I get some help in here?"

The patrolman wiped the stubble on his chin, nodded solemnly, and stepped inside. Lane closed the door to the hallway and began his true investigation.

He got on his hands and knees to look under the bed. Nothing but dust and hair balls from previous guests. The pillowcases were empty of stains; the bed sheets showed nothing special. The bathroom had a used towel over the shower curtain rod that'd since dried, some toiletries rested on the counter and, on the sink's edge, there was a razor spotted with dried shaving cream.

He opened the closet door. Inside was a briefcase.

He brought it to the bed and lifted it open. It was full of clothes; nothing worthwhile. The bedside table was empty except for the Gideon Bible rattling in its top drawer.

Lane grabbed it and held it up.

"Got a favorite passage?"

Hoover shook his head.

"Maybe in the next life," Lane said.

He dropped the Bible back into the drawer and slammed it shut.

The scene clear of any obvious suspicion, it was time to work the body.

"I was Steve's partner for a bit, awhile back," Hoover said, unprompted. "I asked for a transfer back in '62. Was getting tired of working homicide so I had them put me on traffic duty. More stress on the day to day but fewer nightmares."

"I get that," Lane said.

He went down to a knee to examine Harrison's pockets. Empty.

"Always felt like I left Steve holding the bag on a few things," Hoover said.

"That's just the passage of life. We all have those," Lane said. "I'm sure he didn't take it personally. I heard he was a good one."

"Got that right," Hoover said. "My name's Nick."

"Alright Nick," Lane said. "Tell me about your pal."

As Lane patted down the body, Hoover went through their shared history.

They'd met in the army when they were stationed overseas in Germany, and became close once they realized they were both from the city. Back home, they'd decided to convert their newly acquired skills in weapons handling and crowd control into being cops, then moved up the ranks together to the homicide division. They were good at the gig, especially when they worked the scenes together, but at some point the line between policing the public and policing their own got real blurred.

"Any stiff that showed with a red tag on its toe meant to give it the once-over, nothing more," Hoover said. "It meant that someone else, someone above us, had wanted it swept aside. It never sat right with either of us."

Hoover stood there with himself for a moment, working his way through something.

"Another thing you learn in the army is to follow orders," he said.

Lane lifted Harrison's head to examine the bullethole. It had entered at the right temple and exited above the left eye, where the gaping wound had already congealed. Not a perfectly straight line, but all of that bone and brain matter in there will always tweak a trajectory.

Lane smelled Harrison's hand: gunshot residue. He smelled the mouth: No booze.

"Pretty clean case," Lane said as he pulled a cigarette from his pocket and lit up, leaning against the desk next to the body. "Which is why frankly I'm a little troubled, Officer."

"What do you mean?" Hoover asked.

"Tonight, I got the phone call just before dinner," Lane said. "When that happens, it means they need some real help on a case. Get a fresh set of eyes on something that's bugging them, and also has some urgency to it. This just ain't that."

Hoover sat on the bed. Lane took another inhale and aimed a finger out the door.

"I can tell you some of the worst things that eight or nine of those men out there have done in their lives," Lane said through a cloud of smoke. "My job is pretty simple. I'm a detective, but I solve the shit that other cops can't, or won't, figure out. Those red toe tags you mentioned? I clean up some of those messes."

Lane turned to Harrison's body.

"Trouble with this one is," Lane said, "I can't figure out why they brought me in."

The hallway door slammed opened and in waddled Captain Volley.

"Whatcha got, Lane?" Volley spat.

"Clean as a whistle," Lane said, and took another

draw from his cigarette. "It all got too much for your man, so he ended it."

Volley looked at Hoover. He gave him a glare that took Hoover a moment to register, but when he did, he bashfully bounced off the bed and back out into the cacophony of the hallway cops.

Lane and Volley were alone again with the fallen officer.

"Any idea why he'd do it here at this joint?" the captain asked.

"Privacy. Get away from home. Wanted a stranger to find him instead of his kids," Lane said. "Dealer's choice."

"I guess that's that then," Volley said.

"I suppose it is," Lane said.

"Go ahead, roll him out," Volley yelled into the hallway.

Three officers came in. Lane knew them all.

There was Rogers, who beat up a 16-year-old until his jaw needed to be wired shut, and Drake, who shot a pregnant woman in the back, and then finally in walked Glavis, who took a percentage from all the street walkers on 5th.

Lane sucked in smoke as he watched them lift the body on the gurney, and cover it in a white sheet before wheeling it out. He stood up and put his cigarette out on the windowsill, then lifted open the window and flung the stub into the courtyard.

"One more thing," Volley said. "Thought I'd save you the trouble of writing it all out yourself."

The captain took a folded piece of paper from his jacket pocket, set it on the desk, and used his fat hand to iron out the wrinkles.

It was a pre-written report—the official declaration that, according to Detective Lukas Lane, Detective Steven Harrison's life ended via suicide, full stop.

Volley set a pen down next to it.

Lane recalled the gauntlet of officers still in the hallway, still hanging around for some reason, lingering and brooding, as if waiting for one specific action to take place before they could depart. And who were there just in case that action didn't take place.

Then Lane thought about Adele and Johnny back across the river waiting for his return, his turkey and potatoes still being kept warm in the oven.

Without reading the note, Lane signed his name on the dotted line, handed it pen and all back to Volley, and went back home.

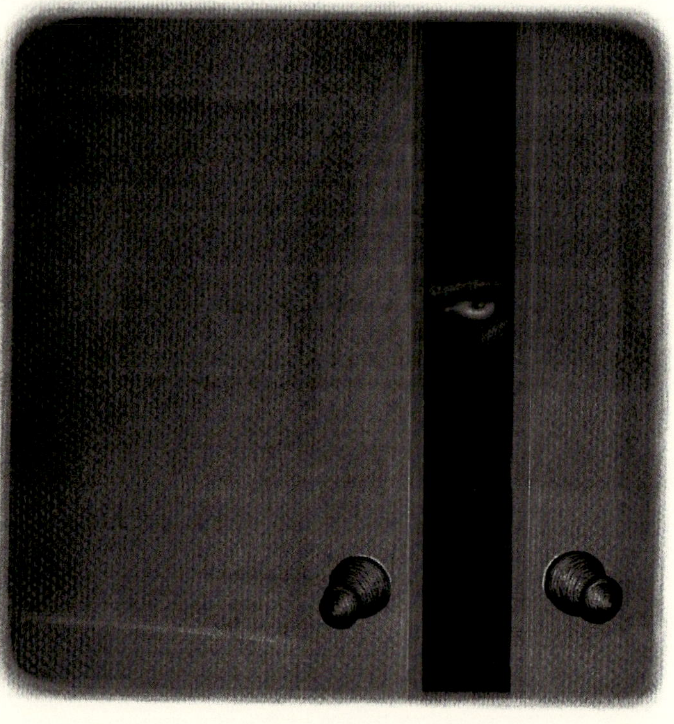

22. Mikey Gets A Scoop.
Room 699

FROM A BOOTH IN THE BACK of The Anchor, Mikey Jervis checked his watch, then stared again at the phone booth in the corner, trying to mentally will it to ring. When his wish didn't take, he returned to his scotch and the conversation at hand.

"Thing with Bobby was that even when he was in full-blown politician mode, there was always that glint in his eye telling you he was in on the charade of it all too," Gary said with a confidence that comes with years on the ledger. "He knew the dance between us guys and folks like him, he knew it was nothing but a show."

It was Gary's last day at The Chronicle after two decades of coming home late every night with ink stains under his fingernails. He and his wife Sam had already made plans to trade in their two-story home across the river for an RV and see what else the country had to offer.

It sounded like a dream to everyone but Mikey, to whom the plan sounded like a long death.

Mikey looked at the phone booth again. Silent.

"Hot date, Mikey?" asked Todd, a copy editor a few years his senior.

"Something like that," Mikey said. "Meeting a source later."

"I thought this wasn't a work night," Todd said.

"C'mon, Todd," Gary droned. "They're all work nights for Scoops Jervis over here. I once had that drive myself."

Gary lifted his glass, they all clinked and drank.

He called over Barbara, the Anchor's young bartender, for refills and, as she headed back to the bar, the phone loudly clanged and echoed through the dimly lit space. Mikey bolted from the booth and picked it up on the second ring.

"Lukas Lane is dead," said a voice, frantic and quivering on the other end.

It was Ginger.

"They killed him," she said. "Called it suicide."

"Slow down," Mikey said, pressing his notebook against the booth's glass. "Are we meeting or is this over the phone?"

"Room 378," Ginger said.

Click.

Mikey got to work. Over the years, they'd established a little safeguard for their meet-ups in case anyone was listening, a simple substitution code that, when he was done marking up the numbers, revealed she was in Room 699.

He went back to the table, grabbed his bag, and downed the scotch.

"Knowing you drunks, I can't imagine I'll be up there longer than you'll be down here," Mikey said, his thin mustache lifting on either side with his smirk.

"We'll be here, unless your source ends up getting other ideas," Gary said with a wink, then turned back to the party. "Which reminds me of another story..."

"You're gonna have to save that one for when I come back," Mikey said.

He gave Gary a loving squeeze on his shoulder, just in case this was indeed goodbye, and walked through the wooden door into the Palmer's lobby.

Behind the desk was Stroud, fucking Stroud, already waving him over.

"Can we help you, Mr. Jervis?" Stroud droned. "Don't see your name on our list of scheduled guests."

"Meeting a friend upstairs," Mikey said.

"Of course," Stroud said, and pulled out a pen. "Just need to sign you in. Room number and name of the guest, if you will."

"You're kidding."

"Can't be too careful these days," Stroud said. "Crime running rampant in our fair city and all, not like it used to be."

"Oh, I just remembered I left something in the car," Mikey said. "Be right back."

Mikey exited through the front revolving door into the night and sped around the corner to the hotel's side door. He pried it open with a pen, walked back inside, and hustled into the nearby stairwell.

It was a little game they played. Stroud knew he couldn't do anything to keep Mikey out for long, what with him moored behind the desk, but at least Stroud could make the scoop hound take the stairs. Around the third floor, Mikey got winded and leaned against the wall.

Lukas Lane. Dead.

Called it suicide.

Mikey had seen Lane now and then, here and there at crime scenes or in those expansive halls of justice. He was a detective from across the river who cut a large, blocky profile. Worked internal affairs stuff for the city, like some outside consultant brought in for an extra set of uncompromised eyes.

He'd be, what, the fifth or sixth cop suicide over the past few months?

Now, there was a story.

Mikey opened the door onto the sixth-floor hallway and rapped his 1-2-1 coded knock on Room 699.

The handle spun, Ginger let him in.

"Fuck, fuck, fuck," Ginger said, cigarette shaking in her mouth with such rapidity that a dusting of ash floated down onto the green carpet.

The door shut behind him, and she walked to the window ledge to blow out another strand of smoke.

"Fuck," she said again.

Ginger had always been unrattled in their meetings together. She'd usually just calmly and succinctly break down who was in bed with whom, lobbing tips to Mikey about which power players were worth snooping into, and for what. Tipsters like Ginger had the kind of value you couldn't buy, and Mikey knew better than to try. All he could offer was a fair shake and to tip her off whenever he heard rumor of an upcoming vice raid.

"It's all bigger than you think," she said. "Way bigger."

She stubbed out her cigarette, lit another.

"I'd seen Lukas a few times," she said. "Nice guy, real gent. Last I heard he was working a case. Big one. Internal stuff. Cops gone rogue in the department, 14th Precinct mostly. Had a code name for it. Sunset."

She crossed the room.

"Last time we met he said that something always bothered him about an old cop suicide," she said. "Someone named Harrison. Ring any bells?"

Mikey shook his head.

"Lane wouldn't off himself," she said, mostly to herself. "Wasn't the type. I know the type. I've been with the type, and he wasn't."

The phone rang, they both jumped.

She looked at it skeptically for a few rings then picked up.

"Hello," she said, and Mikey saw her face blanch white. "Oh, hi. Okay, see you soon love."

She hung up and turned to Mikey.

"You have to go. Now."

"What's up?"

"Captain Volley," she said.

"Volley?"

"On his way up," she said. "How would he fucking know where I was?"

Mikey hoisted his bag over his shoulder. Ginger pulled open the door just as the elevator dinged from down the corridor.

"Fuck," she said, and signaled Mikey to halt.

She stepped into the hallway and turned to the elevators. As soon as he heard the doors whoosh open, Mikey saw Ginger's entire countenance shift at once—from rigidity to a sensual looseness with a shift in her hips, a single leg thrust out. She called out.

"Thought I heard you coming, honey," she said down the hall. "Came pretty quick."

"Hope you don't have to say that again tonight," said a deep voice that laughed at its own joke.

She waved a hand back to Mikey, as if trying to will him from existence. He circled the room, trying to find cover.

Beyond the open window was the fire escape, and also whatever peering eyes lurked in the building across the way. To his right, the bathroom. No go. To his left, a dark closet.

He slunk inside.

Ginger had hung up a variety of dresses, probably 20 in all, like she'd been staying at the hotel for a week or more. He parted them, ducked inside, and closed them in front of him just as the girthy Captain Volley entered and kissed Ginger on the cheek.

207

"Good to see you, dear," he whispered.

Mikey was close enough to hear his guttural tone crystal clear. Through the crack in the door, Mikey could make out Volley's expansive gut and the revolver that hung against its side. He carried an open bottle of cheap red wine in his fist.

"Hope you don't mind I already started on my way up," he said.

He took a swig straight from the bottle and handed it over. Ginger took one herself and Volley set it on the desk.

"Thanks for the gift, honey," Ginger said.

She had a new giddy affect to her voice, entirely different from a minute ago, and led Volley by the hand to the bed, out of Mikey's slivered field of view.

Mikey became conscious of his breath, how quickly his pulse thumped through his temples. His focus on that rhythmic beat was drowned out by the bed frame slamming against the wall as Ginger did her paying gig. This went on for another few minutes, with Ginger's soft voice occasionally offering quiet encouragement, before Volley's wet and rasping final groan.

The police captain caught his breath with a wheeze, and Mikey heard the flick of a lighter.

"So, Captain," Mikey heard Ginger say. "To what do I owe the great, great pleasure of this visit."

A loud shift of weight in the bed, then Volley's loud footfalls as he crossed the room.

"You were just on my mind is all," he said.

Volley passed by the closet door as he stumbled into the bathroom, and Mikey heard his massive feet plop on the tile before dribbling out a staccato flow into the toilet water. When it dissipated to a trickle, Volley hacked up a loud, harsh cough and dropped a loogie in the bowl to follow down the flush.

Volley crossed again by the closet slit, naked and full of folds, and opened the drawer. Inside were two highball glasses. He set them on the desk, his round, fleshy body obscuring Mikey's sightline as he filled them to the brim with wine. He brought them back to the bed.

"Let me ask you something," Ginger said. "I heard that Lukas Lane died."

"That's true," Volley said. "Suicide."

"I liked him," Ginger said. "Helped me out of a jam once."

"He was that kinda guy I heard."

"Do you buy it?" Ginger said, sipping her wine. "That he offed himself?"

"That's a big question," Volley said. "You know, when these things happen, it sends us into all sorts of questions. We see guys when they're logging hours in the office or out in the streets, but only get glimpses of what's actually going on at home. Who's to say what's going on behind those doors."

Mikey reached into his bag and felt for his tape recorder. He pulled it out, clicked a button, and saw the red recording light flash on.

"All we know is that his blood alcohol tested through the roof and he had rocks in his pockets," Volley said.

"That could be someone trying to off him for—"

"Drink your wine and let me finish, dear," Volley said. "He left a letter behind. Nothing in the way of concrete explanations, just personal emotional kind of shit. Just sad is all."

Mikey extended an arm through the hanging dresses to aim his recorder.

"Am I safe?" Ginger said.

Volley let out a belly laugh that echoed through the room, and Mikey watched the needle on his recorder spastically tilt back and forth.

"You got nothing to worry about now love," Volley said.

A long silence. Then a damp, muffled sound that

could only be the two of them starting round two. "They like to have their cake and eat it twice," Ginger had once explained to Mikey.

But then Mikey realized that the sound was all off. Squishier, more frantic.

The bed frame was striking the wall without any sort of rhythm, sharper and louder than before. A minute or so later, he heard a pants zipper and the metal click of a belt buckle before Volley's wide figure flashed past the closet door. He opened the room's door and exited out into the hallway.

Mikey parted the dresses and stepped from his hiding spot, but just as he did, the door burst back open.

Mikey was exposed.

All Volley had to do was take a quick peek to his right, and if the tales around town were true, he'd end Mikey's time in this world with a quick gunshot to the dome. Probably mark the case as a peeping tom caught in the act. Bad legacy to leave behind.

"Forgot something, love," Volley said, then mumbled, "Don't know why I'm telling you."

He retrieved the two wine glasses from the bedside table and brought them into the bathroom to give them both a hearty scrub, then took the one with lipstick still around its rim and put it into his bag. He grabbed the wine bottle from the desk and walked back out the door.

Mikey waited until the captain's loud footsteps faded down the hall, then slowly left the closet to peer toward the bed.

Ginger was gone.

He stepped deeper into the room and noticed that, against the wall on the bar's far side, there was one of Ginger's shoes bent at an awkward angle.

Her foot was still inside.

Mikey gave a wide berth as he walked to the narrow space next to the bed, and there was Ginger alright.

Motionless. Her face was smashed against the wall. It looked like she was melting.

Mikey gave her body a closer look. Her face was a bluish red, and there were claw marks across her throat. He played a hunch and, yep, her fingernails were filled with her own flesh and blood from attempting to excavate whatever poison Volley had given her.

Mikey sat on the bed and considered the angles.

There was no question Volley would make sure the report on this death would cross his desk, and if there was a note in there saying that one Michael "Scoops" Jervis was the person who discovered the body? Well, that'd be too much heat for this intrepid reporter.

No real choice but to scram and let the maid find her.

He searched the room for any trace he'd left behind. He looked under the bed, glanced at the desk, and even opened the nightstand, knowing full well he never used it. Inside, there was only a Gideon Bible.

But before he closed the drawer, he felt a hand grasp around his wrist.

It held it in place, and Mikey saw long red tendrils like fingers appear across his arm. The curtains blew open and he heard a voice whisper and shriek at once.

"Sunset," it hissed.

Mikey stepped back or was flung against the wall, he wasn't quite sure, and then the wind from outside calmed.

He stood back up and held a stillness as he looked once more at Ginger. His source, his friend in a way. Her face held a static look of anguish and fear.

Mikey picked up his bag, the tape recorder's light still shining red, and he made the sign of the cross on his way out even though he hadn't believed in years.

212

23. The Crew's Last Ride.
Room 450

TONY AND JON walked through the dilapidated lobby of the shabby old hotel to the front desk. Behind it was a disinterested woman in her mid-twenties who looked up from her cheap horror paperback. Her name tag read Connie.

"Yes?" she said, exhausted by having to expend the effort.

"A room please," Tony said. "Two, actually—two rooms. On the fourth floor."

Connie looked at the two young men, their faces studded with residual acne. They reminded her of those cartoonish comedy duos with one slim-and-tall (Jon), and one short-and-fat (Tony).

Beyond this oddball pair were the crew's other two members—a boy wearing glasses with thin, metal frames and shoulder-length hair parted down the middle, and a blonde girl with a mousy face who waved back cheerfully.

"I'm Holly," the girl said, putting an arm around the four-eyes. "and this is Martin. Go ahead and wave."

The boy in the glasses did.

"That's wonderful," Connie said. "$59.99 per room. Do you want me to do the math on that?"

Tony had already set a credit card on the desk, so Connie filled out the paperwork and Tony faked his dad's signature.

"Thanks, Mr. Sandoval," Connie said with a roll of her eyes, then reached into the desk's bottom drawer to pull out four sheets of paper. "Gonna need everyone to sign these."

It was the special waiver for those requesting to stay on the Palmer's fourth floor, letting the hotel legally off the hook for any incidents, "physical or mental," that may occur from spending a night on the haunted premises. Something the dumbasses at Lathan had added in desperate promotion for these sorts of thrill seekers.

"Those staying on the fourth floor can examine only their own rooms and the communal hallways," Connie droned from memory, "but if you'd like to take video or EVP or use any other devices to further investigate phenomena, there's an extra $25 charge per room. Cash only for that."

The four friends rustled through their pockets and, between them, came up with $50.

"Do you have a preference for rooms?" Connie said.

Tony set his elbow on the desk and leaned forward in an attempt to present a casual suaveness.

"We were told to ask for dealer's choice," he slyly said.

"Someone told him that was special code or something," Holly yelled from behind, with a roll of her eyes.

"Of course," Connie said, raising an eyebrow.

She reached to the wall of keys behind her, plucked two random keys for no reason other than they were close, and set them on the desk before returning to her paperback.

Tony grabbed the keys and the crew walked into the main hallway, then hung a left to the elevator bank for the South wing.

A car dinged upon arrival.

They went inside, pressed the "4" button—its plastic covering scuffed from years of use—and waited for the lift's ancient engineering to get cranking. The door closed and, after a moment, the carriage stirred as if it was being roused from a long nap before it slowly rose.

"I'm so nervous I'm gonna shit!" Holly shouted.

The others giddily laughed at her outburst.

It was the end of summer, and this was the crew's last hurrah.

In a few weeks, each would scatter off to various points for their next chapters—Holly to private school, Martin and Jon to state college, Tony hanging around the suburbs for a few years at the local community college before whatever was next, which would turn out to be not much. The crew wanted one last overnight road trip, and when Jon lobbied for ghost-hunting at the Palmer, it was an easy sell.

Ever since Tony got a Sony DV camera for his birthday, the crew had been shooting nonstop, which inevitable led to the amateur attempts at special effects. They'd made it look like Holly was getting her head lopped off, jumped in the air a bunch of times so it appeared like they were floating in awkward stutter, even tried trick shots with the basketball hoop before Tony's asshole brother Todd ratted them out for banking them off the windshield of the family minivan.

But it was always their videotaped ghost investigations that were the most fun.

They'd go to noted "haunted" locations around town late at night, shoot as many digital cards' worth of footage as they could, then hunker down in Tony's basement to examine their proof of the great beyond.

They'd see shadows and claim they were demons,

then convince themselves that out-of-focus dust specs were really orbs containing spirits of the dead.

They even gave themselves a name: "The ParAbnormal Crew."

Tony had spat it out one night, and while it wasn't great, no one had any better ideas, so it stuck.

The elevator clanged to a stop and opened onto the fourth floor with a listless ding. The crew stepped off.

This floor had a different feel than the lobby.

Colder. Damp.

The wallpaper was browned and the stained and trampled carpeting was a dark green. The smell of stale cigarette smoke lingered in the air.

The elevator car stirred and then shuffled off to wherever was next, leaving them to stew in a thickening silence.

"Boo!" Tony shouted from the top of his lungs.

Everyone jumped save Jon, whose fear response made him freeze like a possum but always passed it off as having blood made of steel.

"You little shit," said Holly, slugging him hard in the bicep.

Tony winced and massaged where she struck.

"Alright, enough fun, let's go," Jon said.

They passed an alcove where a torn and abused vintage yellow couch sat, and Holly put the back of her hand against her forehead in theatrical exhaustion, spun around, and collapsed back-first onto the couch. With the landing, a massive plume of dust puffed up in her face.

"Bet you wish you hadn't done that," Tony said.

Holly answered with coughs as she staggered back to her feet.

"They really let this floor go, huh?" Martin said.

"Kind of like your mom," Tony said, then immediately, "I'm sorry, I like your mom. It was just reflex."

Martin stared him down for a moment, then offered

a hand. Tony took it and they went through the fourteen sequential steps of the crew's secret handshake.

Apology accepted.

Jon snatched the two sets of room keys from Tony's dangling grip and stuck his once-white Adidas shoe forward out onto the carpet.

"You kidding?" Tony said. "What are we, twelve?"

"Any better ideas?" Jon said.

Jon had lobbed plan for the four to split into pairs, each spending the night in one of the two rooms with cameras and microphones—they'd "borrowed" extra equipment from Tony's jerk brother—in order to give them a better shot at collecting ghost proof. Tomorrow, they'd all go through the footage together. All that still needed to be figured out was who was going with who.

With no alternative method forthcoming, Holly, Tony, and Martin shrugged and stuck their shoes out next to Jon's, who then began the great sorting process.

"Bubblegum, bubblegum, in a dish," he said. "How many pieces do you wish?"

Out went Tony, out went Martin, which meant Jon and Holly got Room 450, while Martin and Tony got 409.

"Okay," Jon said. "Stay safe."

Martin and Tony started down the hallway to their digs, and when they finally turned the corner, Jon reached out to hold Holly's hand.

She clutched it back.

"Did you rig it?" she said.

He smiled.

They'd made out a few weeks ago after Jon had strategically dropped Tony and Martin off first so that Holly could join him in the front seat of his parents' Dodge. As the car idled in front of Holly's house, with the dashboard light shining on their faces, she leaned over for the first kiss, and kept going for an hour until a neighbor knocked on the window and told them to get moving. That was the last time they'd been alone with each other, until tonight.

Jon opened Room 450 and they walked in.

He set his bag on the bed. Holly came up next to him to examine the camera, but before she could, he grabbed her in a bearhug and they fell onto the bed. They kissed for a minute, but when the momentum began to shift into the next gear, she released her arms and placed her hands on his shoulders.

"Alright, buster," Holly said with a smirk. "We have to get to work. I take my ghost hunting very seriously, you know"

She stood off the bed and unzipped the bag, purposefully ignoring Jon's pout, then removed the camera and began examining the room through its side viewfinder.

The phone rang. Jon picked it up.

"Hello?" he asked, then rolled his eyes.

He pressed the speaker button. Holly heard a hissing, wet voice on the other end asking if they were ready to die.

"Good one, Tony," Holly called out. "Very believable."

"So, like, what's the plan?" Tony asked, his voice returning to its normal pitch.

"Did you read anything about where the good hauntings are?" Martin asked over the phone.

"These are all good questions," Holly admitted.

"Just hang out and see what you can find," Jon said.

He hung up and raised an eyebrow to Holly, then patted the bed next to him.

"Maybe this area is worth investigating a little more..." he said.

She rolled her eyes and blew him a light kiss. Jon saw the camera's red recording light blink on.

"Here is Jon on the bed at the infamous Palmer Hotel," she narrated. "Wave hello, Jonathan."

He did so with a plastered smile, then gave her the

finger. She panned the camera around the room.

"There's the wall. Boring. And there's the ceiling. Also boring," she said. "Here's a desk with a lamp on top."

She walked into the bathroom and flicked on the light.

"And here is, you know. And here's the mirror, which means, here is me."

She waved to herself.

In the viewfinder, she lingered for a moment on her eyes, as if attempting to discern what she herself was actually thinking. She returned to the bathroom, panned past the bed where Jon again raised a middle finger, and walked to the window.

"Here is our view from the fourth floor. Which is supposed to be the spoooookiest floor."

Through the viewfinder, a blur of a woman wearing red swept downward and was gone in an instant.

Holly jumped back, the camera shaking in her hand.

"Shit!" she shouted, then winced in preparation for the sound of impact.

"What?" Jon said, standing up from the bed.

Holly dropped the camera to her side and stepped hesitantly to the window to peer on her tip-toes down into the courtyard. When that angle didn't work, she opened the window and leaned out onto the fire escape into the flickering red glow of the rooftop sign.

"What?" Jon said.

"I think I just saw someone fall," Holly said.

"Um," Jon said. "What?"

"Someone fell right past this fucking window," Holly said. "I think."

A knock on the door.

Jon ran to the door and peered through the peephole but saw only empty hallway.

"Very funny," he called through to the other side.

No response.

"I said very funny," he called again.

Still nothing.

He unlocked the door and slowly turned the doorknob so that the latch just barely retreated from the lip, and when it did, suddenly the door pushed open.

Jon let out a loud, sharp yelp at the movement.

Tony's smiling face appeared in the cracked door.

"I finally fucking got ya!" he said.

He turned behind to slap Martin a high-five and they both entered.

"We were bored," Martin said, and slumped onto the bed. "Where's Holly?"

At her name, she ducked back inside from the fire escape and told them what she thought she'd seen.

"What the fuck!" Tony yelled.

"Should we call the front desk or something?" Martin asked.

"And what, tell them we think we saw a person jump off the building?" Tony said. "But they're not down there now?"

They discussed the pros and cons. Martin picked up the camera, flipped open the viewfinder, and began browsing through the footage Holly had shot.

"Guys..." Martin said.

They gathered around.

As the 12:00 a.m. timestamp blinked in the upper right corner of the image, a smudge of red flashed by.

Martin called the front desk.

"Yeah, we get that now and then," Connie droned. "More often these days. I'll look if it makes you feel better."

She called back a few minutes later, saying that all was fine and normal in the Palmer's courtyard, no dead bodies splattered on the ground.

"Can't make any promises for the rest of your night though," Connie said, before adding, "mwahahahaha!"

Click, dial tone.

The clock rolled to one o'clock, then two in the morning as the crew kept trying to figure it out, with the classic skeptic's "tricks of the light" explanation—being argued by Jon and Tony—winning the debate.

Around three, Martin lay face down on the carpet to "rest his eyes," and that was it for him. Holly went next, curling into a ball on the bed, so the crew was down to two.

As dawn painted the sky, Tony and Jon climbed out onto the fire escape and softly spoke to one another as they watched the opposite tower's windows blink away, one by one.

Silence descended upon them as they sat groggy and sleepless until Tony broke it by admitting to Jon how he was feeling left behind, what with everyone going away. Jon said that nothing was actually changing, that they'd all be back for Christmas soon enough, and then the summer. Anyway, they all knew that the crew was too strong to ever break up, but even then he wasn't sure if he was telling a lie.

When the sunlight finally hit to tops of their shoes as they dangled off the edge of the fire escape, they crawled back inside Room 450 and found space on the carpet to get a few hours of sleep before it was time to check out.

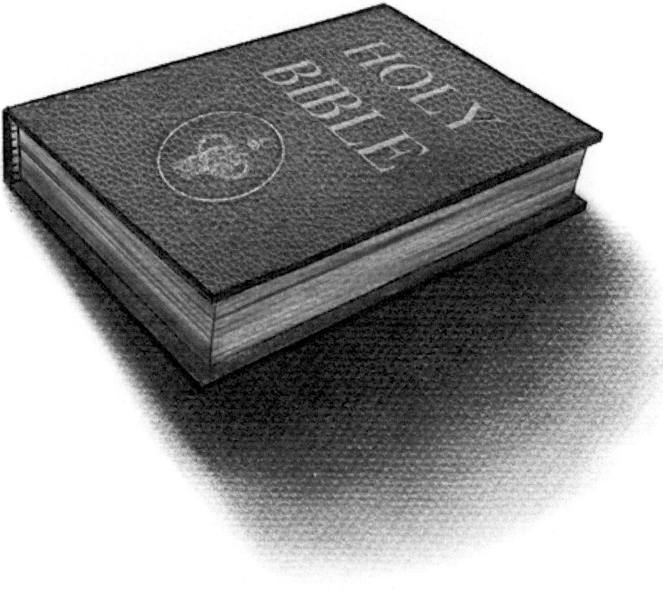
HOLY
BIBLE

24. Abigail Closes the Case.
Room 699

ABIGAIL HARRISON FELT the deadbolt disengage from the frame, and the door rocked slightly as it did. She opened her eyes, twisted the knob, and walked into the room where, she was told, her dad had killed himself.

Sunlight streamed in through a thin part in the curtains and cast a white triangle on the green carpet that ended in a sharp point on the back leg of the desk chair.

The door slammed shut on its springed hinge and she jumped at the booming sound, then took a deep breath and talked herself down. She pulled her overnight bag from her shoulder, set it down, and leaned against the wall.

For some reason, she thought about her Uncle Nick.

He wasn't a blood uncle, but he was closer than any of the ones who were. Nick was her dad's old partner on the force, and after her dad had left Abigail and her mother holding the bag of continued existence, he was the one who swooped in to handle the real shit.

Even before the actual funeral, he'd moved into a nearby motel and spent those long early nights of grief with the fractured family. After, he found an apartment nearby to move all of his shit into, to keep an eye on everyone. When Abigail finally turned 21, she confronted Uncle Nick about fulfilling the promise that she'd made him make when she turned Sweet 16—to tell her everything he knew about her dad.

"He was a good cop, Abbie, and more than that, a good man," he'd told her one night over coffee at an all-night diner. "Stevie Harrison was one of the goddamned best."

Uncle Nick had then detailed one particular case. Stevie had tracked down a serial rapist to his Westside squat, then took part in a chase that went on for hours and hours across three different subway lines before Stevie jumped a full flight of stairs to physically land on top of him, ending it for good.

"Superhero shit," said Uncle Nick, who had himself been off the force for years by then, now working his "retirement gig" of providing security for a downtown jewelry shop. "That was just your dad's style."

Abigail waited for a pause in the conversation to ask the question that she really needed an answer to.

"Uncle Nick," she started, "did he kill himself?"

Uncle Nick rocked back in his chair so only the rear legs touched the linoleum.

"Why would you ask that?" he said.

"That reporter who came by," she said. "He mentioned there were, what did he call it, inconsistencies. Said there were inconsistencies, and then something about a case named Sunset."

Uncle Nick sipped his coffee for what seemed like forever.

"That reporter," Uncle Nick had said in the diner, then sat forward and placed hands on knees like he did whenever he was finishing telling a story.

"Don't you worry about him."

There was a long silence before Uncle Nick spoke again.

"Stevie always worried about family first," was all he said. "Family first. Always family first."

An hour of prodding and yelling and defeated pleading didn't convince him to give any further details, so Abigail cried and told Uncle Nick that he'd gone back on his promise, and he shrugged and said that was all he could do—he couldn't help her anymore—and then he paid the check.

During a patch-it-up call later that week, he gave her two pieces of information: contact info for the Chronicle reporter who'd been digging around, and the number of the room where her dad had died.

"You'd have found both on your own anyways," he said. "You've always been a good snoop."

And so, weeks later, here was Abigail Harrison, inside of Room 699.

She walked to the bed and took off her shoes and socks, feeling the carpet with her bare feet. She stretched her toes out flat, then curled them in as deep as she could while examining the desk from afar.

It was made of dark brown wood and had six drawers with brass handles. Each drawer grew larger in descending order, and the desktop itself was deep and wide. Abigail considered how her dad's body would have splayed across it after he pulled the trigger.

She was 12 when it happened.

She remembered being in the basement, playing with the Erector Set she'd gotten the previous Christmas, when she'd heard a faint sound and noticed her mom in the shadows at the top of the stairs.

Frozen solid.

Abigail set down her wrench and approached to find her mom's face all swollen with a pink hue, her eyes stained red.

Whenever Abigail remembered her dad now, it'd always be dusk and he'd be at the kitchen table with his late-night coffee. He'd look out the window into the backyard at the oak trees against the backdrop of fading blue until the sky darkened enough that the orange ceiling light in the kitchen turned the glass into a mirror, and then he'd turn to the copy of yesterday's Chronicle that he always kept nearby.

She once asked him why he never read that day's paper, why he was always a day behind.

"Other folks want to know the news," her dad had told her. "I already know that. I want to know how they're telling it."

Once she asked him if he'd ever catch her if she became a bad guy. She must have been six years old.

She remembered how he glumly folded up his paper and pushed out the chair, as if taking a meeting with a peer. She climbed on the chair, dangled her feet off the edge, set her elbows on the table, and made a stern, serious look with her face, one that mimicked the ones she'd seen adults try to pull off.

"You won't ever be a bad guy," he said, and gave her a kiss on the cheek. "And that's that."

Abigail realized that her eyes were closed then felt the mattress on the back of her head, and put together that she'd fallen asleep in the hotel room.

She didn't quite know why she wanted to see the room. She knew it wouldn't bring her any closure, whatever that was anyway, because he'd laid it all out in the letter he left behind.

"I've been struggling with this sadness my whole life," he'd written in a script more scraggly than his usual hand. "The work of a tortured man," claimed the medical examiner. "Please know that I tried everything else first," was the letter's final sentence.

Abigail felt her eyes closing again so she forced them open. In the first red of the setting sun, she made herself get up and walk to the desk. She pulled out the chair, sat down, and traced her fingertips along its top. It felt cool and smooth, like a stone carved over the eons by a raging river's force.

Without thinking, she mimed a gun with her thumb and forefinger and put it to the side of her temple. She flicked her thumb and made a soft sound, then turned to see where her dad's brains would've splattered. She felt the grain of the sickly green vinyl wallpaper.

She slumped in the chair, and the desktop reflected the sunset. She watched the colors change from purple to fiery scarlet before darkness, then left the room lights off, so she was lit only by moonlight.

She stretched her arms out to take in the desk's full extent, then rested the side of her face flush against it.

She was at Frank's Hot Dogs, back in their town across the river. It was damp from rain earlier that evening. Storm clouds loomed above, but were disempowered by the pink and purple band painting the sky.

He was returning from the stand, itself shaped like a hot dog, with a red plastic tray in his hands—loaded with chili cheese dogs and fries, packets of ketchup and mustard, two small Styrofoam cups of ice-cold tap water. They ate as the sun disappeared and the hot dog stand's lights kicked in, bathing them in amber glow.

She told him about her day at school—how Joey got kicked out of sex-ed because he started giggling when the teacher described what S-E-X was. That would put her in sixth-grade in this dream, Abigail thought, then she noticed that the taste of Frank's was better than it had ever actually been.

She looked up at her dad. He had a coating of brown chili encircling his mouth like lipstick of a clown. She giggled as he pulled out napkins from the dispenser to wipe it off, then he looked back with stern eyes.

"I'm sorry I left when I did," he said. "I was protecting you. I thought. I knew things you or your mom couldn't, because if you did, you'd be here with me."

Abigail tried to speak past a bite of hot dog, but then she recalled she was in a dream, or at least something like a dream, and her mouth was suddenly empty.

"I know," she said, back in the clarity of her 21-year-old self. "I think."

He leaned back and nodded as if talking himself up the guts to continue.

"You're going to go through many events in your life," he had said, or was saying now, it was tough to know for sure. "It'll seem like I'm not there, that I'm missing them, but while I can't hug you again, not yet anyway, know in your heart that if there's anything you need, I'll be here for you. Right here."

He stretched out his hands and placed them on tops of hers, and as he did, faint electricity sparked through.

The giant red metal hot dog that topped the stand began to glow intensely, then suddenly burst into flames. She felt its warmth and watched the fire glow in her dad's eyes, but then the scene broke away in long strips that peeled and curled and fell from view.

She was in the hotel room staring at the green vinyl wallpaper above the desk, the next morning's sun reflecting off of it.

Her heart raced as she stood.

She spun and found that the bedside table drawer had, at some point, fallen out and landed on the carpet. She walked to it and looked inside.

There was an old Gideon Bible, nothing else.

She grabbed it—when she did, she felt another electric spark.

She sat on the bed and flipped through the Bible, and soon discovered markings throughout, letters that had been circled in a black pen.

She brought it back to the desk, took out a thin pad of cheap stationery with The Palmer's insignia from the top drawer, and began to transcribe the circled letters.

T-H-I-S-
I-S-
T-H-E-
C-O-N-F-E-S-S-I-O-N-
O-F-
S-T-E-V-E-N-
H-A-R-R

That was enough. She slammed the Bible shut.

Whatever was in the rest would put her in harm's way, would undo whatever her dad was trying to protect them from, she was sure of that.

"Family first," she muttered. "Always family first."

She stuffed the Bible into her bag, left the room, and took the elevator downstairs.

At the front desk was the tall, pockmark-faced clerk. Abigail asked for a large packing envelope and wrote out the name of that Chronicle reporter that Uncle Nick had told her about, that fella named Scoops Jervis, then placed the Bible inside. No return address.

She handed it to the clerk, told him this was important to get to its destination, then checked out.

Over the years, Abigail had returned to the Palmer twice more. Once was before her marriage to Frank, and once again, before the birth of her son Jason. Both times she asked specifically for Room 699, and both times she forewent the bed for a night splayed out on the desk, always dreaming that they were back at Frank's Hot Dogs in the pink and purple evening just after the summer rain had passed.

Later on, after mom's death, she'd returned one more time and discovered that the hotel had been converted into condos.

That was okay, she thought. Now at least dad had some company.

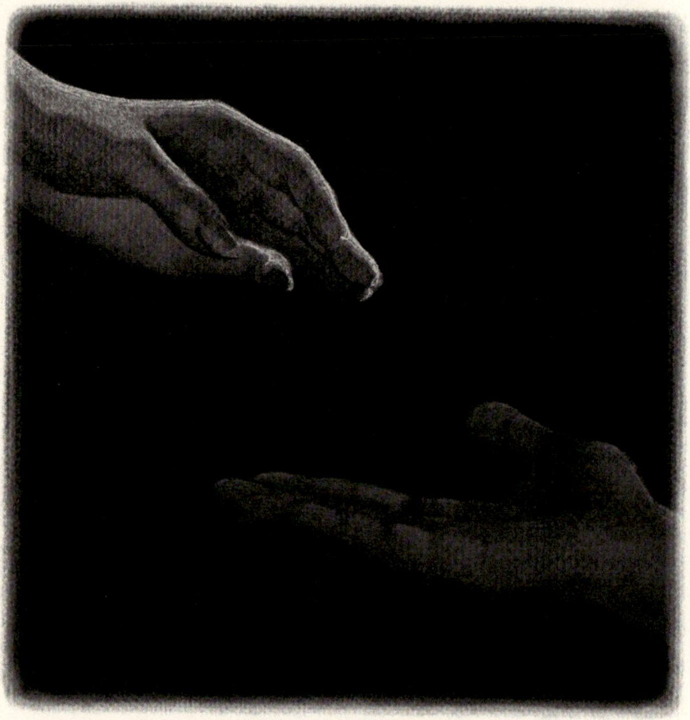

25. Sally's Last Dance.
The Tabor Hall

It was well past midnight when the power drill started taking off the plywood.

It had been tagged so often over the years that it blended into the building's wall under a slick coat of spray paint, but ten minutes and a few dozen screws later, they were in.

The ten of them, all dressed in black, rolled their rusty carts over the door's threshold and filed in. A dank, wet smell permeated the room. The tall, bearded one, Danny, reinstalled the boards behind them just in case a patrol was making the rounds, and the interior was pitched again into darkness.

The crew flipped on their headlamps and streaks of white fanned through the hallways, creating long tunnels of hovering dust. They pushed their carts along the musky carpet, past the bank of elevators, then through a maze of splintered crates and torn boxes that'd been left behind once the owners of the old hotel had decided their attempt to convert the building into something else was a massive failure.

At the main intersection of the ground floor, the group split up. Half walked down the gently sloping hallway into the lobby, a spacious room with soggy furniture and a large grandfather clock. It was wrapped in a sheath of cobwebs and its pendulum inside hung motionless.

Samantha entered the old employee break room behind the front desk and found a locker stuffed with random items. A silver bracelet with "Lila" etched into it, a magician's wand that revealed pink plastic flowers when you pulled its end, a Gideon Bible with various letters circled inside.

She closed the locker, moved on.

The other half of the group had walked up the steps into the old dining hall, a glass enclosure with missing panes that caused the wind circling through the courtyard to whistle as it entered. In the kitchen they found a loose can of beans, a fridge with a molded through interior, and forks resting on the tiles that'd been buried under dust.

They all returned to the main crossroads to gather again.

"So, where are we setting up?" asked Freckles, a short redhead with hair shaved at the sides and a wispy mustache just starting to sprout from his pale face.

A loud creak came from down the hallway. The helmet lights all spun to its source.

Sasha was opening a set of double doors and peering inside. She brought her cornrowed head back out with a bright smile on her face.

"I think I found it," she called.

They sped down the hall to the old ballroom, all playfully trying to get there first. When they walked inside, their footsteps squeaked out annoying cacophony on the scratched wooden surface as their headlamps scanned the room.

It was an open space over two stories high with a

balcony wrapping entirely around on its second floor. Their headlamps reflected against the silver gilding that traced the ornate ceiling decoration high above.

"Looks perfect," boomed Harv's voice from somewhere in the darkness, and everyone mumbled agreement.

They returned to the hallway and rolled in their carts. Spencer came in with a few folding tables he'd found stacked in a closet. They set them against the wall—the starched, yellowed wallpaper crinkling as it creased behind—and began to unload supplies.

Mini-bags of Doritos, Lay's, and Cheetos. Cans of Pringles stacked like palace columns next to a fortified bunker of granola bar boxes. Single-serving cartons of cereal they'd gotten after Eileen had bargained them away from an overnight janitor at the airport. Plastic bottles of brand name orange juice they'd talked someone into considering as a tax write-off. Styrofoam cups, bowls, paper plates, napkins, and utensil packets from friends working at McDonald's and Burger King.

Rabe set the LEDs in the corner and angled them up so they cast into the furthest reaches, and once the space was lit, everyone casually claimed spots on the floor with sleeping bags and pillowcases stuffed with laundry. They'd figure out actual rooms tomorrow in the daylight, when it was safe to move around.

"What do we think?" Pedro said.

His voice carried without force, and when he sat down, his position became the head of the circle just like always.

They began talking about logistics.

For the past few years, the Palmer had been vacant save for the rats that still nested and the ghosts that still lingered, occasionally spotted by curious kids looking to get scared or vagrants needing a place to crash. But it wasn't until two weeks ago, when Pedro heard about the space from Xavier, who'd spent a few cold fall nights inside himself, that the plan of occupation took shape.

Another winter was approaching and, as the train tunnels and alleyways began to fill more quickly than usual, as systems beyond their grasp were accumulating, as power funneled upward, these empty rooms in the twin skyward buildings all remained unused.

Pedro had looked into it some more: Latham, the building's owner, had yet to put it up for sale, let alone close any deal, so the going thought was that they'd be safe well until after the season's cold had come and gone. Maybe even past that. Anyway, a few months inside for folks who'd otherwise be on the street were better than nothing.

In the impromptu meeting on the floor of the Tabor Hall, they began splitting up duties. Who'd clean up where, who'd spread word around to the camps, who'd check folks in and get them situated, who'd list what items were still needed, the process for conflict resolution, security concerns. After the tasks were sorted, the tone shifted and the conversation grew more casual with people drifting away from the circle for earplugs and sleep or flashlights and exploration.

Sally and Simon made eye contact and wordlessly took the stairs. He held her cold, paperthin hand as she gripped the rail to aid her balky knees on their way up to the ballroom's second floor.

They were an odd pair. Sally was an old guard leftist, 70 years young, who'd been involved since the 60s and had the white scar lines in her leathered skin to prove her bonafides. Simon was in his 20s and new to the scene—a foreclosure then a bad fight that sent him couch-surfing, then living in his car that got ticketed and booted until he found himself in the encampment on 8th, where they'd met. Last night, Sally had set up a chair, draped a torn plastic trash bag over Simon's chest, and buzzed his hair and neck, making him look "presentable" for tonight's offensive.

They walked to the front row of balcony seats and Simon's headlamp caught rats scuffling around the floor. Sally had gotten used to them all those years, so she simply set a hand on the seat arm to help lower herself down.

"Give me a second to rest, hun," Sally said to Simon, who took his own seat next to her. "I never told you that I'd been here before, did I?"

Simon shook his head as a big smile ran across his face. He loved hearing her stories.

Sally described a night from 1960. She'd just turned 17, and her school was having their prom right here at the Palmer. She'd worn a blue dress that her grandma had tailored, and her date was a kid named Frankey Pienkowski. She laughed just thinking about him.

"Frankey had this awful cowlick," she said. "Looked like a mouse had taken squatter's rights on the side of his head."

"What else?" Simon said. "Tell me more."

"We went to prom, but that was just a formality," she said. "We didn't spend more than five minutes together. We both just needed a date."

She pointed to a far corner, near the stage.

"All night I was over there," she said, "dreaming with my gals."

They'd gossiped about boys and stink-eyed the clique of girls near the punch bowl. But it was later that night, Sally told Simon, that she figured out the rest of her life.

"I'd gone to the bathroom, and found this flight of stairs, so I walked up it," Sally said.

She turned to her right. As she raised her arm to point, she felt a slight twinge of discomfort, so she just let it fall.

"Over there, out of the light," she said, nodding instead. "I sat for the last half of the dance, watching them all. That's when I knew I had to get out of here."

Sally saw that Simon's eyes had drifted to the ballroom floor where he'd caught sight of raven-haired Monica. She was at the table, sorting boxes of oatmeal. Too long of a story anyway, Sally thought, so she gave him the short version.

She tore up her acceptance letter to University of Wisconsin, moved in with a cousin in Mexico City, and met Carlos. Simon nodded as if he knew the rest, like she'd mentioned it before, but she couldn't have—she'd always kept this to herself.

"Fascinating," Simon said, his attention gone for good.

Sally smiled deeply and set her wrinkled hand on his arm and gave it a squeeze.

"Think I'll sit here a while longer," she said.

He pecked her on the cheek.

"You call me if you need help," he said, and she listened as his footsteps echoed down the stairs.

Sally felt another twinge in her arm, but cast the pain aside, and leaned forward to spy on the burgeoning pair. Without a word, Simon helped Monica sort the oatmeals. He made a soft joke; Monica smiled back. Sally had seen all that before. She knew that'd be that, and silently wished them godspeed.

Her fingers traced the wooden seat's arm, and her thumb found a ripple, a slight indentation. She tilted her head to look and her headlamp illuminated a small carved spiral.

"Can I have this dance?" a voice near her spoke.

She turned with a calm, serene expectation. There was Carlos. Twenty-seven years old, like before.

His head was shaved, and he had that fierceness behind his eyes that made him seem angry, but she knew it was only aesthetic to disguise the teddy bear hidden within.

She'd missed him all these years, and she told him.

"I've missed you too," Carlos said, then grinned and offered his hand.

She felt its warmth. Not like the last time that she'd held it, growing cold as he bled out in Tlatelolco.

She stood with no pain, a new tightness to her skin, a gracefulness in her joints. She leaned and kissed him on the cheek as if it was the most natural thing in the world to do.

Carlos leaned back to take in a better look of her and let out a wolf whistle. She looked down and saw that now she was wearing her old blue prom dress, so she performed a curtsy.

Suddenly, the band onstage played a new song, up-tempo with a fancy beat.

"C'mon," Carlos said, grabbing her hand.

Rather than running down the stairwell, they simply glided over the balcony and floated softly down into the middle of the dance floor.

The rest of the dancers all spiraled around, paying no mind to this couple's late entry, or even the scattered sleeping bags of the occupiers that began to fade on the ground.

Sally and Carlos synched into a two-step. She felt sweat rising on her back, making her dress cling to her body. His smile was deep and wide, every tooth pearly white.

The band's next song was slow, so they danced close in each other's arms. Sally looked past Carlos through the shadows of the flowing, faceless dancers and saw Monica and Simon, still huddled in the corner, speaking quietly next to a lantern light.

Sally lay her head on Carlos's shoulder as they rocked in in rhythm and she told him all about these new friends of hers.

Interlude II:
The Grand Dance.

I SINK BELOW TO THE GRAND DANCE.

The ballroom lights are a low, flickering red, and I'm surrounded by others.

Hundreds in silhouette.

A coolness resonates from them, I hear the deep heaves of their breaths.

I look around.

There's an old man with a glass eye painted blue. There's a gaunt woman dressed in black whose elbow-length gloves sharply contrast with her pale skin. There's a young child with ruby-red lips and, strapped to her wrist, a purple balloon strapped that hovers in eerie stillness.

I see a young man with a hunched back and a thick open gash running down his forearm. It doesn't bleed, but it's not congealed—merely a vertical strip of liquid that floats around exposed bone and muscle.

They all look familiar, but I don't know from where.

They face the ballroom stage with stoic looks and anticipation in their eyes. Their knees loosen and they gently sway, as if in preparation.

I sway as well.

I spin around up into the second-floor balcony surrounding the ballroom. Every seat is occupied. The audience sits silently.

A woman in a white dress with dirty white hair is in a front row seat. A pearl necklace hangs around her neck, pearl earrings dangle from her ears, a pearl bracelet rattles on her wrist. She holds the railing and blotches of white appear in her knuckles as her distressed grip trembles. She looks familiar, too, but I don't know why.

Her eyes look past me towards the stage, as if I'm not there.

It is empty save a chrome microphone that shines metallic in the bright spotlight. A thick purple curtain hangs behind. It begins to ripple.

A simmering energy weaves through the crowd. Odd giddiness creeps into my stomach. Like quivering forced butterflies when you're falling. The curtains part, revealing darkness behind it.

A murmuring din sounds around me, so I murmur as well.

Nonsense words. Nothing of coherence. An incantation of sorts. Lips quivering like a cold night.

Those around me burble similar madness into the air.

Through the curtains, as if beckoned by the crowd, a woman in a red dress walks out. She strolls, one bare foot in front of the other and walks across the stage, her long brown hair bobbing with each step.

Our susurration grows to a higher pitch. I feel the humming vibration in my throat.

It tickles my ears.

The woman approaches the microphone and the spotlight catches her aqua blue eyes. They seem to illuminate the reddened room all on their own.

Our resonant whispers echo against the ballroom walls to such a churning volume that my eyes begin to shudder, blurring the woman into a veiled apparition.

The crowd silences. Expectancy lingers thick in the air. The woman opens her mouth.

Then, she screams.

The microphone amplifies it and the speakers blast shockwaves through my body, or whatever this is. It feels like being struck by a windstorm of heat, of anger. Her shriek forms gooseflesh on my arms, sends a shiver down my vertebrae, and pinches the bridge of my nose so hard that I desperately want to squint, but I cannot.

I'm forced to look.

The woman's mouth closes as she steps away from the microphone, but her scream still resonates. She begins to gently rock, side to side, swaying to some silent music only she can hear.

Those closest to the stage mimic her movements, then the second row, then the third. When the wave finally reaches me, I sway too.

To my left, the old man with the glass eye. To my right, the young girl with the still balloon. They sway as well.

A new presence floods the dance floor. I notice that the balcony has thinned out as they've all begun to stream down the stairs to join us. We squeeze against one another to fit in. Our legs and shoulders rub, our backs and chests brush.

We sway.

We all sway.

The woman in red glares at us with her aqua blue eyes, then she begins to softly twirl in a circle.

All at once, we collectively shuffle, our moves predetermined by some force. We form into a circle with rows between us, and when our transition is complete, the woman halts her spin.

Our voices again quiver in high-pitched din.

The woman walks off the stage down onto the dance floor into our aural bed of lunacy. She walks into the circle's opening and strolls, one bare foot in front of the other, through the corridor that we, her looming dancers, have created.

She follows the aisle, approaching closer and closer to me, and it's now that I realize she's been walking inside of a spiral, and I am at its center.

I feel my heartbeat. I feel my pulse throb in my ears, my neck. The tips of my fingers feel hot and electric.

The woman approaches me.

I reach out my hand, and she smiles and extends hers. I feel the faintest electric spark as we touch. She pulls me to her and we're suddenly in each other's arms. I close my eyes and let her guide our dance.

I feel her warmth, a sensation I haven't felt in however long I've been here, wherever this is. She puts her head on my shoulder and I realize I can smell her hair.

I sense the other dancers moving around us, so I open my eyes. They look at us with smiles of bright white teeth and glowing stares.

The woman removes her head from my shoulder and whispers in my ear. I can't make it out over the music.

"What?" I ask her, but realize my voice has thinned into silence.

She whispers her mysteries again. Still, I can't hear.

The woman tenses in my arms. The smiles from the other dancers now seem strained, forced. They're pulled back in torturous pain, their reddened unblinking eyes staring back as desperate pleas.

The woman pushes away from me as a look of horror grows on her face. Some new realization has entered her mind.

I float away from the grand dance,

and then I open my eyes.

26. Jimmy Price Cleans Up.
Room 584

FRECKLE-FACED, WILD-EYED Jimmy Price looked at his hand.

10 of hearts, 10 of diamonds, 10 of spades.

This meant the sweat-sheened giant to his left named Mouse should have bupkus—soon confirmed by his glum-faced fold.

"Bullshit," Mouse huffed.

"Gonna raise," Jimmy Price said.

He took fifty from his stack of chips and threw them in the pot.

"Call," said Puggy, the bald, heavy-browed Lithuanian seated across the table.

Jimmy Price knew Puggy had two pairs, Kings over Queens, just enough justification for him to see this hand through to its conclusion. As long as Jimmy played it right.

"Fold," said Walter, the bespectacled thin man to his right.

Now this, this was unexpected, and that in itself made the act worrisome to Jimmy Price.

If Jimmy had stacked the deck properly, and he always did, that meant Walter just folded three nines, a sort of hand someone didn't just muck.

Not unless they felt like something was off.

A hot flash shot up through Jimmy's chest but stayed tucked below his t-shirt's neck line. He'd been in enough situations like these that he'd developed a mental trick to alleviate the pressure of getting caught in a scam. All he had to do was believe in his heart that he wasn't full of shit, that he wasn't a lousy cheat.

Justify your actions enough to yourself and your conscience allows for anything, he'd learned. Absolutely anything.

"I'll take one," Puggy said, and hurled a spinning card that landed face down.

Jimmy delivered the next card—which he knew was an ace. Puggy's face remained stoic upon seeing it, which happened to be his tell.

Jimmy traded in a five for the seven he had waiting, locking him into the full house that'd be just good enough to take the hand.

"Hundred," Jimmy said, raising the pot.

Puggy called, raised another hundred.

Jimmy winced, the way he did whenever he was trying to give the impression he was deep in thought. It was usually a planned feign, but this time he had real things to worry about.

Did Walter's early fold of three nines suggest that he suspected Jimmy was using a loaded deck? Was he mucking this hand to test out his theory? Was that what Walter meant earlier when he told the story of Turtle, the East Side card sharp?

If Jimmy got caught messing with the deal, well, with this crew, he'd be lucky to get out of the room with any of his slippery fingers still attached.

"Too rich for my blood," Jimmy Price said, and folded his winning hand.

Puggy flashed his hand as a taunt then stacked his new chips in front of him.

"Good fold by me then," Jimmy Price said, then mixed his cards into the deck, gave it a quick shuffle, and the deal shifted to Mouse. Jimmy rocked back in his chair and pulled out a cigarette.

This many packs into the night, a persistent smoky haze hovered in the room, blotting out the smell of fresh paint and upholstery that it'd had when they first walked in hours ago.

Tonight was the new North wing's grand opening, the end of a long process that capped off Jonathan Palmer's vision for the land his father had left him. And for those who made sure these final steps went as smoothly as possible—with the city's red tape when it came to new construction, with the workers complaining about having to clock in overtime—they all got first dibs, on the house.

But while the big guys got the new upstairs suites, down here on the fifth floor was reserved for their goons.

Jimmy Price, Mouse, Puggy, and Walter all knew each other, but only loosely, having lingered together in the shadows for any number of basement meets and alleyway payoffs over the years. Which is to say, they weren't what you'd call co-workers and weren't what you'd call friends.

Jimmy was Hog Williams's man, Mouse belonged to Mr. Thompson, and Walter was Frank Constantine's longtime right hand.

Puggy, meanwhile, had recently been brought into the employ of Sammy Gratzie after his previous boss had been laid to rest.

This new transition of employer is what brought on Puggy's new, unfortunate line of questioning.

"Whaddya mean, what cut do I get?" Mouse said, shuffling the deck. "That's none of no one's business."

"You tell me, I tell you, and we all get to know who's getting fucked out there on the streets," Puggy said, re-stacking the chips he'd just won.

"I'll show you mine, you show me yours kinda thinking," Mouse chuckled. "What is this, recess at St. Mary's?"

He finished shuffling, offered a cut, retrieved the deck, and dealt.

"What you're speaking of is communism," Walter said softly, his thin fingers striking a match against the tableside. "Which would be a problem when it comes to the people in our line of work."

Puggy closed his mouth and Jimmy Price looked at his cards. Four suited, nothing higher than a six. The definition of junk.

"You guys figure it out on your own," Jimmy Price said as he stood up from the table. "I gotta go take a leak."

He left for the bathroom and flicked on the light switch. It cast orange on the pristine surface.

He shut the door behind him and Jimmy heard a higher-pitched plea from Puggy saying he didn't mean nothing at all by that talk.

"Dumb son of a bitch," Jimmy thought to himself, and lifted up the toilet seat with his polished black Florsheim. He pissed with a force that splashed over the rim and onto the tile, then he flushed.

From the other room he heard a deafening barrage of gunshots and screams.

He flinched and ducked down instinctively, then clumsily pulled out his revolver, before jumping into the bathtub, yanking the shower curtain over—as if that'd offer any protection—and aiming vaguely at the door.

Jimmy tried to recall the number of gunshots. Maybe four, but they were rapid, too close together for just one gun.

Then screams.

Then nothing.

If it was a group of assassins they'd still be out there, waiting for him to step out.

The bathroom light suddenly went out, plunging the room into pitch blackness except the sliver of light streaming in from under the closed door. Jimmy felt his own quivering breath bounce off the shower curtain and back against his face. It rippled the vinyl and made a crinkling sound, so he closed his mouth and held his breath.

Heat and heaviness invaded the room, and he felt hot breath on the back of his neck.

Then a whisper.

"Cheat," it hissed in his ear.

He spun around and his revolver smacked against the wall tile and dislodged from his hand. It fell with a rattling din into the tub, then slid to a cold stop.

Jimmy Price heard only his heartbeat in the enclosed space.

"Thief!" a voice echoed in the shower.

He swept open the curtains and bolted from the tub, then out of the bathroom, slamming the door behind him, holding its handle to keep whatever was in there from breaking through.

He realized that he smelled gunpowder in the air, then looked over his shoulder and found the ghastly tableau of a gangland massacre.

Contorted and awkwardly bent bodies, splotches of red and pink where faces once were, a clump of wet flesh surrounded by scattered poker chips and cash.

The hotel's new carpet, already soaked with blood.

Walter was face-down next to the bed, an exit wound in the back of his skull. Puggy was still in his chair near the window, a hole right between his confused eyes. Mouse slumped against the far wall, a river of blood where his left eye once was.

Jimmy let go of the bathroom door and leapt towards the open closet. He hurried inside, shut his eyes, and reached to his chest where his pendant of Saint Christopher hung.

He quickly said a prayer even though he hadn't believed in years.

When he opened his eyes, he was looking at a bag on the floor.

Brown, leather.

A wet, sickly gargle came from the other room, and Jimmy slunk his head around the corner. The gargle came again, and he realized it must have been coming from where Mouse's body rested against the wall.

He carefully gave the scene a wide berth, and there was Mouse, alright. His left eye was gone, but his right eye was open, glaring at Jimmy.

He was still alive.

The fat man coughed blood down onto the white t-shirt that clung to his swollen beer gut. It raised and lowered, raised and lowered with frequent, panicked breaths.

"Mouse?" Jimmy Price asked. "What happened?"

Mouse's right shoulder jerked and settled on the carpet, then jerked and settled again, as if he was having a seizure, or maybe trying to perform some action but failing in its attempt.

Jimmy followed the shoulder to his hand, where Mouse's hand still clutched his gun. He was trying to defend himself, but his brain wasn't in command anymore, so the gun merely lifted a millimeter, then settled back down on the ground, then lifted again, stuck in this spiralling movement.

Jimmy crawled over to it and unfolded Mouse's fingers from the handle then took the gun for himself.

"Thief," Mouse hissed. "Thief."

A loud sound in the hallway.

Someone was door-knocking a few rooms down,

and someone else quickly answered.

Jimmy stood and ran to the door, but as he did, his foot caught Walter's splayed arm and he fell face first into the carpet. Mouse's gun dislodged from his hand and flew into the bathroom, spinning against the tile before colliding against the tub's edge.

Jimmy pushed himself up and heard another knock outside in the hall. It was the one room over, and it was soon followed by a short inquiry asking if anyone had heard a loud noise.

Other mob goons on the fifth floor, trying to figure out what had happened.

"Cheat," a voice whispered behind Jimmy.

He spun around, but the bodies lay where he'd left them. Even Mouse was still, his remaining eye now closed for good.

A loud knock on the room's front door, right behind Jimmy.

"What is it?" Jimmy called through.

"We heard a loud noise," one voice called. "A few of them. What's going on?"

Jimmy stood in place and thought through his story. He was in the bathroom, and there was some argument, and the three of them shot each other to death, he had nothing to do with it all. Maybe they'd buy it, maybe not, but what choice did he have but to tell the truth on this one.

He opened his eyes and the brown, leather bag on the closet floor caught his eye again. He crept in and peeled it open with his Florsheim.

Inside was a jackpot.

Expensive watches and gold jewelry on a bed of thousands of dollars.

"Well," Jimmy Price shouted through the door. "Who are you?"

"You gonna open up or what?" boomed from the hallway.

He grabbed the bag and searched for anywhere to hide it. Under the bed, no good. Out the window, he could be seen. He thought about entering the darkness of the bathroom for about one split-second before those disembodied voices spooked him out of that option.

His eyes landed on the metal grate near the nightstand, hanging by a single screw. Mouse's body must have dislodged it.

Jimmy dove to the grate, spun it open, stuffed the bag inside, then ran his fingers across the carpet to find the other bolts.

"Coming, coming," he shouted, as he screwed the bolts back in with his fingers.

Another loud bang on the door.

"Do we have to break this fucking thing down?" a voice said.

"Coming, coming!" he yelled, stood up, and opened the front door.

Two goons on the other side. Max Grouse and Paulie Barone, both with wild glares. They looked past Jimmy to the sprawled, bloody display on the floor.

"You boys got here just in ti—" he got out before Max shot Jimmy Price twice in the chest.

He huffed air through his nostrils, smelled smoke and burnt flesh as his body slunk to its floor, then felt a pain in his back like an itch he couldn't reach. His front was cold and wet.

He faced the darkened bathroom as the two hoods stepped over his body.

"Where's the take?" Jimmy Price heard one say.

But that was no real concern about it all by Jimmy Price anymore. He felt a blissful lightheadedness as his eyes closed, then a faint voice in his mind whispered to him that it was time to rest, that he had to sleep in order to regain his strength. He shut his eyes.

And then, from the bathroom, Jimmy Price heard a soft rustle.

He forced his eyes open and in the darkness could see only the closed shower curtain.

It billowed gently, almost as if it was breathing.

Behind it, he saw a dark shadow with eyes that glowed fiery red.

Long, wrinkled fingers caressed down the curtain's side and grabbed its end into a bunch.

"Where the fuck is it?" he heard one of the goons, it didn't matter which really, yell to the other. "Did you check the bathroom yet?"

And then, Jimmy Price saw the shower curtain slowly pull open, and he decided right then that it was best to listen to that voice in his head.

That he did, in fact, need to get some sleep.

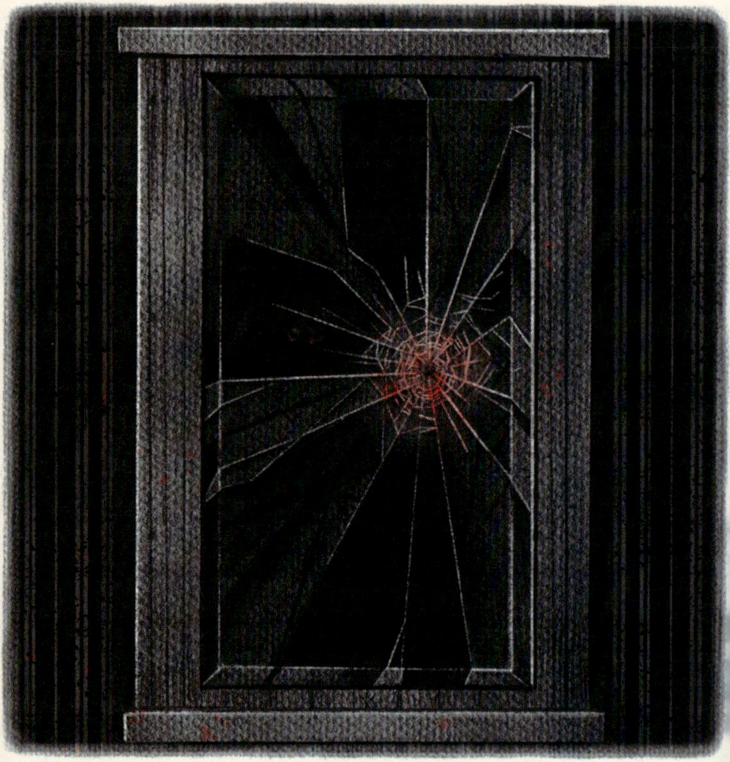

27. Wendy Learns an Old Trick. Room 650

WENDY SCREAMED IN FRUSTRATION as she flung the cards across the floor, and as they scattered in disarray she punched the mirror she'd leaned against the wall.

It spiderwebbed and a central spiral of blood spread through its new cracks. She looked her hand over and found a ragged cut on the edge of her pinkie knuckle.

"Dumbest motherfucker on the planet," Wendy muttered to herself. "Real smart shit, you asshole."

She sucked on the cut and tasted the iron, and let her auburn hair fall down in front to make a small cocoon for her face, a private space that let her block out the world and gave her mind some time alone. It was an old trick she learned from she forgot who.

Wendy breathed deeply in for a long few seconds, then recalled how little time she had left to get this trick just right.

She flung back her hair and stood with enough force to topple the chair onto the carpet, and stormed into the bathroom where she put her hand under the running faucet.

As she let the cold water wash out her cut, she examined herself in the mirror.

Her outfit—the forest green dress she'd wear tomorrow—fit loosely around her body, but it was her face that captured her attention. There was her latest forehead wrinkle, a yellow splotch along her cheek, her brown eyes now dry and reddened, and a newly burgeoning mole near her temple. Time was unfair to all, but she felt it was especially so for her.

She pulled her fist from the water and tore off a piece of toilet paper to set on her cut, then watched the blood expand its borders in an oblong circle, gluing the paper in place. She took one last look in the mirror at this aging monster before her, then it was back to the bedroom to work on this fucking stupid card trick again.

It was nearing midnight the night before her big audition for The Herman Marcuse Show.

A few months back, they'd lost one of their main acts, The Great Fraust. The rumor was that it was a positive HIV test. Sad stuff and all, but the real news—the current big to-do in the magic industry—was the void it left behind.

See, Marcuse was one of the few network showcase spots out there, and now it was up for grabs. Merely a season on that show was enough to guarantee sell-out performances for the rest of your showbiz days.

Wendy had known she'd been ready for prime time for years, but she also realized she was attempting the impossible: entering an old boys' club.

If they were going to go with a woman magician, they wouldn't want her, no matter the skill level. They'd want someone younger, more attractive, tighter in all the places where the TV cameras would be picking up.

They'd want a girl.

Not Wendy.

Still, these chances didn't come around often, if ever, and when she called her dad for advice, he said she had to try, if only so that when she made it big, they'd have to live with having said no. When he bought her a plane ticket and a night's stay at the nearby Palmer, then told her they were both non-refundable, she had no real excuse left to give him.

Wendy's audition trick was something she called "Lucky Sevens," and it worked like so.

She'd shuffle the deck, have a member of the audience cut it, and fan all 52 cards face-up in a seemingly random splash. Meanwhile, her keen eye would pick out where the sevens landed. As she collected and shuffled the deck, she'd tell the story.

This rendition was about "a friend of hers" named Alfred, a day trader who'd only ever buy stocks whenever their listing showed a seven in its price. It was a compulsive quirk he picked up after not going with his gut on a big buy years back.

"Maybe you heard of it," she'd tell the audience of Marcuse scouts. "A little company called Energizer."

She'd pause for their giggle of recognition.

"Alfred couldn't stop thinking about how much money he lost because of that single decision, so he vowed to never let it happen again," Wendy would say. "And every time a seven came along that ticker, he bought. So today, in Alfred's honor, we're going to keep an eye on the sevens."

While she told the story, the real deception would occur.

She'd shuffle and reshuffle then reshuffle the deck some more until the sevens she'd picked out were all lined up in a row. It took countless hours of practice to make this subtle ordering appear like random chaos, even longer to do it while she was telling the story, but that part she was comfortable with.

It was the next step that still stumped her.

When the story was over, she'd have someone cut or tap the deck. She'd make it their call—the trick seemed more spectacular that way. If they tapped, her job was over, the set-up already having been completed.

But audiences rarely did this.

She'd found that observers couldn't resist having a say in the outcome, and if they cut the deck in just the right spot, the trick was fucked—anywhere in the middle third, and it'd be necessary for her to reorder the sevens again.

But with a close-up trick like this, mere inches away from the crowd, all eyes would be on her hands, making it nearly impossible. What she needed to do instead was simply counter the cut by placing the halves back in their rightful order. This moment was make-or-break for the trick—and where the real thing called "magic" actually was.

What Wendy couldn't figure out was how to make it work.

She'd tried slipping her wrist in front to block their line of sight, but that was clumsy, and often drew further attention. She tried scratching her opposite arm as a red herring for those expecting such an obvious distraction, but that gambit sometimes led people to focus their attention elsewhere, maybe finding her attempt to clandestinely stack the sevens in the process. She thought of going with a meta "hey, look over here" bit to break the tension before pulling it off under their noses, but that just wasn't the right tone for Marcuse.

Back from the bathroom, she got on her hands and knees to pick up the flung cards, then reorganized the deck.

The chime of a clock striking midnight came through the hotel courtyard, and she walked to the window to find out from where.

As she approached, a blur of scarlet fell past.

It was gone in an instant.

She opened the window and leaned out to inspect below, but nothing caught her eye. The only thing out there was the courtyard lit up radiantly—white from below mixing with red from the rooftop's ancient sign.

It must have been a trick of the light, she thought.

Then, a sudden movement from across the way.

A curtain had pulled open, and standing in front was a young blonde girl, probably six or seven years old. She pulled the curtains behind her to create her own hidden, private space.

"You're up late, sweetie," Wendy muttered.

The girl had blonde pigtails that hung at her sides, her eyes stretched wide open as she pressed her forehead against the glass. Wendy watched her mouth the word "wow" as she looked in awe at the complexity of the world outside of that window.

Wendy put her own forehead against the glass and felt the cool of the outside. The movement caught the girl's attention.

Wendy gave her a little wave, and it took the girl a moment to figure out the proper response, but when she did, she raised her hand back. Wendy took the wordless conversation up a notch by placing her lips flush against the window, then blewing until her cheeks bubbled like balloons.

The young girl giggled.

Her face contorted into an expression of curiosity, as if asking "can I do this too?" Wendy answered by removing her lips, then slowly and expertly restarting the process, trying to teach her the steps as best she could from the distance.

She opened her mouth and the girl across the way opened hers, then she placed her mouth against the window, and the girl followed suit. Wendy blew so her cheeks filled up, and the girl tried as well, but instead of inflating her mouth a cloud of hot breath dusted the window on either side of her cheeks.

Wendy laughed, and seeing this reaction, the girl laughed too.

Then all at once the window split into long strips that warped the courtyard into odd, funhouse-mirror distortions as the screen of reality fell apart and Wendy was in the way back seat of her family's old station wagon, shuffling a deck of cards to pass the time.

They were on a road trip to the House on the Rock. She was six years old and sitting next to her cousin, Amy, whose habit then was sticking the ends of her pigtails into her mouth and licking them into points like painters' brushes.

Both were their family's only children, born a day apart.

"One day older, one day wiser, a whole lot blonder," Amy always said.

They were basically sisters.

The road stretched out far behind them. On that trip, Amy had snatched the deck from Wendy's hands and taught her how to blow raspberries on the back window as they passed cars.

"Give them something to remember us by," Amy had said with a wink.

Then, suddenly, this vision from the way back seat was cut into strips again and peeled away. Wendy and Amy were older and sitting at the townie dive named Fish's.

They used to sneak in as high schoolers, but now, they had long left that era behind them, and were both back home for grandma's funeral. At Fish's, they'd run into some acquaintances who still lived back in town, and after a few drinks, Amy had unbuttoned her top. Soon enough, the guys were stumbling over each other to buy their next rounds.

"Gotta work with what you got," Amy had said, pulling her blonde hair into a ponytail to show off her bare neck.

The bar scene stripped and peeled again and now Wendy was at Amy's funeral.

Dead at 32.

Cancer.

Came on fast, then it was all over. One of those things.

Wendy blinked and was back at her sixth-floor window, looking out.

The window where the young girl had been was now occupied only by curtains that gently swayed side to side, as if someone had just brushed past them. The sound of light rain began to patter against the glass.

Wendy spent another few minutes looking for another figure in the Palmer's windows across the way—anything to give her some distraction away from the task at hand—but when nothing fit the bill, she returned to the desk and tried again to perfect her misdirection.

She thought of Amy again and set the cards aside, then stood so her full body appeared in the cracked, leaning mirror. It was still marked with a circle of blood from her knuckle.

She looked at her loose forest green dress then undid the top few buttons to considered how it'd look to the old boys' club.

28. Hoight Dies.
Room 809

HOIGHT WOKE UP on the last day of his life in the same room where he had spent his first.

The dawn hit his wrinkled, ashen face, and he rubbed his eyes as if to push the light away, but quickly relented and twisted himself out of bed. This blast of early morning light was why he'd kept the curtains open. He had a lot to get done on his birthday, after all.

His knees worked out the aches of their 65 years as he crossed the floor, then squatted down to lift up the pumpkin he'd pre-gutted and left on a thin layer of old Chronicles he'd laid out on the desktop. He plunged a serrated knife into the pumpkin's flesh and carved out the eyes first, just like Aunt Harriett, no blood relation, had taught him decades ago.

"The eyes will tell you what it's thinking" she had told him, "and from there, you just carve how it tells you."

Aunt Harriett and Hoight's mom, Alice, had been maids at the hotel under the first Mr. Palmer—Mr. Jonathan, that is.

They'd mopped floors and cleaned out ashtrays and otherwise catered to the many needs of the countless thousands of guests who'd flowed through the doors to write their names on the ledgers.

Sometimes, those needs went beyond what was in the job description.

Alice had a long night back in '35 with a man passing through, and nine months later, she was leaving this world screaming in pain as Hoight was bursting into it crying. He'd only met her for a few moments before she passed on, but believed that he still knew her smell.

Right away Aunt Harriett had taken over his official stewardship, but it was more of a family affair, with most of the hotel staff pitching in, everyone using their breaks to dote on the tiny orphan. Mr. Jonathan had set Room 809 aside for that purpose indefinitely, which turned out to be longer than anyone would have guessed.

When Hoight turned 18, Aunt Harriett sat Mr. Jonathan down after hearing rumors about his passing the hotel's ownership down to his son, Mr. Jack. She had the boss put it all in writing, telling him that the maids would drop their brooms if he didn't, and with that leverage Mr. Jonathan relented. The contract said Hoight couldn't sell or rent the room, but he also couldn't get kicked out of it either, no matter who took over, which ended up meaning Mr. Jack, then Ms. Jacqueline then Mr. Joseph, then those outsiders with all the money.

The room was his. All he had to do was stay working at the Palmer.

Hoight made alterations to the room over the years. He stripped the wallpaper and put up wood paneling, tore up the carpet and added Persian rugs, installed shelves, put in a hotplate, and added thick green drapes that he usually kept open as he slept. He always liked drowsing off to the city night trains as they clattered on by.

Over his long career of carving Jack-o-Lanterns, only twice had Hoight made anything other than a proper face.

One time was in honor of Sneezers, the kitten he'd found in the kitchen one late fall night who stuck around a few seasons before disappearing again, as street cats do. A few years back, he tried out a design of the hotel itself as a gift to new management, but he'd misjudged some angles and it collapsed in on itself before he could present it. He'd only done faces otherwise.

Hoight finished with this year's smile—making the fangs sharper than usual, since that's what the eyes told him to do—then set it aside to get ready for his real work at the front desk. He didn't officially start until six that night, but Hoight liked going down early to soak in the "happy birthdays" from co-workers and guests.

He walked to his closet and pushed his front row of civilian clothes to the side so he could access the rear, where all of his bellhop outfits hung.

For a long while, he had donned actual costumes for the Halloween holiday, but Latham made a policy against that—something about not wanting to give off the wrong impression—so those were out of the rotation.

Instead, it was another day in his standard bellhop outfit. But while he mostly wore off-black or brown, sometimes a purple if he was feeling frisky, on this special day he brought out something from the back of his closet—the burnt orange one, the one that really popped.

Hoight knew his uniforms were perceived as a little strange these days, but so what—they made him feel comfortable. And more than that, they set limits between when he was on the clock and when he wasn't. If he was in his bellhop uniform, ask away for some assistance, and if he wasn't, keep on walking. As the Palmer's only permanent resident, this distinction was important.

Hoight went to his mirror and adjusted the uniform so it sat crisply on his shoulders. He ran his fingers over his collection of oval felt hats that hung from a row of pegs and snatched up the orange one. He straightened it on his head and lifted the pumpkin in his arms. He looked into the mirror again and saw looking back the damn President of Halloween, so he gave himself a wink and then departed his room.

He entered the elevator and already inside was a couple who looked like they'd gone a few rounds with each other overnight, and with some bad results. The man gritted his teeth; the woman stared off into the corner. Hoight had seen all this before. Late night joy swapped for early morning regret.

"Y'all heading down I hope?" Hoight asked.

They nodded and rode the rest of the way in silence.

The doors opened onto the ground floor and the pair walked outside to their separate cabs. Hoight approached the front desk where Stroud was watching his shift tick away on the grandfather clock.

"They look like they had the wrong kind of fun," Hoight said, lifting his pumpkin onto the desk.

"You don't know the half of it," Stroud muttered.

Stroud was always an enigma to Hoight. Despite working together for three decades, they'd only ever bonded once—when new management came in. But even that conversation, over a few rounds in The Anchor, felt to Hoight like Stroud was sizing him up, like he was trying to find weaknesses.

Hoight dipped his cap goodbye and walked into the hallway storage closet. In back was his bucket of decorations—fake cobwebs and cut-outs of skeletons, witches, and black cats. He pulled them out and started pinning them along the hallway walls, spending hours to place them just right, pausing whenever the elevator dinged with another guest's exit to doff his cap and bid each one "a pleasant journey."

When the decorations were to his satisfaction, he walked up the short staircase into the dining room for his late birthday brunch of black coffee, eggs benedict, and a morning paper. For dessert, the kitchen staff—Harvey and Georgia were working today—brought out a muffin with a lit candle on top. He blew it out and devoured it all in two bites.

There were a few hours still left to go until his shift, so he walked back into the lobby, now bustling like just about every Halloween at the Palmer. Maybe even more so now than before, somehow.

Hoight passed Stroud, who was handling the influx and outflux with his standard mechanical demeanor, and opened the wooden door with the anchor carved into it. He stepped into the darkness of the bar.

"My birthday boy!" Barbs called, wiping down the bar.

They hugged and she sprayed soda water into a glass, dropped a few ice cubes in, slid it across, then poured out two shots of whiskey.

"Here's to another year," she said.

"One more down," he smirked.

They tapped their glasses on the bartop and threw them back. Hoight closed his mouth and exhaled from his nose, feeling the whiskey burn deep in his throat. He didn't usually drink on workdays, but he learned to make an exception for his birthday.

They bullshat another hour—complaints about new management, a couple's loud dispute on the 9th floor that Stroud had to break up, fresh development happening around the city, a new constant they were still getting used to.

The clock ticked to five—Hoight's cue to head out. He kissed Barbs on the cheek and walked out into the evening's chilled air.

A train car clinked overhead as he turned the corner and crossed the street into Lou's Candy Shop. He set an elbow on the glass case and shot the shit with Lou for a little while—that shooting last night across town, the dreams of the ball team's chances next season.

"They got a shot if everyone stays healthy," Lou said.

"Like any of us," Hoight replied.

When they were done, Lou lifted the giant sack of candy onto the counter and Hoight set down two $20s in return, but Lou only took one like always. Hoight said goodnight and cradled the bag as he hauled it back to the Palmer.

He walked through the front revolving doors just as Stroud was walking out, the two nodding curtly to each other through the glass dividers as they always did at shift change, then Hoight walked through the empty lobby and ducked into the break room to grab a metal bowl. He filled it with candy, set in on the desk, lit the candle inside the pumpkin so its spooky face came to life, then waited for the best part of his birthday every year.

The trick-or-treaters.

It was another old tradition that new management wasn't fond of, something about insurance concerns, but he'd be damned if he was going to send those kids away.

The first came in around seven.

A tiny tyke dressed like a ghost, the tried-and-true classic of two eye holes cut into a sheet. However, the flowers on the linen of this particular outfit made it all appear somewhat less chilling than intended.

"I got a joke, kid," Hoight said, leaning across the desk. "Knock, knock."

The kid behind the sheet stayed quiet until his mom, a short woman with a brunette bob, nudged him.

"Who's there?" the kid said from behind the sheet.

"Interrupting ghost."

"Interrupting ghost wh—"

"Boo!" Hoight shouted.

The kid shrieked and giggled, candy spilling from his pillow case. Hoight let out his barreling whopper of a laugh and it echoed through the lobby, then he pushed the bowl of candy forward. The kid grabbed a handful and they were off to the next score.

The next hour was spent alternating check-ins with trick-or-treaters until Hoight ran out of candy, this year's lot being particularly greedy. With Lou's closed at this hour, he put up his handwritten "Back in 5" sign and went into the hallway closet to dip into his auxiliary stash. As he refilled the bowl, Hoight heard a deadened metallic clank down the hallway.

He looked down the hallway and saw that the door to The Tabor ballroom was cracked open, its stopper caught on a piece of carpet. He walked over and peeked inside, and for an instant saw faint light being cast from under the stage. Suddenly, it blinked out.

Hoight mulled over the ramifications of leaving the front desk empty for more than his promised five, then considered the possibility of an electrical short under the ballroom stage, then couldn't think of anything else except how such ancient wiring could make the whole old place go up at any moment.

He crossed to the stage and dipped into a crouch, his muscles aching with the motion, and he discovered a loose panel at the bottom. He shifted it aside, flicked on his small flashlight, and scanned the crawlspace, finding nothing out of place until his roving light caught a metallic glint that hung from a concrete slab.

He looked closer and saw it was a small ring, and it quivered, as if it'd just been struck by some hidden breeze.

"Ah, hell," Hoight said.

He considered getting someone else to cover for him at the desk, or at least dip into The Anchor and let Barbs know.

Or, shit, maybe he'd just head upstairs, take off his uniform, and tuck himself into bed for a long sleep before finally escaping this place entirely to begin some new chapter in his life, however late in the game it now was for him.

But he knew that wasn't a real option, not after this many years.

"Ah, hell," he said again.

Hoight took off his orange cap and laid it down to protect it from whatever dust he was about to encounter, then ducked into the crawlspace.

The musk of stale mold stung his nostrils and made his eyes water as he examined the metal ring in his quivering flashlight.

It was small, like the tab on a soda can. There was an insignia etched onto it, too. A circle, maybe some kind of spiral.

Hoight flicked the tab with his finger and a soft ping hummed in the crawlspace for a moment before settling back into silence. He grabbed at the tab and pulled, and the wall slab moved toward him on some kind of hidden hinge.

On the other side of the slab was a corridor, narrow and dark, with wooden beams jutting out amidst broken cobwebs like wisps of an old man's hair. Empty wooden chairs lined one side.

Hoight thought once more about crawling out and taking the next train out of the city.

"Ah, hell," he said begrudgingly.

He crawled deeper into the passageway.

His arm brushed against something—it rustled, and a shiver went down his spine. When he discovered within him the guts to turn and look, he saw that a notebook had been pinned to the wall.

He angled his flashlight—108 was scrawled on the cover.

Inside was a collection of dates and names and descriptions, but nothing that made much sense. Looking up from the pages, he saw a small hole of light coming through the wall. As he leaned forward, he heard a clang from further down the corridor.

Hoight flashed his light into the darkness searching for the sound's origin. More chairs, more notebooks, more pinholes of light, then another corridor to his right, the end of which held a half-circle of orange light that filtered in through some kind of frosted glass.

He crept to it one slow step at a time and soon could make out the hotel lobby's ornate ceiling through the other side. He quickly realized that he was looking in from behind the face of the grandfather clock—the one that'd been ticking away in the lobby for as long as he could remember.

No one was at the front desk except his lit Jack-o-Lantern, smiling devilishly back at him.

A notebook hung near the glass. Nearly every page was scrawled with tight, tiny penmanship. He flipped to the beginning, and his eyes happened upon his own name:

October 31st, 1968
Hoight dressed & acting like a child.
Again.

He let the notebook swing on its string and retraced his steps back into the original corridor, turned right, and at the end he saw a metal ladder that stretched up far up past the reach of his flashlight beam.

"You dumb motherfucker," Hoight said to himself as he set a foot on the ladder's first rung, then began to pull himself up.

He clambered one foot over the next until he came upon a round portal that glowed between gaps in the ladder's rungs. It was a small window that looked out into the courtyard; white light from the dining hall blared in. As he climbed, he saw that every floor in this vertical tunnel had such a portal; the white from below giving way to the red of the rooftop sign the further he ascended. A number was carved next to each portal, growing by one each level.

When he got to **8**, he twisted his body to step over the small gap from the ladder into the corridor.

The red light of the rooftop sign was shorting out again, and it flashed behind him like a strobe. Hoight recalled his constant requests to management to fix the loose connections, but put it out of his mind as he approached the pinhole of light marked 809.

He peered into it—sure enough, there was his room.

His bed was made, his closet door opened to reveal his row of unused bellhop uniforms. On the desk was the balled-up newspaper that still held bits of pumpkin gore and seeds.

He opened up the notebook that hung nearby and read its most recent entry:

October 31st, 2000
Carves pumpkin, orange uniform today.

Hoight flipped back to the first page:

December 1st, 1967
Wakes at 5am, blue uniform.

He heard a shuffle behind him and the flickering red light disappeared.

"It's not my fault you're the most boring motherfucker in this place," Stroud croaked.

"You've been busy," Hoight said.

"Could say that," Stroud said, stepping to him. "I imagine you're not going to forget about all of this."

"Don't see that happening, frankly," Hoight said.

Stroud nodded curtly, then reached into his pocket and pulled something out something shiny. Hoight countered by holding out his flashlight.

"Better than nothing I suppose," Hoight muttered.

"What do you think would've happened if you'd have found these passageways first?" Stroud said.

Hoight knew he wasn't exactly expecting an answer, so he kept quiet.

"I picture you cementing the door shut the next day."

"Don't think you'd be wrong," Hoight said.

"That's your problem, Hoight," Stroud said, taking a step. "Can't tell a good thing when it falls in your lap."

Another step.

"Depressing to consider—you giving up all this power, all this freedom."

"And what power and freedom do you mean?" Hoight said.

"Power over those who control this city," Stroud said. "And so with that, the freedom to do whatever I want."

Hoight remained silent.

"Need a ticket to a ballgame to show off to a client, I can call in a favor to Harry Drake with seats behind home plate. Had an affair in Room 309. Want to haul yourself up the public office ladder? Got a fixer who spent nights in 487 shooting up black tar heroin," Stroud said, close enough now that Hoight could make out the pockmarks on his face.

"Need someone killed on the cheap?" Stroud said. "Got a few guys for that. This is true power."

"And what did all that freedom get you?" Hoight asked.

Stroud lifted a foot to take another step, hesitated, then set it back down.

"What did it get you?" Hoight calmly repeated.

"Anything I wanted," Stroud said.

"And working here for the past thirty years was what you wanted?" Hoight said. "Got nothing much else to show for it than that."

"At least I'm not stuck here," Stroud said.

Hoight inhaled deeply and raised his forearm in defense as he gripped his flashlight, feeling its heft, imaging how it'd feel to bring it down upon Stroud's bony head.

"Aren't you though?" the old bellhop said.

Stroud lunged.

His knife caught Hoight's forearm and carved through flesh, muscle to bone. Hoight swung his fist and felt Stroud's cheek give way, then a hot flash of pain in his own stomach. Hoight stepped back and grabbed at his belly—he felt hot liquid and slimy viscera pouring through his fingers.

Stroud stood back with his shattered face as Hoight stumbled and fell to his knees. He wiped his bloody knife across the front of his pants.

"Do you want company or privacy?" Stroud asked, his cheek already puffing.

Hoight smirked.

"Always liked my alone time," he coughed.

Stroud stepped back into the darkness and Hoight heard the clang of the ladder as his executioner departed.

Hoight sat, bleeding out on the corridor's wooden floorboards. After he built up enough energy, he crawled to the ladder with vague notions of finding safety or help, a trail of blood slicking in his wake.

All at once he felt exhausted, and his head fell. He noticed a pinhole on the ground.

~~750~~ was etched next to it.

Too exhausted to call out, he lay face down and started tapping out in desperation.

tap. tap. tap.

His thoughts went to his mom, to Aunt Harriett, to Barbs, to everyone else he'd known and loved in the Palmer all those years.

Tap! Tap! Tap!

He slept and woke, slept and woke again, and somewhere in between consciousness and whatever was next, he felt presences surrounding him.

They were angry.

They wriggled and squirmed, squeezed and grabbed, trying to consume him, to absorb him into their dead flesh, their wretched selves.

Seized by terror, Hoight found a reserve of energy to lurch out of their grasp and crawl to the corridor's end, to the portal into the courtyard.

It was a peaceful night sky, with red flickering against the iron of the fire escape.

Hoight then felt their clammy hands grasping at his ankles, his calves, his thighs. He took in one last gasp, then unleashed a scream that made the windowpane quiver as they dragged his body back down the corridor and off to some world other than our own.

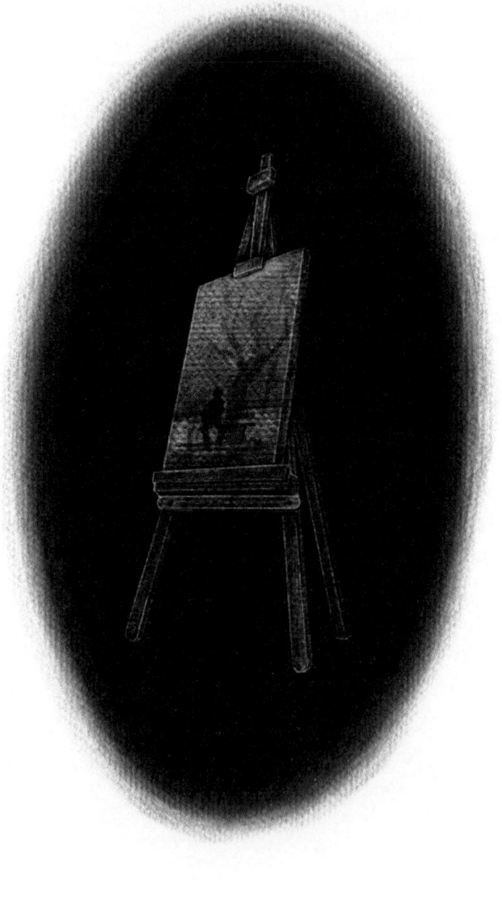

29. Gertie Paints Her Masterpiece. The Penthouse Suite

THICK RAINDROPS THUDDED against the penthouse window panes.

Gertrude Wagner brushed her blonde hair away from her forehead and looked into the sky, hoping for at least a small clear patch, however narrow in aperture, but there was only a looming slate of grey.

It was the third day in a row Gertie's view had been blotted out.

"Shoot," she said. "Shoot the dang boot."

Gertie gingerly strolled past the piano and clumsily struck a few keys with her knuckles. The dissonant notes echoed through the wide-open space and faded away as she approached her easel.

White cloth was draped over its front. She flipped it over to confront her painting, unfinished and taunting.

It was an old man on a park bench in twilight. In one hand, he gripped a newspaper with fat fingers that also held a cigar, its end smoldering in amber. The paper's other end, however, held the real intrigue.

Its corner was folded back, revealing the old man's inquisitive eye as he gazed toward some place far outside the canvas's purview. This is what had caught Gertie's attention.

The scene was inspired by the last city she visited, before arriving here. It was just a thing she saw one sunset night from her own park bench, a random image that caught her intrique long enough that she wanted to capture it forever.

Like usual, she'd made a quick sketch with the man's outline and newspaper, and a first attempt at his curious glare, skeletal outlines that she'd fill in with other details drawn from inspiration she got from wherever her next destination happened to be. She enjoyed this method of picking out specifics from a variety of locations and times and smashing them all together.

Later critics would call this "Gertie's Collage Period," but for now, it was just how she liked doing things.

Her week at the Palmer had begun productively enough thus far. She'd taken a discarded newspaper from the lobby to fill in details for her painting, choosing a ghastly story about a German killer executed by guillotine that, she felt, somehow fit the theme. The next day she used her penthouse view of the purple evening sky to fill in the space behind the old man. But there was still one key element missing from the scene she wanted to capture—a group of fireflies floating above the man's right shoulder, hovering in radiant blue-white glow.

On Monday, it started to rain and never let up. Three evenings at the Palmer without those fireflies she wanted to consult.

Three evenings wasted.

She glanced down into the courtyard and saw a tall, drooping canvas tent tweighed down by puddles, installed to protect the ongoing construction of the hotel's new glass-enclosed dining hall. A man was nearby, sitting on a wooden crate and he held a coat over his head to protect him from the downpour.

That's when she got her bright idea.

No reason to waste the night. She'd, instead, find someone that would help her complete the old man's leering eye.

"Lawrence!" she called out.

A short, bald man waddled in from the next room and stood at attention.

"Take me to where the people are," she told him.

Lawrence wracked his brain for a moment, then mentioned a speakeasy across town, but that wasn't quite what she had in mind.

"Not a party," she clarified. "A place to see people. Normal people."

"Well, there was a crowd downstairs, and—" Lawrence started, but before he'd finished, Gertie had already run into the bathroom to get herself fixed up.

An hour later, the penthouse's private elevator opened on the ground floor to a hallway filled with people—mostly single men, some couples—waiting to make their way to check in. When Gertie and Lawrence turned the corner, they saw that the grand lobby was an absolute madhouse.

Despite its tall ceilings, the room felt cramped and cluttered. Sweaty faces huffed in loose order, winding like a snake from the front desk. Couches and chairs and even tables were occupied. Suitcases stacked waist-high turned the floor into a maze. A cloud of cigarette smoke hovered in the air.

Gertie pulled excitedly on Lawrence's sleeve.

"This is perfect," she whispered.

"If you're happy, I'm happy," Lawrence said. "If you don't need me anymore, ma'am, I'd like to step outside. I don't do well in enclosed spaces."

Gertie gave his sleeve another pull, made her giddy, affectionate squeak, and leaned to kiss his cheek. He blushed then wove through the crowd and out the Palmer's revolving front door, and she strolled the lobby with her hands clasped behind her back, grinning as she examined the faces.

Most were bored, some were near rage, all of them tired.

Her attention landed on a large man who was halfway to the front of the line. He had a bald head and cherubic face, and fanned himself with a train ticket.

"Hello!" she said enthusiastically.

It took him aback.

"Hello?" he responded.

"What is it that you do?" Gertie asked.

"I'm a judge," he said. "I'm staying here for a case."

Gertie cocked her head to the side, closed an eye, and looked him over from top to bottom. At this silent examination, the judge gave a look of confusion, then he sucked in his belly and thrust up his chin before spinning left to present what he'd heard was his best angle.

"Oh, honey," Gertie heard a nasally voice say nearby.

It was from an older woman in a peach-colored coat and flower skirt. She rolled her eyes and shook her head at the display, and the judge suddenly glowed a bright red.

Gertie looked over the judge once more, then rested a gentle hand of consolation on the woman's forearm. She pursed her lips and squinted like she'd just tasted something sour.

"Not what I'm looking for, darling," Gertie said. "Don't worry."

She continued making her way through the crowd.

Gertie's eye caught another man. Skinny and wrinkled like a prune, he was alone and holding a small black case at his side. He wore a priest's collar.

"A priest!" she exclaimed.

"I help?" he said in a thick accent, maybe Austrian. "I do what?"

But Gertie knew right away that he wasn't quite right either. His eyes were too round and wide. She needed something more striking, sinister even.

"You looking for someone, miss?" a smooth baritone voice spoke from behind her.

It came from an older man seated next to the lobby's grandfather clock. His head rested against its mahogany side, his kind eyes watching her with a drowsy curiosity. His sideburns had greyed, but his face was free of wrinkles.

"You don't seem worried about your place in line," Gertie said.

"No point worrying," the man said, tilting his head off the clock. "Fretting won't make the process go any more quickly."

He smiled, and when he did, his eyes shone in the light and seemed to pull back into twin points.

Sharp, sleek.

Just what Gertie was looking for.

"What kind of work do you do?" Gertie asked.

"Oh, this and that. Stocks, investments," he said. "Do you really care about that?"

"Not really," she smiled.

"Thank god," he said. "That conversation is always such a bore."

A few more niceties and Gertie told the man that he wouldn't have to wait in line anymore if he went upstairs with her to sit for a painting she was working on. He said he'd love to—that, as a matter of fact, he used to dabble as a painter himself.

The man stood, favoring his side as they walked through the milling crowd to the penthouse's private elevator. As the doors closed, he introduced himself as Graham.

They rolled to a stop, and the cage opened into the small private hallway before they entered through the double doors into penthouse's expansive room, Graham's heels echoing against its wooden floor as they strolled the space.

Gertie explained to Graham what she was looking for, then showed him the painting thus far.

"It's lovely," Graham said with admiration.

He slumped down into the chair, and Gertie walked to the easel, lifted her paintbrush of Kolinsky sable, and began trying to translate Graham's eye onto the canvas.

"You must be new money," Graham spoke.

"In a way," Gertie said. "Had a thing go my way years back."

"Funny how these things just kind of happen," he said.

Gertie would always have these conversations with her subjects to make the situation less awkward, but at some point, she'd begun learning how to use them to guide their emotions. If there was a certain expression she wanted out of them, she'd find the subject's trigger point and try to tweak it in a certain direction. It was like directing an actor, but with the actor unawares.

"Do you come from money?" Gertie asked.

"In a sense," Graham said, smiling. "Owned land nearby, but lost it all in a bet. Another one of those things that just kind of happens."

His eye made another slight twitch—just the gaze she was seeking. This is what she'd press him on.

"Do you regret it, that bet?" she asked.

"What is there to regret?" he said. "It was a thing that happened."

"But you could have said no to it."

"Some things are simply fate," he said.

"Tell me about that," she said as she painted. "Tell me about fate."

Graham let out a giant laugh that boomed through the room.

"What is there to tell," he said. "We are hurtling through time in whatever direction we are, without any real choice or say in what we do."

There it was—that perfect tinge in Graham's eye.

"Tell me more," she said.

"Think about the concept of choice—it's an illusion," Graham began his speech. "Any number of infinite decisions, or cultural and social shifts, all that occurred well before you ended up here inside the penthouse at your easel. Similarly, infinite decisions made by structural forces were determined well before I ended up downstairs in the lobby to where you found me, my head resting against that clock."

"But what about my decision to paint you?" Gertie asked. "And your decision to say yes?"

"Ah, but these are merely the expected decisions that come from the happenstance of our own lived experiences," Graham said. "We exist in a certain place, at a certain time, and we've siphoned ideas, opinions, and morals from those around us, as if through osmosis. They fight and wrestle and destroy one another until a decision gets made, but our conscious mind has nothing to do with that process, it is nothing but constant battles raging within us, out of our control."

"That sounds bleak," she said.

"Not to me," Graham said. "It's freeing. We're just a marble dropped from the top of an embankment, without much say in which way we're headed, just knowing it's down there somewheres."

The rest of the conversation went on like this.

He opined on the state of the universe, and the events, familial or societal or structural, that had led to this, their single shared moment together in the Palmer Hotel. As he spoke, there was a gregarious wonder in his eyes.

Meanwhile, Gertie nodded and laughed, but kept mostly a frozen smile as she cast brushstrokes against the canvas.

"Just think—if you hadn't seen that man on the park bench," Graham said, "we never would have met."

"Just think," she said, mostly dismissively, and stood for one last look at the eye she'd painted. "And I think we're done. Thank you so much for your time, Graham."

She extended a hand—and he suddenly lunged and grabbed her wrist.

His nails dug deep into her arm's flesh.

She felt a shock flush up into her face as she tried to understand this new violence coming from this man's blissful face, still in awe at the world.

"Now, imagine the events that led me to this next decision I'm going to make," Graham whispered. "Whether I should let you live or die."

A flash of light swiped in Gertie's periphery, and she felt the cool blade of a straight razor pressed against her neck.

"You have no say in this, just like the rest of us nearly all our lives," Graham said. "It's all chance."

He stayed silent as if he was processing some emotions, his eyes fluttering as he contemplated some hidden question. Gertie thought about the odds of anyone reaching her in time before a quick flick of his wrist opened her jugular.

"Right now, it seems I have autonomy," Graham said, mostly to himself. "It feels that way, to me at least. But is that accurate. Do I really? Or am I simply a product of the conditions that have led me here? And will they dictate to me that I should cut your throat and let you bleed out on the floor?"

He took a fistful of her hair and breathed in deeply, then pushed her slightly away to take in the view from the bank of penthouse windows, wistfully looking out at the city landscape.

"We used to have so much fun here," he said gently, as if she wasn't even in the room. "It used to be so much better, before they all ruined it."

He removed the blade and Gertie fell to the floor, a light trickle of blood coming from her neck. She scurried into the room's corner in a panic, closed her eyes, then tucked her head protectively into the crooks of her elbows.

Moments later, she heard Graham's bootheels echoing away as he exited into the penthouse foyer, slamming the door behind him. A moment after that, Gertie heard the ding of the elevator as it was called. She waited until she heard it descend, then ran to lock the door.

She slumped against the wall and sobbed.

Lawrence came back an hour later to find Gertie silently staring at her painting, complete now save for those missing fireflies.

"It's lovely, ma'am," he told her.

She spoke in a flat voice, never taking her eyes from the painting as she told him it was time for them to go to wherever was next. They would be checking out from the Palmer that night, she'd decided.

"Very well, ma'am," Lawrence said. "I will pack the painting.

"No," she said. "Leave it behind. A gift to the hotel."

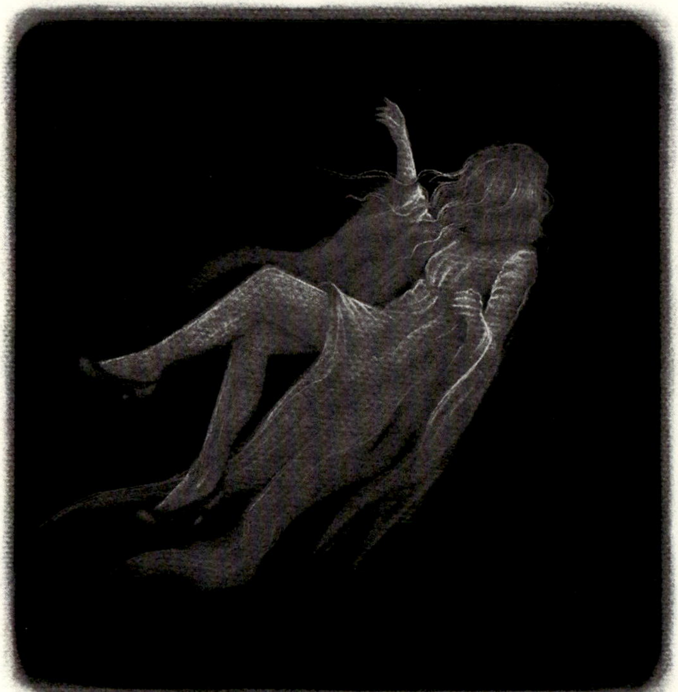

30. The Séance.
The Lobby

THE NIGHT'S FIRST RAINDROP formed in the grey clouds and fell.

As it descended, it reflected the red of the sign that, for one more night, broadcast the hotel's name out to the city and even beyond to the flatlands across the river.

The wind shifted and the thick orb angled toward a group of six who examined the sky from the rooftop, then gained speed as it hurtled towards a woman who was all dressed in white. It struck her forehead with a wet smack.

Maude leaned forward to let the cool liquid run down her nose and her coif of snow-white hair, fortified by half a can of hairspray she'd applied before arriving, remained perfectly still. She felt the next few raindrops on the back of her neck, then looked up to see a streak of lightning ignite the clouds a brilliant blue glow, like floating lanterns in the sky, before they all heard the tremendous boom of thunder.

The other five participants in that night's séance—some wearing masks to thwart the spread of the ongoing pandemic, some not—turned to the woman in white for guidance.

"Let's go down," she said.

The wind picked up as they crossed the rooftop and Maude's loose white dress billowed behind—she looked like some stubborn soul who wouldn't stand still for a daguerreotype. She opened the rooftop door into the stairwell and the others followed behind just as the downpour began.

This was for the best, Maude thought. The feel was off up there anyway. And if there was one thing Simon had taught her that'd actually stuck in her brain all these years later, it was the importance of atmosphere.

They descended down to the 7th floor, where Maude opened the door to the strums of acoustic guitar and dim chatter.

In the hallway's alcove, a moldy green couch that the Society had pulled up from basement storage was set up as a makeshift stage. A long-haired man stood on top and tuned his guitar in front of scattered, silhouetted partygoers who sipped from their red plastic cups as they waited.

Near the back, Maude found tall, bespectacled Patrick Jacobson, wearing a black tuxedo with long coattails hung to his knees.

Maude grabbed his sleeve.

"Not gonna work, huh?" he said.

Patrick was president of the Palmer Preservation Society, and the rooftop séance had been his idea. He thought it'd add a nice intrigue—whipping wind, dark skies, the group bathed in light from the rooftop sign that they'd wired to a generator to give it one final night of life.

These hobbyists always thought they knew best, Maude thought.

What he didn't know—what none of them knew—was that you didn't need much for a successful séance. A dark room, the more enclosed the better, somewhere that your voice would boom against the walls. The rooftop was anything but that.

"Too stormy," she whispered. "Going down to the lobby."

He nodded, glanced at the guitarist who'd launched into an out-of-tune ballad, and said that, on second thought, he'd join them. The group, now seven in all, continued down the stairwell.

On the way, Simon popped up into Maude's thoughts again.

They were rehearsing, years back when she was beginning as his apprentice and he still wore a trim mustache and long black hair. From her hiding spot in the closet, she could see the crow's feet around his eyes deepen in anticipation, and then he scrunched his nose—the signal she was waiting for—and she slammed her fist against the wall.

He dissipated from Maude's memories as the group reached the 4th floor.

Patrick held up a finger for the group to wait, then opened the door.

"—more than a few dead bodies were discovered in these rooms," said a woman's droll voice in the hallway. "And also more than a few old people who fell asleep and forgot to charge their hearing aids."

The woman chuckled to herself.

Maude peeked through the door and saw a small tour group in the shadows lit by a faint LED lamp that was being held by a short, red-haired woman wearing a mask. Patrick took her aside for a few whispered words, and she turned back to her group to made an announcement.

"A change in plans," the woman monotoned. "We're going down to the lobby for a fun little séance."

As they descended again, Maude calculated the portion of ticket prices—minus the cut going to Joey, her assistant—that she'd be getting from tonight's show. It was a good score, and would let her take the next weekend off entirely, a rarity in her career.

An older man from the group sidled up next to Maude in the stairwell.

"You're leading this show, huh?" he asked through his mask.

She nodded, and he introduced himself as Mikey.

"Know much about this old place?" he asked.

On the way down, Mikey told Maude some broad strokes of the building's history that he'd learned. He was writing a piece about tomorrow's demolition for the Chronicle. As a matter of fact, he was just on his way home to finish it up—it was a shame he couldn't stick around for the séance.

She made a mental note to ask Patrick for his name and contact information later. Tips from old city reporters like these always came in handy. Simon always preached the importance of these encounters.

"If you're in this profession, you're never off the clock, never on vacation," he'd told her. "When you least expect it is when you find the good stories, the ones that change the show from mediocrity to something people tell their friends about. That's where the real money is."

They exited on the ground floor to racket of a generator rumbling in the ballroom, and followed the orange extension cords down the hall and into the lobby.

Maude had been given a tour of the space yesterday as Society members were frantically restoring it to its original, pre-conversion look, filling the room with torn, scuffed furniture that Latham had kept in the basement. Now, a crowd milled in soft kaleidoscopic haze from mismatched lamps that'd been placed throughout.

Their dress styles were a mix—suits and gowns, jeans and T-shirts. Some in the crowd wore masks, but most didn't, or had them tucked under their chins. Dim blue lights from vapes flickered like digital fireflies.

The Society wasn't going to throw anyone out tonight. This event wasn't strictly legal anyway, and they didn't need any extra attention.

The rooftop group turned to Maude for guidance, and she instructed them to move the furniture against the walls, except for one large circular table, which would be set in the center.

They pulled up only enough seats for the original six—her and the customers who paid a premium. She announced that the others could stand around and watch as long as they kept quiet.

Maude took one last look around and made a slashing motion across her neck to those near the lightswitch and the bulbs all quickly cut out. The nine-armed candelabra at the table's center cast a quivering orange haze, and conversations of the partygoers died into expectant silence.

"It is now eleven o'clock," Maude projected theatrically. "Will all of the participants please take their seats."

She sat as a soft rumble of thunder vibrated the glass of the revolving front door.

The other five from the rooftop took their seats, and Maude shifted her hands so they flowed freely through the ends of her long white dress. She raised them face-up and began to softly hum.

"We begin as we begin them all—with a prayer to our Mother Spirit," Maude said. "To watch and protect us in this liminal realm between the life being lived and what's next for us all."

She closed her eyes and began her incantation, some bullshit about the veil between this and that, she didn't even think about the words anymore.

Joey, her silent partner who leaned against the dusty grandfather clock, pulled down his mask to sip his drink and released it, letting it smack back into place. He never paid much attention to this crap Maude was spilling.

He had a more important job to do.

He scanned the crowd for skeptics, specifically those who might get mouthy. If they did, Joey's duty was straightforward: shout down the troublemaker quickly and powerfully, and if that didn't work, grab him—it was always a him—by the arm and offer to show him something outside.

Tonight's group didn't seem to be a problem, Joey thought, what with them being there more for the building's last night than Maude's performance.

Maude finished her bullshit and extended her hands in either direction. The man to her left and the woman to her right took them, then offered their own opposite hands. Soon, the circle was complete.

A thick anticipation filled the room. It was the part of the show Joey never got used to. He knew all of Maude's tricks, hell he'd designed most of them himself, but there was still something eerie about this moment before it all began.

"Tonight, we are guests at the Palmer Hotel," Maude said. "One last group before the hotel leaves us for good. But before it does, we must make sure this structure has been cleared of those who have been left behind."

A long roll of thunder sounded from the storm now fully raging outside.

Maude scrunched her nose.

Seeing that signal, Joey pressed the button on the remote in his palm.

A blast of air came from a ceiling vent. The candles flickered, their flames trembled.

The show had now truly begun.

Joey examined those outside of the central circle. They consulted their partners with widening eyes, wordlessly asking if they saw that flicker too. This trick always worked like a charm.

"Guests of the Palmer Hotel," Maude spoke in a somnolent drone. "If you are present, make yourselves known."

Heavy breaths of anticipation, another roll of thunder. Other acts would use this beat to "send another sign" that the spirits were around them, but that move was for amateurs. This first call-out to spirits, you let slide without interruption. It gave the ones that were answered later a little more legitimacy.

"Perhaps they're shy," Maude said in a cheerful voice. "Why don't we try again?"

Chuckles through the crowd, smirks from those seated. It was always a crowd-pleasing moment, and an important one. You break the tension so it could then be ratcheted further.

"Are there any guests left in the Palmer!" Maude boomed.

The new caustic tone to her voice always caught the audience off guard, and tonight was no exception. Joey saw the partygoers tense up as Maude's voice dissipated in the quiet of the lobby, and then he pressed another button on his remote.

A loud thumping came from the darkened hallway somewhere past the front desk.

It was a modified kick-drum Joey had rigged in the closet, angled so that it struck the side wall.

Everyone swiveled to look, everyone except for Maude.

She shut her eyes and breathed in heavily through her nose, as if beginning a mystical transition. As soon as the jump-scare from the hallway dissipated, the crowd would recenter their attention back onto her.

And she'd be ready.

"We are here, we are here!" Maude boomed, her facial features creating dramatic, dark shadows in the candlelight. "We are not intruders, we are friends. We wish to help you pass to the next realm."

Silence.

"Do you want our help?" Maude asked.

Joey pressed a button and the thump came from the hallway again. Fewer heads glanced toward the noise this time, most focusing on the woman in white at the head of the table.

"We need to know how to help," Maude said, the first bead of sweat forming at her hairline.

Now it was all Maude's show. Joey just rested against the clock and waited to trigger the finale.

"Did a murder occur?" Maude asked into the air, frantically searching the corners of the lobby. "Were you murdered in here?"

A subtle creak came from somewhere in the room.

"That is a yes," Maude concluded.

It was a subtle form of improv Maude had perfected, using each new creak or bump to develop the atmosphere and further the narrative. In a room this big, in a building this old, with this many people stuffed inside, there'd be no shortage of odd sounds. Once, Maude turned a stomach grumble into a spirit coming to terms with being spanked by their father as a child.

Over the next twenty minutes, Maude wove a tale of someone named Jones, murdered in this very room. Their corpse was in some unmarked grave far away, but they'd left something behind. A special token.

"Heartfelt," Maude said, pretending to hear Jones's plea. "Gold."

It was all building to a search through the room that, inevitably, would lead some lucky person to the gold necklace concealed on the grandfather clock's pendulum. Joey had placed it there earlier in the evening. When it was found, the finale would begin.

Joey would press the button that'd create a giant gust to puff out the candles, then would come the sound effects in the ceilings and walls he'd spent hours setting up late last night, then silence, before Maude would relight the candles and deliver her closing spiel to inevitable applause.

Later, Joey would retrieve his special effects as the partygoers came down from the excitement—usually, he'd wait until the scene was clear, but the building's demolition tomorrow was a hell of a strict deadline. Later in the week, he'd swing by Maude's to get his cut of the take, and spend a quarter of it at the corner bar near his place that night.

Joey was thinking about drink number three when he felt a hard knock against his shoulder.

He shifted his weight and looked at the grandfather clock. Maybe someone had just bumped it on the other side. He rested against it again.

Another knock, ore forceful.

As Maude continued, he stepped slightly forward to examine the clock's interior. In the candlelight, he made out the gold necklace spiraled around its pendulum. Nothing unusual, everything in its right place.

"We will help you," Maude pled to the spirit. "We will find the item you left behind, then you'll be free of your burden. Is that what you want? To be free?"

Joey leaned back against the clock.

"I said, is that what you want?" Maude said. "Do you want to be free?"

A boom in the clock, this time loud enough to get the entire room's attention.

They all looked toward Joey and he looked back. Past them, he saw Maude's eyes snap open and glare in his direction, and he slowly raised his hands and eyebrows in a mixture of apology and confusion. They turned back to see how the medium would react.

A new look suddenly emerged on Maude's face.

Her mouth dropped open. An odd, wondrous smile formed as she released the hands of those at the table then slowly stood up.

This was a new bit, Joey thought.

"There, there!" she screamed, pointing to Joey.

The entire room's gaze swung back to him and he raised his eyebrows even further.

"In the clock!" she shouted. "Don't you see? Don't you see?"

Joey stepped aside and the partygoers shifted into a tight half-circle so they could examine the clock themselves.

Maude approached, and the crowd parted for her.

"He's there! He's there!" Maude shouted. "Don't you see? The bellhop! The bellhop in the clock!

There was something off about her voice, Joey thought. It was a tone he'd never heard before.

And then she leaned forward to the face of the grandfather clock and whispered something so quietly only the damned could hear.

tick. tick. tick.

A gasp went through the crowd as the grandfather clock suddenly came to life, then began to speed up.

tick.tick.tick.tick.tick.tick.tick.

All at once, Maude was lifted from her feet and thrown through the air, her body flung into a group of people near the table. They fell in a mass of arms and legs, and the grandfather clock began to tick away even louder.

Tick! Tick! Tick!

Joey ran to Maude and bent down on a knee.

"Are you okay!" he shouted over the clock.

TICK! TICK! TICK!

In the dim light he saw a welt forming on her forehead, purpling at an incredible rate.

"No," Maude said.

Joey couldn't hear her.

"No!" she screamed.

TICK! TICK! TI—

The noise stopped.

A quivering stillness came over the room. Slowly, the partygoers turned back to the clock. Its pendulum was halted mid-swing.

Joey turned to Maude.

"What is this?" he whispered.

"I think we're in trouble," Maude said with a startling clarity that turned Joey's blood cold.

A new sound from above.

Thunder, but near.

Constant.

An earthquake from the hotel's higher floors.

Everyone looked up as if they could see through the ceiling to its source, and the noise grew louder, closer, like an avalanche falling down toward them.

But then, not just from above. Somehow from the sides, as well. And below, too.

It was surrounding them.

The lobby's original ceiling lights came on, casting the group in a flickering orange strobe, and the partygoers scanned each other's faces for solace but found only halted breaths and searching eyes.

The grandfather clock's pendulum began to sway again.

Back and forth. Back and forth.

Its ticks were drowned out by the raging noise.

And then the clock struck midnight, chiming with deafening intensity.

The partygoers clasped their hands to their ears and began to scream. The volume only grew with each new toll of the bell.

Joey squinted through tear-filled eyes at the frenzied chaos. Some in the crowd clawed at the side of their heads with a ferocity that left their ears bloody and torn, those in masks coughed out droplets of spotted blood, painting Rorschach tests in deepening shades of red.

Patrick Jacobson had somehow procured a sharpened edge from a piece of furniture and, without hesitation, stuck it in his carotid and jerked across like he was pulling a rip-cord. His body sprayed the grisly, writhing carnival of anguished partiers in an arching crimson drizzle, then he fell in a clump. A moment later, the mass strained toward his hand, scratching and clawing and biting one another for the prize of using the edge next.

Joey felt pressure in his ears, then a painful pop. He winced and new dampness ran down the sides of his neck.

He turned to Maude.

Her face had begun to peel away in vertical strips, each new fillet of skin rolling down it revealed a fresh layer of wet red behind it. Still, she was somehow serene.

Maude pulled him gently by the back of his neck to bring him closer, and he saw strings of muscle where her cheeks and lips once were. They tightened and shifted like a cluster of maggots as she spoke.

He couldn't make out what she said.

She pressed a finger to his ear to aid her voice, and blood flowed down her wrist, staining the sleeve of her white gown. She spoke again, and this time he could make out her voice over the lobby's horrific orgy of sobs and screams.

"Joey," she whispered. "This is the en—

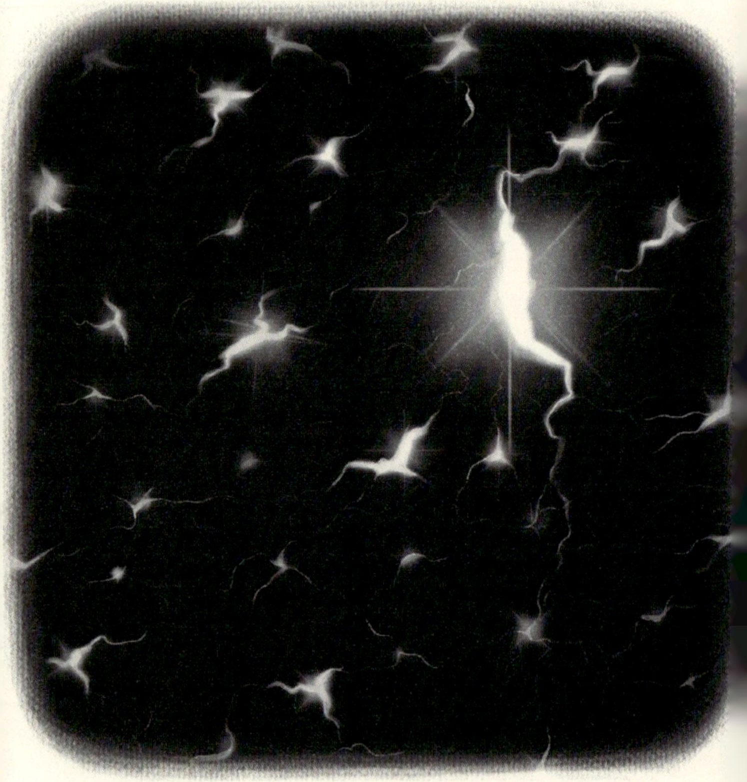

31. Hoight's Long Night.
The Palmer Hotel

I SINK BELOW TO THE GRAND DANCE and twirl for a while, then I float away and open my eyes.

I make out the lobby through the half-circle of glass at the end of the darkness, and hear the echoing ***tick-tick-tick*** of the clock's pendulum.

Between the hour and second hands, I see the man who killed me.

He taps his finger to the pendulum's rhythm on top of the desk as he stares at the clock, but not into it, not at me, whatever I am, here on the other side. Only at the time.

I hear the squirming coterie approach from behind, and I'm enveloped within its tendrils. They feel warm and slick as they form around me to control my arms and legs, my head, fingers, and eyes.

They're inside of me too, puppeteering whatever's left in there.

They spin me away from the lobby into the hidden corridor and pull me past the hanging notebooks that all remain unmoved by my presence. Then through the wooden chairs laid out against the corridor walls. Then to the dead end, then up the ladder, rung by rung. Through a portal I see the courtyard bathed in moonlight and flickering red.

The limbs move me down a corridor dotted with pinholes of light and bring me to the one marked 809. They push my head forward, force me to look inside.

My furniture is gone, the carpets removed, my closet empty. Paint buckets, rollers, and sheets of torn plastic have been left behind.

I hear a noise behind me: the coterie twists me around and I see my assassin's faded outline.

A dark aura with fuzzy borders and a jittering interior. Its movements blur as it approaches, then I feel the sharp pain in my guts, the stabbing deep within me, fresh like the first time. My assailant disappears.

The limbs make me stagger down the corridor, then force my hand to *tap-tap-tap* against the ground. They hoist me to look through the portal into the courtyard's glow, almost as if they're taunting me with a view of the world that I've been torn from.

I see the faint outline of a woman's face, diffusing into tufts of gossamer.

She's barely there.

The limbs squeeze my insides and force me to scream, so I do.

The woman falls.

My eyes close.

I sink below to the grand dance and twirl for a while, then I float away and open my eyes.

Through the half-circle of glass I see someone new behind the front desk. A stranger. Short, red hair. She thumbs through a paperback as a guest patiently waits to check in.

The slick limbs approach and enter me and spin me around, through the corridors, up the ladder to the eighth floor, lit in flickering red.

There is Stroud on his night shift, still a being of flesh and blood, stooping in a chair as he leans forward towards a pinhole. He backs away, scrawls in his notebook, peers again.

I pass into his body and am struck with a feeling of simmering rage. It wafts into my nose like burnt engine oil, then the limbs carry me through to where he sits to *809*. They make me look inside.

My room is no longer my room. Gone are the shelves, gone are the drapes, gone is the hotplate. A man sleeps in my old bed. His feet stick out from the covers. He snores.

The limbs spin me, and I see my assassin's jittering shape again. It's Stroud, but also not. It approaches in a blur.

It passes through the corporeal Stroud who still sits taking his notes—the two entities blend momentarily together in shimmering solidity—then I feel the pierce of my stomach. An awful, shocking new pain.

The limbs drag me to the floor to issue my ***tap-tap-tap***s, then to the courtyard portal where that woman's face appears again, still faint but now clearer than before.

Long brown hair, aqua blue eyes, wrinkles of worry on her forehead.

My insides compress like a squeezebox to make me scream, and I do.

The woman falls.

I close my eyes.

I sink below to the grand dance and twirl for a while, then I float away and open my eyes.

A man stares back through the half-circle in the clock. He presses at the corner of his mustache, then turns around to see a woman in red behind him. She's familiar somehow, but I can't recall why. The man turns back with a smirk and pulls his mustache off. I know him as well, but don't know why.

The limbs spin me, float me down the corridor and up the ladder to the pinhole into my old room, now empty. They spin me to my shaded killer and I feel that ghastly pain, searing and crisp, then they make me strike my *taps*, then push me to the courtyard portal.

The woman's face beyond is now clear and real—actually there, I can feel it—in the flickering red strobe of the broken rooftop sign.

She's hesitant in her steps, worried about falling. She can see me, I can tell.

I try to remain silent, but the tendrils clamp down on my insides and urge me to scream. I hold out as long as I can, but it's a fool's errand, so I do. I watch the woman's eyes widen with fear as she steps back off the fire escape.

Then I watch her fall.

A moment later, another figure falls past, thinking of what a strange world it has been. I hear a grotesque sound of shattering bones and splattering flesh. I close my eyes, now filled with tears.

I sink below to the grand dance and twirl for a while, then I float away and open my eyes.

Over and over I cycle through the Palmer, forced to obey the orders of the greasy arms and legs that slither through the interior corridors, dragging me from clock to corridor, up the ladder to my stabbing, down to the floor to issue my *taps*, then finally to view the courtyard portal.

And every time at the end of this cycle, the woman in red glares back with mounting fear. Every time I'm forced to scream, and every time she falls.

I begin to notice some new awareness growing in her blue eyes with each cycle. Confusion, pleading, acceptance, hope, then acceptance again. But nothing changes in our routine.

The limbs make me scream, she falls, and we do it all over again.

I sink below to the grand dance and twirl for a while, then I float away and open my eyes.

The lobby is full of commotion this time. Another cycle, there are fewer guests. Then, it's empty save the red-haired woman with her paperback. Then, she's gone and no one's left. Later, there's a flock of roving headlamps perched on top of shadows wheeling in carts of supplies. Then, it's empty again.

Later still, the lobby is lit brightly with new furniture. A large man stands behind the front desk dressed like a security guard. He buzzes people in through newly installed glass door.

I feel the corridor shake and watch the guard bolt from his position and out through the revolving front door. In the empty lobby, lamps topple from their tables and crash to the floor. I hear silence and realize that the grandfather clock has stopped ticking.

The gelatinous limbs drag me back down the corridor.

I sink below to the grand dance and twirl for a while, then I float away and open my eyes.

Through the half-circle, the lobby is now candlelit. Shadowy figures roam about. I see a table in the center occupied by a circle of people, finely dressed and holding hands. There's a strange electricity in the air.

From the table, a woman in a long white dress shouts an incantation. Confusion suddenly grows on her face and she rises toward the clock, toward me, stuck here on the other side.

She peers through the glass. She can see me, I can tell.

She whispers to me, telling me to be free. I've never thought of this before, so I take her up on it.

Before the squirming coterie can grab me, I reach out to this woman in white. As I do, I feel a flash of hot energy spark through the air, then see the woman ejected away, as if struck by a thunderbolt.

She crashes violently into the crowd. Everyone screams.

I pause within the lobby, free from the writhing captors on the clock's other side. The partygoers freeze in a tableau of intertwined limbs and strained expressions. A diorama of preserved horrors, their screams still faintly lingering in the air.

And then the pageant strips away and in its place before me opens up the entirety of my past.

It's an expanse of pure black speckled with slim fissures of light.

Millions of them.

A wall of stars.

They shine in varied rhythms like lights from a disco ball. One pulses brighter than the others, and so I step into it.

I'm in Room 809, but it is not yet my home. I'm being held by my mother. I know her by her smell.

Dimples form in her brown cheeks, then her eyes wince with pain and blur with tears.

I've seen enough.

I withdraw from this fissure. Another star pulses brightly in the wall, so I step in.

I'm at the corner table of the hotel's dining hall, across from Mrs. Abernathy. I still remember her name.

She holds a rose I'd just given her, and I speak in my prepubescent voice telling her that her boy will be back soon. I see a thankful look appear on her face.

I withdraw to the wall of stars.

It pulses in a pattern that I cannot decode, so I randomly try another.

I'm in the hidden eighth floor corridor.

I feel the stab wound in my belly, the warm liquid as I bleed out into the wood. I pound on the floor in desperation, and then I find myself at the portal, staring out into the courtyard. The outline of the woman's face is there, barely, in the flickering red.

I desperately want to scream—for help, for pain, to make one last sound before the life flows out of me forever—but instead...

Instead I use my remaining strength to bite my lip, to swallow my pain, to stay silent as a mouse.

The dim figure of the woman descends down the fire escape to safety.

I withdraw to the wall of stars.

Beyond the veil past the wall of my life's moments, the bodies in the lobby remain frozen in time. But something has changed now. Some of the stars have blinked out, others pulse brighter than before.

I remain still and examine the wall in this place between time.

After hours, or years, or perhaps all time all at once, I learn how to read them.

I know precisely where each star leads, to which moment of my life within this hotel that the fissure will transport me. I ponder this knowledge for hours, or years, or perhaps all time all at once, and then I begin my plan.

I return to a day in 1962. I'm behind the front desk, checking in an old man with a nervous girl on his arm who's old enough to be his granddaughter. Twin streaks of blue eyeshadow run down her cheeks.

I remember when this had first happened, years ago. An ambulance had showed up hours later to take her away in a stretcher.

This time, in this new trail I've created, I tell the man that the hotel is booked up. He glares at me and I hold my ground, and he delivers a great big huff before he takes her by the arm and they spin around and exit through the revolving doors back out into the city street. I feel some some type of satisfaction.

Maybe it will make a difference.

Maybe not.

I withdraw to the wall of stars.

I return to a day from 1983. I'm outside of the front of the hotel, holding a picket sign. I see a man approach, old and angry and muttering under his breath. He looks into the lobby and I follow his gaze to see Stroud—that bastard Stroud—on the door's other side. He waves the angry man around.

I follow the man down the street this time, screaming as I do. Screaming bloody murder. I call him a piece of shit, a fucker, a scab.

On the side of the hotel leaning from the open door I see Stroud, that bastard Stroud. I see the wheels spinning in the angry old man's head as I scream at him, then something suddenly clicks. He crosses the street and heads for an approaching train, forgoing the Palmer entirely.

Stroud closes the door with a grimace and retreats inside, and I rejoin the picket out front.

I withdraw to the wall of stars.

During these journeys—as I step through into my past, shifting the course of events before retreating again from the time-bound realm of the living to my wall of stars to do it over again—I notice something peculiar.

Now and then, I see other figures lingering throughout the hotel. They are faded silohettes, some of the shimmer as they move. They spiral as well, going through their own cycles through the hotel's rooms and hallways and corridors, or twirling in the ballroom, as I once did.

Souls imprisoned.

As I once was.

While the woman in red has been freed from her cycle, all of these others—hundreds, thousands, maybe more—they all go through their tortured routines, grasped by the slippery limbs, forced to their fates by the puppeteering entities that reside within this cursed structure.

I stand in front of the wall of stars again, the partygoers all still in their frozen moment of time, and I contemplate my options.

After hours, or years, or perhaps all time all at once, I recall an entry from Stroud's notebook that hung near the grandfather clock:

October 31st, 1968
Hoight dressed & acting like a child.
Again.

I formulate a plan.

To kill two birds with one stone.

I return to a day from 1957. With no one around, I wheel a metal cart into the ballroom, then down to the hidden space below the stage. I load the cart with concrete blocks to weigh it down, making it immobile. It sits there, unremarked and unmoved, for over a decade.

I return to a day in 1959, and I order a shipment of ammonium nitrate. Then, weeks later, I return for the package's arrival. I haul it under the stage and maneuver it deep into the hidden corridors, making sure it's out of sight.

I return to a day in 1960, and I bore holes through the face of grandfather clock and run wicks inside.

I traverse the years, entering the stars to times in my past when no one is around—often in the middle of the night, awakening in my room—to hurry down to the ballroom and disperse the explosive materials throughout the labyrinth of the corridors.

When my plans are complete, I enter the stars and leap to Halloween night, 1968.

I wait behind the front desk in my costume, handing out candy next to my lit Jack-o-Lantern, until I see a flash of white from within the grandfather clock.

That's Stroud making his mistake, bobbling his flashlight, sealing his fate.

That's my signal to finish my job.

I sprint to the ballroom, crawl under the stage, and brush the cobwebs from the metal cart that's been ignored in the corner. I remove the bricks I'd placed on it a decade ago, push it in front of the concrete slab door, and weight it down into immobility.

No one will be coming in or out of the corridors anymore. It's been sealed.

I spend the rest of this final journey winding my way through the hotel. I knock on every door and tell every guest that there's a bomb threat, or provide them with some other message of imminent danger, anything to get them out.

They trust me. The bellhop uniform comes with a certain authority.

When The Palmer Hotel is clear, save that one dark soul in its guts, I finally return to the lobby.

I use a small hammer to smash in the face of the grandfather clock. On the other end, I see Stroud's eyes staring back.

"Do you want company or privacy?" I ask.

He remains silent.

I light the wicks that I'd planted beside the clock's pendulum, and I watch the flames flow back through the hidden corridors. Stroud's shadow scurry off down the corridor, towards what he believes to be safety.

I know better.

I take one last look at the grandfather clock, then at the empty lobby where I'd spent so much of my life, and I leave all of that behind as I push through the front revolving doors with enough force that they keep spinning long after I cross the street to the train station.

I can see the hotel as my elevated train leaves the city, and in an instant, its windows shatter in immense concussion. As the train crosses the river out of the city, the crossbeams of the rooftop sign become engulfed in flames, giving the overcast sky a halo of orange.

I turn forward in my seat and ignore the distressed comments from the gawking passengers as I begin to consider where my next journey will be.

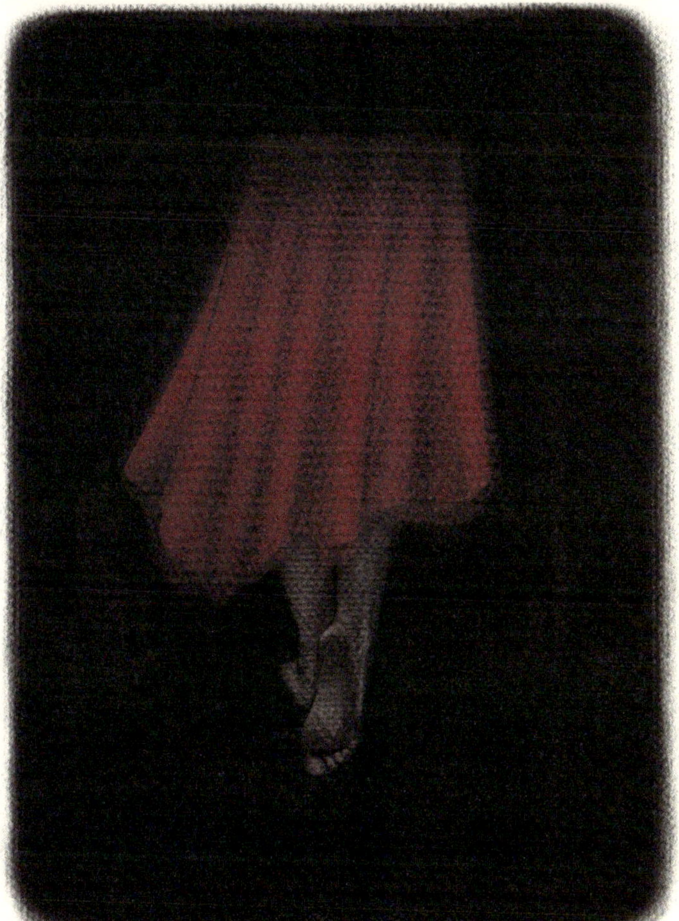

Overnight Fire Guts Palmer Hotel

by Gary D'Angelo, staff writer

DOWNTOWN, November 1st, 1968

Firefighters spent Thursday night putting out a blaze that damaged much of the historic Palmer Hotel.

No casualties have been confirmed, although a representative for the fire department estimates it will take crews weeks to comb through the wreckage. Sources familiar with the situation have told The Chronicle that arson has not been ruled out.

Experts who have examined the smoldering structure from afar expect that much of the building's exterior will survive, but that the interior will require extensive rehabilitation before resuming operations.

"I was woken up around midnight and told there was a bomb threat," said Barry Kind, a guest at the hotel who was in town for a convention. "I gathered my things as quick as I could, and I'm sure glad I did!"

The Palmer Hotel dates to 1898, when, as local legend goes, local entrepreneur Jonathan Palmer won the building in a bet. Previously named The Winthrop, the hotel became a destination for tourists and investors in the burgeoning city. In 1910, the location's success led Palmer to add eight more floors, and, in 1929, a second ten-story tower was built on an adjacent plot of land.

The fire was largely confined to the older, southern wing of the hotel, but the newer, northern wing suffered some damage as well.

While no one from The Chronicle has yet been able to personally inspect the devastation, sources have confirmed the famed glass-enclosed dining hall in the courtyard, a power lunch locale for many of the city's political elite, has been destroyed. The hotel's long iconic rooftop sign was also lost to the flames.

"It hurts, it really does," said Jacqueline Palmer, the hotel's current owner. "But we'll find a way to fix it and get back on our feet. Any city worth its salt needs a hotel like the Palmer."

1. Mary Wakes Up.
#750-S

MARY WATTER WOKE to a tapping sound that rattled around and around in her brain.

She sat up in bed in a panic as the sound faded away, then huffed deeply, in and out, in and out, in and out. Her face flushed a tingly hot red, and she put a hand against her chest to feel the frantic flutter of her heartbeat. It pounded against her fingers as if it was trying to burst through, then slowly settled. She set a hand down next to her and felt that her sheets were all drenched in sweat.

She recalled a few flashes from her nightmare.

She was falling in a flickering red light, the wind blowing through her hair with deafening power. She looked skyward into the starry night and then suddenly the sky became blacked out.

From this pure darkness came twisted limbs—slick arms and legs chaotically intertwined. They were reaching down for her. In her dream, Mary somehow knew that succumbing to their grasp was more to fear than the ground that was approaching from below.

The purple haze of the new November dawn streamed in through Mary's windows, and the horrific feeling from the nightmare slowly faded away.

Mary turned to her bedside table and saw her clock. The digital numbers said it was 6:12 a.m.

"What the fuck was that all about," she muttered to herself..

A flicker of white light caught her eye, and she found that the flat-screen bolted to the wall was still broadcasting a commercial for some slick new generation of smartphones. She must have left the TV on overnight again.

The commercial concluded and on the screen came the image of an attractive woman in a blue dress. The shot expanded and showed that she was next to a grotesque older man in a black suit. They sat, side by side, behind a news desk.

She snatched the remote off her bedside table and pointed it at the TV. She pressed OFF, but her finger hit MUTE instead. The voices from the talking heads blared through the speakers.

"—e'll see here," she said, "a graphic that is surely on everyone's mind."

The next image showed an electoral map of the United States split between blue states and red. It was previewing this week's presidential election between the beloved incumbent and the no-buzz nothing contender.

The news heads said some words about the big show to play out in the ballot boxes, hyping it like boxing promoters even though everyone knew it was a foregone conclusion. Like uncles around the barbecue bullshitting their way through quantum physics, Mary thought, and turned off the TV.

She got out of bed and walked barefoot on her Persian rugs to the window and opened her curtains, white and printed with flowers.

She'd found them at a thrift shop years back, browsing while high—her preferred method of shopping. As soon as she saw them, she knew she had to have them. They spoke to her in some strange, mystical way.

She peered out of her view from the 7th floor.

The courtyard of the structure that Mary had now called home for a decade-plus was empty. The rectangular expanse of grass below was dotted with soccer balls, mitts, and other detritus left behind from the kids playing last night after dark.

Her neighbors had yet to stir this early in the morning, except, she saw, Woodrow in #690-S. He was having his morning coffee and cigarette before heading off to start his day behind the wheel of a city bus.

The movement from Mary's curtains caught Woodrow's eye, and he raised his mug and waved a morning salute. Mary smiled and waved back.

Through the window on her metal fire escape that she'd painted a vibrant red Mary noticed something between the empty pots that were out lining the stairs, waiting for next spring. It was a mug, the one into which she'd poured a sip of whiskey last night. She must have left it out while listening to the "trick or treats!" echoing against the brick walls of the courtyard.

Jerome's call was the loudest, as usual. He had a few years left of being cute in him before hitting the inevitable awkward teenage stage. She remembered holding him as a newborn; now he was over five feet tall. Last month, he showed her a magic trick where he presented her with a red rose seemingly out of the air, a verifiable wonder seeing that kind of sleight of hand act coming from someone she'd known since birth, in a way since even before.

Time works in odd ways, she thought. What a weird world we have.

She cracked the window and walked out to the fire escape to grab the mug, then carried it to the sink in

319

her small corner kitchenette. The mug, she noticed, was branded the logo of her old job at that tech start-up.

It was a long time ago, seeming now to her like an entirely different lifetime. They'd closed a few months after their massive Halloween party boondoggle they had on that party boat. After they'd folded, with some getaway money in her bank account, she'd flown here into the city and lucked into this spot.

It was one of the thousands of new units in the neighborhood, part of the new administration's massive public housing plan. With rent no longer a worry, she bowed out of tech's bubbles and bursts for good. That wasn't really for her anyway.

Mary twisted on the kitchen faucet and filled the mug with water to soak out the leftover whiskey taste, then crossed back to the bed. She passed the full-length mirror outside her bathroom and paused to look at herself.

She ran her fingers through her long brown hair, a few more strands a shade greyer, it seemed, every time she looked. She examined the cobwebs of wrinkles that flanked her aqua blue eyes.

But she also noticed a glow to her skin. She realized that, despite the early wake-up call from her nightmare, she didn't feel exhausted for once.

The lethargy was one of the ways the sickness had affected her.

Mary was an early positive case in the worldwide pandemic. Everything had shut down quickly as treatments and a vaccine were designed. It was now under control, but still, she had to spend the past month in recovery.

Today was the best she'd felt since it began.

Mary took her early wake-up call as a sign to get her day started. She showered and cycled through her closet, ultimately landing on a long red dress she hadn't worn in years.

She put it on, took the elevator downstairs, wished a good morning to Clive at the front desk, and exited out of the front revolving doors.

She went for a morning stroll through the city as it awoke, meandering through the stream of commuters before buying coffee and a danish from her favorite stand, then enjoying her breakfast from a riverside table as she watched the sun finish coming up.

She took the train to the botanical garden, free to enter for years now. She took notes on soils and plants that she'd want to try next spring when her fire escape garden was again open for business, then she walked to the park to clean up some trash before a quick happy hour pint with Joel.

He was a friend of a friend she'd met at a party a few weeks back and had started seeing. It'd been going well enough, with no immediate red flags, but she still liked her alone time, so she kissed his cheek and they separated for the night. She went to the grocery store for pasta, tomatoes, parmesan cheese, and arugula, and then walked back home.

When she was done with dinner, the sun was beginning to set. She gathered her paint supplies and headed down into the community center, the former ballroom of the old hotel. There was a metal plaque outside that detailed a bit of the building's history, but she hadn't read it yet.

Maybe tomorrow, she always told herself.

Over the past few months, she'd commandeered a small section of the center for a little project of her own: painting portraits of every tenant in the building.

She was a quarter of the way through now, and had improved so much that she felt bad about the first dozen neighbors she'd subjected to her artistic whims. Her portraits hadn't really started to resemble their subjects until Raymond in 320-N.

Tonight, it was Maude from 482-S's turn.

Maude was in her early 30s, relatively new to the building. Mary didn't know much about her other than she had a kid named Simon, after his father, long out of the picture.

The kid was presumably being taken care of during this session by Maude's mom, Grace, who lived down the hall. Maude had tanned skin dotted with brown freckles, a short crop of hair that she'd dyed ocean blue, and she spoke in a powerful voice. She wore a white t-shirt and white jeans.

"Just sit here?" Maude asked Mary.

"That's right," Mary said.

Maude sat on the wooden chair and Mary began to sketch.

These sitting sessions were just about gathering the subject's basics. Eyes, nose, the shape of their faces, then some paint to capture their hair color and skin tone. It usually took an hour. After, she'd take the canvas upstairs and fill in the rest on her own time. No need to make her neighbors sit through it all.

When Mary was done, she thanked Maude for her time and they ended with a hug. Mary lugged her materials back upstairs to her place and set the new canvas in the corner to dry, grabbed the mug from the sink, dumped out the lingering water, and poured in another whiskey shot.

She went to the window and stepped onto the fire escape. Below, the sounds of the courtyard kids echoed up into the night. Mary could make out Jerome's voice clearly, even this far up.

"What a day," Jerome's voice boomed through the courtyard, before he let out his trademark steamboat whistle.

Across the way, she looked at the grid of windows. They were lit in the static blues and reds, or beiges flickering in the shadows of swirling ceiling fans, or the staccato whites from flickering TVs.

She watched her silhouetted neighbors move through their bedtime rituals between walls of framed family photos and artwork that presumably meant something special to them. And then she watched them untie their bowed drapes, which fell and obscured her peeping.

There was Woodrow again, having his nightly drink and cigarette after his long day on the bus. He flicked his stub and its orange amber spun down into the yard. He waved goodnight, and Mary waved back.

Mary finished her whiskey and set the mug down on the fire escape. As she began to climb back inside, she heard a noise.

tap. tap. tap.

It came from somewhere within the wall.

Soft.

Like someone tapping on glass.

Tap! Tap! Tap!

She examined the brick exterior wall but found nothing. She climbed up the fire escape stairs, hoping to find the source.

The wind swirled around the courtyard, and then billowed directly towards her, blowing her off her footing. She gasped and clutched the railing, steadying herself.

Mary decided it was best to let these eerie sounds be and just head back inside, to leave the mystery to someone else. But then the moonlight caught the faint hint of something etched on the brick wall, so she leaned forward to inspect it.

Someone had carved directly into the brick itself. It was a ragged design.

A spiral.

She leaned forward further, her face nearly flush against the brick wall. Another loud wisp of wind came from behind, and it picked up speed as it swirled through the courtyard.

And then, after what felt like hours, or years, or perhaps all time all at once, Mary's eyes suddenly filled with tears and she shivered uncontrollably with a new realization that couldn't possibly be put into words.

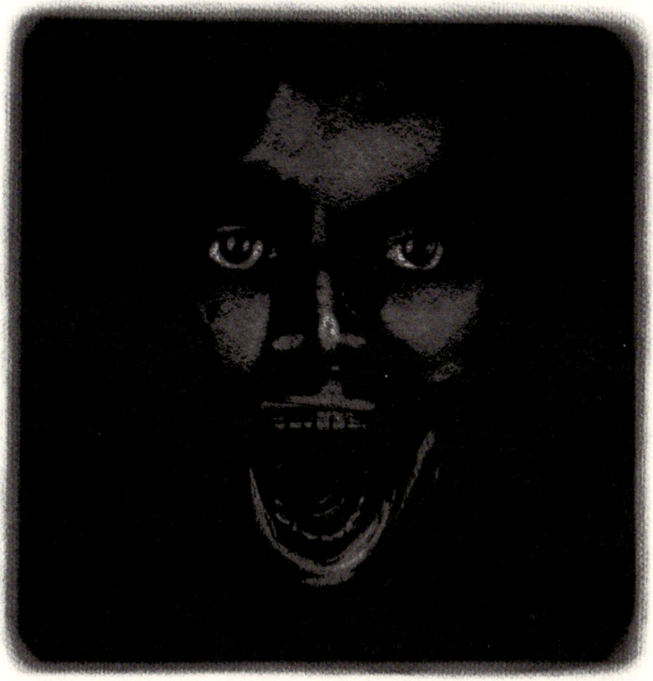

The author can be reached at rickpaulas@gmail.com

The artist's work can be found at Instagram: @tiffanysilverbraun